The world spins, the stars shift
and I can't see anything except his smoky
gray eyes gazing into mine.

You scare me, whispers
From my mouth across his.

Good, he breathes into me.
I need you to save me.

Praise for TAKEN BY STORM

"Passion, pace, pizzazz and a perfect finish—What more can you ask for?"
—Tim Wynne-Joes (*Rex Zero*)

"A debut novel that is satisfying on every level."—Ron Koertge (*Stoner & Spaz*)

"Fans of Meyer's TWILIGHT will enjoy this non-vampiric tale with similar
romantic chords." —Amber Gibson (TeensReadToo)

"Unflinching, honest, and sometimes sorrowful, *Taken by Storm* is a novel that is
not only romantic and entertaining, but thoughtful and moving.
Morrison is a bold and talented author to watch." —The Compulsive Reader

"Angela's writing is stunning." —Kathi Baron (*Shattered*)

"Beautiful, heartwrenching, romantic. It made me laugh and cry.
I couldn't put it down!" —Chan (Always Something to Read)

"Engrossing, honest and edgy." —Susan (Bloggin 'Bout Books)

"*Taken By Storm* showcases characters' fervent hopes and desperate needs
heading for inevitable collision in its pages."
—Uma Krishnaswami (Writing with a Broken Tusk)

taken by storm

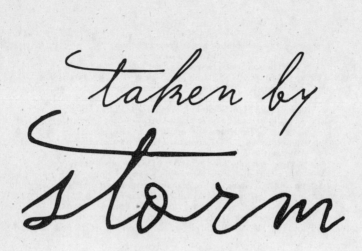

taken by storm

by Angela Morrison

razOr
bill

An Imprint of Penguin Group (USA) Inc.

Taken by Storm
RAZORBILL
Published by the Penguin Group
Penguin Young Readers Group
345 Hudson Street, New York, New York 10014, U.S.A.
Penguin Group (USA) Inc., 375 Hudson Street, New York, New York 10014, U.S.A.
Penguin Group (Canada), 90 Eglinton Avenue East, Suite 700, Toronto, Ontario,
Canada M4P 2Y3 (a division of Pearson Penguin Canada Inc.)
Penguin Books Ltd, 80 Strand, London WC2R 0RL, England
Penguin Ireland, 25 St Stephen's Green, Dublin 2, Ireland
(a division of Penguin Books Ltd)
Penguin Group (Australia), 250 Camberwell Road, Camberwell, Victoria 3124,
Australia (a division of Pearson Australia Group Pty Ltd)
Penguin Books India Pvt Ltd, 11 Community Centre,
Panchsheel Park, New Delhi – 110 017, India
Penguin Group (NZ), 67 Apollo Drive, Mairangi Bay, Auckland 1311, New Zealand
(a division of Pearson New Zealand Ltd)
Penguin Books (South Africa) (Pty) Ltd, 24 Sturdee Avenue,
Rosebank, Johannesburg 2196, South Africa
Penguin Books Ltd, Registered Offices: 80 Strand, London WC2R 0RL, England

10 9 8 7 6 5 4 3 2 1

Library of Congress has cataloged the hardcover edition as follows

Morrison, Angela.
Taken by storm / by Angela Morrison.
p. cm.
Summary: When Michael, a deep sea diver whose parents have just died in a hurricane,
arrives in town, Leesie, a devout Mormon, falls in love with him as she tries to help him
overcome his grief, and then they must see if they can reconcile their very different beliefs.
ISBN 978-1-59514-238-2 (hardcover)
[1. Grief--Fiction. 2. Deep diving--Fiction. 3. Mormons--Fiction. 4. Dating
(Social customs)--Fiction. 5. Conduct of life--Fiction.] I. Title.
PZ7.M82924Tak 2009
[Fic]--dc22
2008029000
Printed in the United States of America
Razorbill Paperback ISBN: 978-1-59514-274-0

To Allen,
my storm forever

prologue

LEESIE'S MOST PRIVATE CHAPBOOK

POEM #24, WHAT DOES IT MATTER?
What does it matter if
another jock pinches me
as I walk down the hall to physics
and high-fives Troy, celebrating
like he just scored
the season's first touchdown?

As I stalk past
the architect of my torture,
I'm frozen, a block of ice—
not a single drop melts.

All hail the Mormon Ice Queen.

What does it matter?

I know the commandment,

but I don't even consider
turning the other cheek.

And yes, it hurts, but
life without pain
isn't much of a test.

This feeling can't be lonely—
I'm not alone.

I walk with His hand on my shoulder,
His voice whispering in my soul,
His love soaring in my heart,
His suffering
my
salvation.

What else could possibly matter?

BEFORE

MICHAEL'S DIVE LOG—VOLUME #8

Dive Buddy: Mom	
Date: 9/2	Dive #: 748
Location: Lighthouse Reef, Belize	
Dive Site: Corky's Wall	
Weather Condition: cloudy	Water Condition: flat calm
Depth: 107 ft	Visibility: 100+ ft
Water Temp.: 88°F	Bottom Time: 4 min. FREE DIVE

Comments:

The dive starts perfect. Perfect water. Perfect sky. Perfect wall. The ocean, warm, flat, perfect. I leave my wet suit drying on the *Festiva*'s dive deck. Salt water slips silky over my skin like Carolina's caress.

Jeez, I miss her. *Caroleena.* She insisted on Spanish pronunciation. I thought this trip would help, but I can't forget lying in the sun, curled together, my face lost in her thick black hair, holding on. Three months. Every day. More when she felt like it. I always felt like it, but I didn't want to use her.

She dumped me on my butt when I took off to dive all summer at the condo. I wanted to bring her to Florida. Keep her close. Keep her safe. But she had to stay in Phoenix and work. Her family's got nothing. And Mom flipped when I mentioned it was a shame the sofa bed in the living room would be empty. Dad was cool with it. He's cool with everything. It should have been Carolina and me all summer, diving.

The creep b-ball jock she's with now is after one thing, as much as he can get. Possessive, too. Freaked when I called her from the Keys. And when we were all back at school, she wouldn't even look at me. Dad knew something was up, let me cut a week for the club's annual "hot deal" hurricane season trip. So, I'm scuba diving my brains out, free diving whenever I can get a spotter, trying not to think about that jock pawing my Carolina.

Love. Makes me crazy. All of it. You get so close, like she's part of you. And then she's gone. You ogle the smiling waitress on the boat, who has your girl's hair and wears a loaded bikini top and a sarong slung dangerously low. You appreciate the view while she serves you a virgin piña colada, but you still ache inside because now you've got a hole in your rib cage that won't fill, a gash that heals way too slow.

Salt water's my therapy of choice.

I swim my makeshift free-dive raft, Dad's old scuba vest packed with everything we'll need, out to the wall. Mom's late.

Lame. I know. Diving with Mommy. But she's missing her scuba dive with Dad this a.m. to lie facedown on the water all morning watching a breath-holding fanatic sink headfirst into the ocean. I got to give her props for that.

Spread out, Dad's BC, the scuba vest, makes a decent place

to hang between dives. I blow air into it until it bounces on top of the water and wonder if I'll get that dive kayak I want for Christmas. I tie my diver-down flag to the BC raft and hook it all up to the buoy marking the edge of the reef. The ocean floor drops off hundreds of feet here, forming a sheer coral wall. Still no scary pink slashed shark bait wet suit jumping off the *Festiva* and finning toward me. It's okay. We've got all morning.

Good old Mandy in Florida used to spot me. That was in no way lame. I faked shallow-water blackout all the time so she'd have to swim down, wrap her sexy body behind mine, pull me to the surface, and resuscitate me. Mandy. Another hole in my guts.

Suddenly, I'm tired of waiting. I sling my weight belt around my hips and cinch it tight. A few more pounds of muscle mass to my core and I won't need the weights. I've got my body taut and toned. I can hold my breath forever. My heartbeat even goes slow-mo when I free dive. Total control.

I pop a quick sixty-footer down to the reef, bop with the juvie fish—yellow and black, blue, purple. Wish I could shrink down to their size and dart in and out of a coral mound happy, careless, flitting, free. Easy to be a fish. I wouldn't make a freak of myself like yesterday when I finally talked to that waitress. She looks eighteen, twenty tops.

I took my drink to the bar for a refill. "You want to hang out with me on your break?"

Chicks usually say, "Yes." Babes hit on me way more than I hit on them. Even the older ones. I think it's the hair. Boring brown, but it went wavy post-manhood. I keep it long. Girls can't resist. I don't take up their offers as much as I could. Mom's got this thing about respect.

But my waitress didn't say, "Yes." She pushed her own thick, black, sexy hair that whispered, "Carolina," out of her eyes and smiled to let me down easy. "I don't think so."

"Come on. There's nobody up on the bow. You could work on your tan."

"Tan?" She's Hispanic, gorgeous golden all over.

"Pretend." I ran my finger down her arm. We both felt it. That charge when it's right.

She didn't get uptight and jerk away from me. I was getting to her. "And what will you do?" She blinked slow. Her mouth opened slightly as she exhaled.

I traced her fingers. "I'm pretty good with lotion."

She laughed again, throaty, teasing. "Sorry." She pulled away then. "Next break the captain lets me call my kids."

No lie. She handed me a picture. Three brown faces tumbling over each other. They stay with her mom up in Belize City. She misses them pretty bad. I felt sorry for her. Wanted to do something. I mean here's this young, beautiful girl stuck serving drinks to creeps like me until her looks go. I wish I could get Dad to hire her, but I don't think she types. I laughed it off, hung out with her while my drink melted. The whole thing made me feel useless.

So much easier to be a fish.

I leave the juvies playing hide-and-seek in the coral's tiniest caves and swim over to the wall for a look. Nice. Steepest one we've been on. Blue, deepening to bluer, deepening to a thousand feet of blue. Perfect. I know I can break a hundred. Today.

Every time I tried at the condo last summer, either the waves were too high or the currents too strong. That's the Keys.

None of that here. I turn away from the promising depths and swim toward sunshine.

When I break the surface, Mom's all over me. "Dammit, Michael, you're supposed—"

"Just warming up. Not a real dive." I suck up. "Never without a buddy." I duck under the BC raft, grab the weight belt I brought for her from the vest's pocket, and surface.

"It looked like a real dive to me." Mom fastens the belt, kicking slow to stay afloat.

I grin and give her a saltwater kiss on the cheek before I move out along the line stretched between the buoy and raft, positioned so I can dive straight down the wall. I float on my stomach, blow through my nose to clear my mask, shoot a spout of water out of my snorkel, and inhale—fill my gut, hold it a few beats, then blow it out nice and slow, expelling CO_2, the waitress, Carolina, Mandy, even Mom through that handy tube stuck in my mouth.

"Take it easy this morning." Mom treads water instead of taking up her spotting position. "Don't go too deep."

I keep venting, soaking up the blue world under me, eager to immerse myself in it again.

"No blackout today, right?" She says that every dive. I was ten that one time. Get over it.

A pair of painted angels drift over the top of the wall, their fins waving in time to my slowing heartbeat. I blow up my chest and gut, nine more mesmerizing cycles.

Mom maneuvers into position, facedown on the other side of the line.

I advance to super-vents, stretch my head back so I can drive air into every chamber of my skull and torso, filling my throat and nasal passages again and again until my fingers tingle perfect breathe-down. O_2 maxed, totally zoned.

I inhale one last time, packing every crevice, and then pack more air and more. Mom bumps my leg. Doesn't matter. I'm Mr. Zen of the Deep. Nothing can penetrate this lean mean free-diving machine.

I slip the snorkel out of my mouth, bend at the waist, kick my massive free-dive fins skyward, and shoot down through the water. One kick, two. My buoyancy slides negative at fifteen feet. I streamline it, conserving my hoard of O_2. Don't need to kick now. Pinch my nose and clear my ears—easy. I zoom past the top of the wall, equalize my mask, glance at the dive computer strapped to my wrist, seventy feet, clear again, eighty. The deeper I go, the faster I fall. I blow past ninety. Hit a hundred before I know it. The water's so kicking clear.

I pull up hard, flip so my head points skyward, and work my fins to stop sinking. I want to celebrate. Kind of a deadly idea. A massive crab, all blued out, sits in a crevice sliced into the wall. He waves his claws in my direction. It took less than a minute to get down there. I have plenty of oxygen packed in my body, but I need it all for the ascent. No time for underwater fans.

I begin kicking for real, powering my giant fins back and forth. Don't go anywhere. Freak. Ditch my weights? No way. Dive won't count. My depth gauge reads 99 feet. Good. I'm moving—just doesn't seem like it. I paste my eyes to the blaring pink triangle that is Mom and kick harder. Ninety feet, eighty.

I make the top of the wall with upward momentum. Acid scalds my leg muscles. My lungs weep for air. Still, I don't chuck the weights. I keep eye contact with Mom so she won't think she has to save me and wreck this dive. My chest vibrates with the effort of holding on to the last dredge of O_2. My legs get stiff. I force them to keep wafting my heavy fins back and forth.

The drowsy warmth of blackout creeps over me at fifteen feet, but I don't give it any room. I blow my CO_2. Positive buoyancy propels me to the surface. I blast through, plastering Mom. She squeals.

My starving lungs kick back mounds of fresh salt air.

"Your lips are blue, baby." Her eyebrows draw together.

I suck O_2 to my brain and stick my computer-strapped wrist in her face.

107 feet. Perfect.

"Whoa." She doesn't yell it and give me skin like Dad would have. "From now on you're going to need a lot better spotter than me." Mom starts untying the diver-down flag from the buoy. "Let's head back."

"We've still got tons of time." I fin over to her. "I'm going again in a few minutes."

"No way." She struggles with my knots.

"Yes. Way." My mask fogs up. I rip it off my head. A few strands of wavy brown chick-bait hair come with it.

Mom gets the rope loose. "You need to work on your knots."

"I just got started." I hock a ball of slime into my mask and rub it around with my finger. "What am I going to do back on the boat?"

"You've got yesterday's dives to log."

"I'm staying." I swish my mask around in the water.

"Not without a spotter." She winds up the rope and hands it to me.

I hook the scuba-vest raft with an elbow. "Then spot me." I put my mask back on, mess around clearing it of my wild hair, remembering how Carolina clutched at it the last time we were together.

Mom turns her back on me. "You're diving way out of my league." She unlatches her weight belt, lifts it out of the water by one end, and sets it on the BC raft. "You know I'm lucky if I free dive to thirty."

"This is stupid. You always spot me."

"Not anymore."

"One more dive. Just to the reef. A baby could make that dive."

"Can I trust you?"

How can I answer? We both know I'll be down that wall again—freaking *should* be down that wall again.

"I'm not going to lie there and watch you drown. End of story." She pulls her still pretty face into a crease. "You're not free diving unless you've got a qualified spotter at the surface and a scuba spotter at depth."

"Give me a break." Nobody does that for a hundred feet. "It's not like I'm riding a sled to 450."

"Don't give me nightmares."

Right on cue, like Mom foresaw all and paid off the captain to get her way, the horn on the *Festiva* blares, over and over.

Mom frowns back at the boat. "Let's go." She starts swimming.

I hang back.

"Get a move on," she yells. "They don't blow that thing for nothing."

MICHAEL'S DIVE LOG—VOLUME #8

DIVE BUDDY:

DATE: DIVE #:

LOCATION: DIVE SITE:

WEATHER CONDITION: WATER CONDITION:

DEPTH: VISIBILITY:

WATER TEMP.:   BOTTOM TIME:

COMMENTS:

MICHAEL'S DIVE LOG—VOLUME #8

DIVE BUDDY:

DATE: DIVE #:

LOCATION: DIVE SITE:

WEATHER CONDITION: WATER CONDITION:

DEPTH: VISIBILITY:

WATER TEMP.:   BOTTOM TIME:

COMMENTS:

chapter 2

AFTER

MICHAEL'S DIVE LOG—VOLUME #8

DIVE BUDDY: blue pills	
DATE: like i know	DIVE #: never
LOCATION: Belize City	DIVE SITE: hospital
WEATHER CONDITION: raining	WATER CONDITION: don't know
DEPTH: 0 ft	VISIBILITY: none
WATER TEMP.: don't know	BOTTOM TIME: forever

COMMENTS:

When i ask for clothes, the nurse opens a drawer in the nightstand and pulls out my dive-club jacket and pants. This log was in the waterproof pouch. Must have stashed it there on the way to dinner. The thing is totally dry. The ink didn't even run.

Wish i put my wallet in there. It's wrecked—salvaged the plastic—my license, dive card, and a condom. The picture of me and Mom and Dad smiling on a dive boat together is ruined. The Belize money fell apart, but my U.S. dollars dried out. They're salty, but they survived. Guess breathing isn't an issue if you're a dive log or a dollar or a stupid condom.

i keep forgetting how. To breathe. Three, four minutes go

by and i realize i'm doing it again. Holding my breath. Good thing i'm not hooked up to those monitor machines. The alarms would be buzzing all the time.

There's an old guy across the hall. Must be close to toast. Bells go off seems like every ten minutes. Nurses run in there. A doctor or two show up. And then i hear that steady bleep, bleep, bleep. And i'm glad the guy's still with us—some shriveled-up old Belize man i don't even know.

The nurse says they're going to call me a taxi in a couple hours, so i shower. First time in days. Get dressed. Maybe somebody laundered my clothes. They don't stink. No mud, salt.

i don't think i have shoes. i limp out into the hall to ask where i can buy some sandals, and the nurse leads me back to my room and makes me get in bed. The sun is shining in my eyes. No blinds. Hurts. Wish i could turn it off.

MICHAEL'S DIVE LOG—VOLUME #8

DIVE BUDDY: solo	
DATE: 9/7, ticket says	~~DIVE #:~~
LOCATION: Belize City	DIVE SITE: airport
WEATHER CONDITION: sunny	WATER CONDITION: don't know
DEPTH: 0 ft	VISIBILITY: nil
WATER TEMP.: don't know	BOTTOM TIME: one hour to take off

COMMENTS:

i'm checked in. No luggage. The nurse gave me a pair of gigantic green flip-flops from the lost and found. You think they're some dead guy's? Am i wearing a dead guy's flops? The airport's got a junky-looking trinket shop and a place to buy drinks and stale sandwiches. Maybe sandals. Not. That would mean standing, moving, talking. My lime flops will do—go great with the gauze and white tape the nurse wrapped around my foot.

i can't remember much about the past week. A lot of blue pills. A punctured arch and a tetanus shot. A hospital ward i didn't care to be in. Questions i didn't care to answer.

Some trauma shrink told me to talk about it as much as i can. Who am i going to talk to? Not him. He said something about processing. That's how i feel—numb, mechanical, processed—like a jar of nasty yellow cheese.

i like the pills, though. The shrink gave me an extra bottle to take—i was going to write home. With his pills dissolving in my gut, my brain mucks into the quarry back in the Keys. Water fog. Shifting grayish green. Freaked me when i was a kid. Now, though, i want no vis. When the pills wear off and reality tries to sneak back in, i'm twelve-year-old me fighting blind terror, trying to keep myself from tearing to the surface and blowing the dive.

The plane finally takes off. Loading all the coffins took a while. i watched from the terminal window. Eighteen. i counted. The coffin i bought for Mom looks nice. i think it's cherry. She liked cherry. Our house is full of it. And pink. Pale pink satin. Not in our house. In the coffin. They didn't have any hot pink with white fish blowing bubbles. She wouldn't have liked traveling in gray plastic like they stuck the guys in.

i have to leave Dad here. They still can't get him out. Fuel leak. Too toxic, even for dry suits. Maybe the stink of the gas will keep the sharks out of there—

Freak—i think i'm going to puke again, and the chicks

with the drink cart are coming with their complimentary sodas, blocking the aisle. My seat's barf bag is stuck together with gum. Hurry, chicks. i need to wash down two more of my complimentary pills.

Breathe, that's it, just inhale, exhale, long and slow. Inhale again. Hold it. Let that O_2 feed your brain. Do it again. And again. Pack. Hang on for a few. Swallow the pills dry. The movie sucks, but the pills work. i'm sinking fast. i won't notice the tanned woman with gold bracelets sitting next to me who's about my mom's age. i won't hear the loud lady behind me condemning everyone i loved, everyone i lost. When i close my eyes, i won't see Mom twirling in her pink sundress for Dad. i won't smell her gardenia perfume. i won't watch Dad smoothly catching her arm and herding her out of the cabin. i won't hear him crack open another crab claw.

i won't remember Mom screaming my name.

MICHAEL'S DIVE LOG—VOLUME #8

DIVE BUDDY: Gram

DATE: 9/15   DIVE #: freezing

LOCATION: Teacup, WA (Tekoa, but Mom always called it that)

DIVE SITE: Gram's

WEATHER CONDITION: freezing   WATER CONDITION: freezing

DEPTH: freezing   VISIBILITY: freezing

WATER TEMP.: freezing   BOTTOM TIME: freezing

COMMENTS:

i can't get warm. Too cold here for Arizona blood. Maybe i should go home to Phoenix—wander around that great big house by myself. Right. It creeps me out staying here, sleeping in Dad's bed from his glory high school days, but our house full of their socks and shoes and underwear—no way. Gram's place is my only option.

Stan, the dive club's treasurer, met the plane in Miami and claimed all the bodies. Guess lawyers are good for something. He took Mom, too. Handed me a one-way ticket to Spokane and a duffel full of my stuff from our condo on Duck Key, thumped me on the back, and said, "Be strong, kid."

Gram met my plane, her face wet and crumpled. Since i got to her sugar-cube house in Teacup, Washington, all i've done is eat blue pills and lie in Dad's old room with that quilt Gram made from pieces of his worn-out jeans pulled over my head. At night, when the pills wear off, i stare at the glowing dial of a clock radio shaped like a football until the nightmares start. i'm on deck thinking how cool it is. Rain like i've never seen. Debris pounding like hail. Then Isadore arrives packing a thirty-foot surge. Mom screams, "Michael, get down here. Michael."

i wake when the wave takes me, shaking, nauseous, covered in sweat, tangled in the pants quilt. i pop more pills, grit my teeth, and wait. She should have made it. i did. i kept telling the helicopter guys to look for a pink sundress, but nobody listened to me. They left her out there too long. So she screams until the pills kick back in.

There's a spidery-thin crack in the wall Dad's old bed is shoved up against. It disappears behind a faded Pink Floyd poster but re-emerges and keeps snaking down the wall until it vanishes behind the bed—right where my pillow is. i take down the poster so my eyes can trace the lines of that crack while the fog settles back down around my ears.

Stan phoned. Was it yesterday? No, two days ago. Gram got me out of bed for the call.

"We all got together Sunday for a memorial dive."

All?

"We dove the Thunderbolt and then went over to the barge."

"Cool." i feel cheated. The T-bolt's the first deep wreck i ever dove. Dad took me.

"Be strong, man."

"Sure." They had no right to remember my parents without me. i'm the one who was there—on that boat. In that storm.

"Are you still there, Michael?" Stan's voice scrapes my senses.

Where else would i be, Stan?

"I need to talk legal stuff with your grandmother."

i hand off the phone. Like Gram can deal with anything more than fixing me endless plates of French toast. Legal stuff. He'll freak her for sure.

Stan must have said something about getting me into school. Gram started in on me as soon as she was off the phone. i can't blame her. She's got to be tired of watching me pick at her thick, gooey, cinnamoned French toast, tired of hearing me retching it into her pink toilet bowl whenever i choke a plate down. That stuff used to be my all-time favorite food. When i was a kid and we visited Teacup, she could get me to do any-thing for a plate of it. Even go down the hill to church with her on Sundays and let the minister pinch my cheek and mess up my hair. Must kill her to hear me vomit it away.

Food and my stomach don't remember how to get along. Getting along with Gram. That's another challenge. i don't know how much longer i can take her tear-stained face hovering over me all day, her shaking finger touching my cheek like she needs to check if i'm real. Maybe she thinks i'm Dad. She stares at me and then the eyes overflow and she disappears into her bedroom. She keeps wanting to change my bandage—like i can't do it myself. Her house smells nasty now. Not that candy scent i remember from visits before she started coming to the condo with us.

School? Sounds even worse.

chapter 3
EVERYBODY'S TALKING

LEESIE HUNT / CHATSPOT LOG / 09/18 7:52 P.M.

Leesie327 says: We're supposed to get a new guy. Senior.

Kimbo69 says: Too bad for him.

Leesie327 says: So cruel.

Kimbo69 says: You're always complaining about how Hicksville it is. Why would you wish that on anyone for their senior year?

Leesie327 says: It's not a big Spokane high school, but the teachers are pretty good.

Kimbo69 says: All six of them.

Leesie327 says: Hey, Mrs. D got me into that poetry workshop where we met.

Kimbo69 says: That MY school HOSTED.

Leesie327 says: Well, they're good teachers. Don't forget my 33.

Kimbo69 says: If you throw your ACT score in my face again, I'm going to puke.

Leesie327 says: Okay, Miss 32. I won't mention it.

Kimbo69 says: I dare you to take the SAT.

Leesie327 says: No way. BYU doesn't want it. You rule that thing.

Kimbo69 says: Coward . . . so this new guy . . . scale of Donne to Byron . . . how hot is he?

Leesie327 says: You're saying Donne's the bottom? Don't dis my boy, Donne.

Kimbo69 says: The man was a preacher.

Leesie327 says: Doesn't mean he wasn't hot.

Kimbo69 says: Not Byron hot.

Leesie327 says: "No man is an island." That's hot. Bet you can't quote a line of Byron.

Kimbo69 says: Just a sec . . .

Leesie327 says: Cheater.

Kimbo69 says: I've got him on my wall . . .

Leesie327 says: Give it up.

Kimbo69 says: Okay, you score . . . back to the new guy . . . report.

Leesie327 says: Haven't seen him yet. He's staying at his grandmother's. Rumor is he's too wasted to come to school.

Kimbo69 says: Druggie . . . what a drag.

Leesie327 says: Not that kind of wasted. His parents were eaten by sharks.

Kimbo69 says: Sharks? Seriously?

Leesie327 says: That's what DeeDee's spreading around. Don't think it's true. Something awful happened. All I know is they both just died.

Kimbo69 says: Intriguing . . . my poet senses are tingling.

Leesie327 says: Remind me not to tell you about any personal tragedies.

Kimbo69 says: What about your grandma poem? See . . . material is material . . . get him to spill his guts on your shoulder.

Leesie327 says: I haven't even met him.

Kimbo69 says: If he's got Byron shoulders . . . go for it.

Leesie327 says: What would I do with Byron shoulders?

Kimbo69 says: You sad, sad, girl . . . a new guy begging for comfort drops in your lap, and you don't know what to do with him . . . what a waste.

Leesie327 says: He's not exactly in my lap.

Kimbo69 says: The point is to get him there.

Leesie327 says: Not my point. You know I don't go out with guys who aren't Mormons.

Kimbo69 says: Then don't go out . . . just get it on . . . you can't stay Virgin Mary forever.

Leesie327 says: I plan on doing it lots after I'm married.

Kimbo69 says: You'll have to do it twice a day to catch up.

Leesie327 says: Is it a race?

Kimbo69 says: Of course.

Leesie327 says: I'm going to stay married forever, so I'll win easy.

Kimbo69 says: You still writing your mission boy?

Leesie327 says: He's not mine. Jaron's got six old girlfriends writing him. I'm just a friend.

Kimbo69 says: Check out the new guy then.

Leesie327 says: DeeDee will take care of that. She always does.

Kimbo69 says: Poor new guy.

Leesie327 says: Small town. What can I say?

Kimbo69 says: But you're out of there soon.

Leesie327 says: Eleven months, one week, three days until blastoff.

Kimbo69 says: Hear anything about your scholarship?

Leesie327 says: Too soon. The essay questions aren't even online yet.

Kimbo69 says: But you'll get it. A 33 ACT . . . you can go anywhere . . . you should try Stanford or Harvard or something big like that.

Leesie327 says: BYU IS BIG! HUGE. GIGANTIC. You know how many thousands of kids don't get to go there? I've dreamed of this my whole life. I don't even mind not having a guy like your Mark because I've got BYU to sigh over.

Kimbo69 says: You wouldn't say that if you had a real boyfriend.

Leesie327 says: How can you not get it? Try to imagine what this means to me: roommates who don't drink or sleep around, professors who not only respect but embrace my beliefs, and thousands and thousands of the hottest guys on the planet who all live by the same rules I do.

Kimbo69 says: Ugh . . . sounds like torture . . . cruel, maniacal torture . . . I'd die for sure.

Leesie327 says: BUT I WILL BE IN HEAVEN. I had a nightmare last night that they wouldn't let me in. I had to go to WSU. I woke up shaking.

Kimbo69 says: Don't dis WSU . . . that's my third choice . . . Mark's second. Hey . . . how's your mom dealing? Is she any better these days?

Leesie327 says: I found her yesterday afternoon with a half-peeled potato in her hand, tear tracks on her face, and the sink flooding over. Taking care of Grandma was hard, but it's way worse without her. I feel it, too.

Kimbo69 says: That's so sad . . . what'd you do?

Leesie327 says: I hugged her, and we cried together.

Kimbo69 says: I thought you didn't cry.

Leesie327 says: That's my rule for school.

Kimbo69 says: Get your grief in the poem about your grand-ma . . . that's what it's missing.

Leesie327 says: You're right. I'll try that.

Kimbo69 says: Crap . . . look at the time . . . I gotta shave my legs . . . sleepover tonight.

Leesie327 says: Have fun.

Kimbo69 says: We'll have a lot more than fun . . . my mom's out on a date, so we can really go for it . . . oops . . . sorry, PG girl . . . are your cheeks burning?

Leesie327 says: After wading through make-out central every day at school, it takes a lot more than that to make these cheeks burn.

Kimbo69 says: Well, it is Friday night . . . what have you got going?

Leesie327 says: Physics.

Kimbo69 says: Trust me, hon . . . biology's way better.

LEESIE'S MOST PRIVATE CHAPBOOK

POEM #26, BIOLOGY

Nuclear equations fall
prey to my calculations,
speed of light fairy-tale power:
E equals MC squared absorbs
whispers of peptides joining in the dark.
I reign over forces that always react equally.
Don't face me with biology:

the pulse, the hum, the empty
nameless yearning for a shoulder, a hand,
a whisper that knows my name alone,
the mystery of being someone to someone,
feeling whole instead of half,
loved—not harassed—far away
from wheat-covered hills
on an endless, rhythmic roll,
our cathedral barn Mom's
grandfather built, the squeal
of hogs, the sizzle
of bacon, white flowers
that scent the night air
swirling through my window,
ruffling the faded pink curtains
that frame my white chamber,
my princess bed,
my pillowed head
that prays for recess from
biology.

chapter 4

NEW KID

MICHAEL'S DIVE LOG—VOLUME #8

Dive Buddy: SOLO	
Date: 9/21	~~Dive #:~~
Location: Teacup	Dive Site: stupid school
Weather Condition: sunny	Water Condition: none
Depth: none	Visibility: none
Water Temp.: none	Bottom Time: 397 minutes

COMMENTS:

The football alarm rings. i'm still awake. Out of pills. Way wired without those little friends. i know every twist and turn of the crack in Dad's wall. i should fix it. Mom hated cracks. i always helped patch our textured walls down in Phoenix. i'm a master at Spackle—even smooth flat walls like Gram has. Some fresh paint and you'd never know. It's just a stupid crack.

i reach out and run my finger along the jagged line. Press my hand to the wall and remind myself to breathe.

"School today." Gram tries to sound cheerful, but she doesn't quite carry it off.

i actually remember how to shower, get dressed. Shaving

is beyond me. i don't seem to have a razor anyway. Did Gram pitch it? Does she think i'll cut myself? i study the grim face looking back from the mirror. The scruff look goes great with the dark circles under my eyes. My hair is gross. Didn't i see my baseball cap in the duffel bag?

"Your foot all right?" Gram calls through the bathroom door.

"No big deal." The arch is still tender, but i'm down to two crisscrossed regular Band-Aids. i open the door. "i need some more pills, though. Can you call the doctor?"

"I'll get right on it." Gram holds out an old pair of sneakers i left at her house when i was fourteen. They almost fit.

"I can drive you." She reaches for her keys that dangle on a key chain hosted by a crocheted pink bunny.

The school's three blocks away. i shake my head. "i can manage."

i do, too. i manage to walk up the hill without limping, push through the double front doors into an open space with a stage on one wall and cafeteria-style serving windows along the other. i manage to ignore the kids sprawled on the stage wearing jeans and T-shirts, even the chick making out with her boyfriend. She's got Carolina's eyes and forehead, the same thick, black hair.

i manage not to see the picture of my dad bulked up with football pads, his helmet under one arm and a cheerleader under the other, hanging in the office. i manage to send the principal-by-day-football-coach-by-night a blank stare when he asks me if i want to practice with the team after school. i manage to slump in a desk with my head down on my arms like a grade school kid in trouble when the English teacher hands me a stack of books on grieving. i manage it all until physics.

Somebody who reeks of smoke sits next to me, bumps my arm. "Hey."

i'd grabbed a seat in the back and assumed my position. i lift my head. Smoke Chick is leaning over so i get the full effect of her skimpy black tank and push-up bra. Cs at least. Quite a show.

"I'm DeeDee. You must be Mike."

"It's Michael." Dad was Mike. i bury my head in my arms again. Not even a twinge from that firm flesh waving in my face.

"Hello-oh." She slides a physics text under my arms. "Anybody home?"

i look up, and she's squatting down beside my desk, her cleavage in perfect position again. She has the sleazy look down. Tan from a bottle. Shagged-out hair dyed too blond. Heavy eye makeup. Red lips and nails. Not pretty enough to be popular but packed sexy tight in clothes that barely cover her assets. i can't eat. Fine. i don't sleep. So what. But a flesh parade like DeeDee is putting on should trigger animal instinct firing on automatic. She's easily good enough for that.

i sit there, numb, wondering what she'd look like lying on a dock with a white sheet pulled over her face. Am i inventing new stages of grief or did the shrink in Belize leave this one out?

The seven other students in the room stare.

"We're on page fifty-two."

i sit straight, push my chair back, fold my arms across my chest, and pull my cap down over my face.

DeeDee perches on the edge of my desk, smack in front of me. "I heard about your parents. If you need someone to, um"—she leans over and drops her voice to a stage whisper everyone can still hear—"talk or—something—I'm always around."

"Get away from me," i snarl at her. Rude, sure. But she is scaring me way more than she knows. i mean, am i broken? i don't want to toss the football around with these hicks or write a research paper on grieving, but you'd think a good night with an easy girl would be just what i do need to start plugging the crater my guts have become. The thought of letting DeeDee comfort me makes me nauseous. i should call Carolina. Her voice always used to do it. Crap. What if it doesn't? i bet the pills would help.

i look away from DeeDee pouting and catch the only other chick in the class staring at me. She looks down fast. Embarrassed red stains her farm girl cream cheeks. At least she has the decency to hide behind her physics book. DeeDee retreats into the desk beside mine. i can still smell her gaudy perfume.

i make it through the class without hurling, then bolt down to Gram's for lunch. "What did the doctor say?" i hope he's called in a prescription. i want a gleaming bottle sitting on Gram's melamine kitchen table.

"I'll make the call after my nap."

Crap.

i hide out in the guys' john while DeeDee hunts for me before afternoon classes start. The john is a real treat. Designer haven. Two urinals. One stall. The place smells like decades of guys missed the mark. Layers of obscene graffiti cover the walls. DeeDee's name takes up some major space. While i'm in there, a blond guy comes in, scribbles something on the wall over the urinal next to me, and leaves. i examine it. Somebody actually painted out a fresh "page" on the wall. *Best Butt* heads the white space. Five girls' names follow. DeeDee tops the list, but the chick who has the most tally marks by far is named Leesie. Guys signed their names all around hers. i'm pretty sure what that must mean.

Looks like DeeDee has some competition for Queen of the Skanks.

chapter 5

DROOL

LEESIE HUNT / CHATSPOT LOG / 09/21 10:39 P.M.

Leesie327 says: The new guy came to school today. Michael Walden.

Kimbo69 says: And he's totally ripped and you got off staring at him all day.

Leesie327 says: I did get a good look at him in physics.

Kimbo69 says: And...

Leesie327 says: He makes me ache he's so sad.

Kimbo69 says: But is he worth aching for?

Leesie327 says: His eyelashes are.

Kimbo69 says: Spill it. Every drop.

Leesie327 says: He hid under a black baseball cap with some kind of exotic fish thing embroidered on the front most of the day.

Kimbo69 says: What did it say?

Leesie327 says: I didn't get that close. He's kind of unnerving. We don't get guys like him in Tekoa—ever. He's good-looking, but not in that pink cheeks pretty boy way Troy is. He got this guy, almost man vibe going. And then there's the eyelashes. Long. Black against his tan.

Kimbo69 says: Tan? Nice. Go on.

Leesie327 says: He huddled in an expensive-looking windbreaker with the same fish as the hat. Kept it on all day.

Kimbo69 says: So you didn't get to see if he's ripped?

Leesie327 says: He doesn't carry himself like a muscled-up guy. He's tall. Six foot easy. I'd call him lanky.

Kimbo69 says: Lanky? What kind of a word is that? You've spent way too long studying vocab.

Leesie327 says: I'm a poet! And it fits. He's got long fingers, and the bones in his wrist jut out.

Kimbo69 says: Oh, wow. I'm so glad you noticed his wrist.

Leesie327 says: Everyone here pales—literally.

Kimbo69 says: Did you check his teeth?

Leesie327 says: He's not a horse. This is a person. A beautiful, hurting person.

Kimbo69 says: Good butt?

Leesie327 says: Kim, please. But yeah. New jeans. Too tight.

Kimbo69 says: Even nicer.

Leesie327 says: His legs look really powerful.

Kimbo69 says: Miss Prissypants examined his thighs?

Leesie327 says: Stop it . . . I didn't look at his thighs.

Kimbo69 says: Don't lie to me . . . you can't even do it online.

Leesie327 says: Great. Now that's all I can think about. I got to go wash that image from my brain.

Kimbo69 says: Not so fast . . . how are you going to make your play for him?

Leesie327 says: Hello, I don't think he's a Mormon. Besides, he's not looking, especially at me. With DeeDee doing her act, I don't have a chance. She makes me so sick. She kept bugging him all day. I wish there was something I could do for him.

Kimbo69 says: I've got it...go for the friend angle...your church can't say anything about that...you could scrape him off the side of the road like that guy in the Bible.

Leesie327 says: The Good Samaritan?

Kimbo69 says: That's him . . . aren't you always doing good deeds?

Leesie327 says: Service projects?

Kimbo69 says: He could be your new project.

Leesie327 says: This is a person we're talking about—real feelings here, real pain.

Kimbo69 says: Better than leaving him for DeeDee . . . she had strangely prophetic parents.

Leesie327 says: Double Ds? Her real name is Diane. But she was DD by seventh grade. Some girls get all the breaks.

Kimbo69 says: You can't really think that...I thought she was ... let's say, well used by all.

Leesie327 says: Yeah. She is. I should feel sorry for her, but I'm just not righteous enough for that.

Kimbo69 says: Leesie's human . . . at last I have proof. Does anybody know what really happened to this Michael guy's parents?

Leesie327 says: Nope. I mean who would have the cheek to go up to poor old Mrs. Walden and ask her for a play-by-play?

Kimbo69 says: I want to know the scoop...snoop around.

Leesie327 says: Like I should Google the guy?

Kimbo69 says: Or use your charm.

Leesie327 says: Let's see. I got a bunch of hits for his dad. Same name. Looks like the guy was Mr. Real Estate.

Kimbo69 says: Look for an obit.

Leesie327 says: There's like twenty thousand hits. Maybe Michael's on ChatSpot.

Kimbo69 says: Watch him . . . he's got to drop a few clues here and there . . . and we'll have him.

Leesie327 says: You sound like we're tracking a murderer.

Kimbo69 says: Maybe he is . . . both parents mysteriously dead.

Leesie327 says: You're psycho. Have a little respect.

Kimbo69 says: Sorry.

Leesie327 says: I Googled him. That's creepy, too.

Kimbo69 says: He sounds mesmerizing. Should I come for a visit?

Leesie327 says: Down, girl. You've got your man.

Kimbo69 says: I thought you weren't interested.

Leesie327 says: I just feel sorry for him.

Kimbo69 says: Come off it . . . you're seething jealous that DeeDee came on to him because you don't have it bad for him? Please.

Leesie327 says: I can't have it bad for him.

Kimbo69 says: How can you help it? Falling for a guy isn't something you can control.

Leesie327 says: You think so?

Kimbo69 says: Close your eyes and leap . . . at least talk to the guy.

Leesie327 says: I don't know if I can. Even broken and bruised, he's—breathtaking.

chapter 6

GHOST SCENE

MICHAEL'S DIVE LOG—VOLUME #8

DIVE BUDDY: solo

DATE: 10/1

LOCATION: Teacup	DIVE SITE: Gram's
WEATHER CONDITION: sunny, cold	WATER CONDITION: rained once
DEPTH: NA	VISIBILITY: NA
WATER TEMP.: NA	BOTTOM TIME: 14,400 minutes

COMMENTS:

The school's English teacher/librarian/volleyball coach, Mrs. D, is making us read *Hamlet* out loud. Kiss of death boring. She feels compelled to explain what's going on after every stupid line. Everyone would much rather just watch the movie—even that four-hour marathon one—except the staring chick from physics. Staring Chick is way into it. She reads that archaic gibberish out like the words mean something. Mrs. D gets her to play Hamlet every day. At least the woman doesn't torture us by making one of the jocks read it. Or call on me.

After the scene with the ghost, poor Mrs. D tries to provoke the class into a discussion. "Is the ghost good or bad?"

Nobody says anything.

"Should Hamlet obey it?"

Staring Chick puts up her hand. She's wearing her hair down long today. Looks lighter, more sun-streaked, than when she hides it in a ponytail. The teacher nods for her to begin.

"I think Shakespeare messed up with that ghost."

Mrs. D grins at her. "Do you think the Bard messes up often?"

"No. Look at Romeo and Juliet. He totally tapped into the innate desire everyone has for a passion so consuming you'd rather die than live without your beloved."

DeeDee snorts to a football jock drooling next to her. "Like she knows anything about passion."

Staring Chick's cheeks go red like when i catch her staring at me every freaking day. "The ghost just isn't convincing. Spirits aren't like that. They are bright and beautiful and emanate goodness."

DeeDee's jock, i think his name's Troy, snorts. "You been holding séances?"

Mrs. D ignores him, focuses on Staring Chick. "So Hamlet is right to doubt?"

"I guess so." She purses her lips. Thinking? Pouting? I don't know. She could be getting ready to kiss the teacher. Or spit at that jock. She's got nice lips. Full enough. I don't like skinny lips. If you're into someone, it probably doesn't matter if her lips don't look pink and wet like Staring Chick's, but it helps.

Mrs. D is droning. "So you are saying Hamlet is right to doubt and wrong to act? Is he wrong to avenge his father?"

"It just leads to a pile of dead bodies." The sun from the classroom window makes Staring Chick's hair glow.

DeeDee frowns. "Hey, don't ruin the ending."

Mrs. D walks over to Staring Chick and stands right in front of her desk. "But isn't this a tragedy?"

"Okay." Staring Chick shakes her hair back and gives the teacher a friendly grin. Makes her pretty—that smile. "The ghost serves a dramatic purpose, but—"

The teacher raises her eyebrows, takes a step back to include the rest of the class.

Staring Chick continues. "Hamlet and Ophelia were in love." Her eyes look blue today. "Maybe as much as Romeo and Juliet."

"Cool, do they get it on?" Troy flips ahead in the text searching for a skin scene.

Staring Chick turns away from him like he's garbage on the roadside. "The ghost ruined that. They didn't get to marry and have children." Her voice is intense. "Hamlet could have been a great king."

"Tragic?" Mrs. D delivers the winning blow.

Staring Chick drops her head. Her hair curtains her face so i can't see if it's even pinker now.

Mrs. D moves in for the kill. "So Shakespeare didn't mess up?"

DeeDee and Troy smirk. Everyone else is zoned.

Mrs. D raps on a desk for attention. "Anybody else want to weigh in?"

DeeDee raises her hand. "I loved a guy like that for two whole weeks. It is pretty cool. Especially the passion."

"Ouch, you're slaying me, Dee." Troy winks, and she licks her lips like she wants him for lunch.

Mrs. D's losing the class. That's what she gets for turning

on Staring Chick. They're usually allies. Remind me not to dis the Bard around her.

"Let's get back to *Hamlet*." She dumbs it down. "Ghost: good or bad?"

Troy doesn't bother to put up his hand. "I think the ghost was good. He wanted justice. That's good. Hamlet should do what he says. Anything else is wimping out. Getting even. That's what it's all about."

Staring Chick's head goes up. Her mouth is set in a firm line. "Regardless of the consequences?"

"Who cares about consequences?" DeeDee jiggles for Troy.

"Michael." The teacher catches me sitting up, listening. "Did you want to add something?"

i shake my head and put it back down on the desk trying not to think about consequences and what they've done to me lately. To my parents, my dive buds, even that waitress i barely knew. That night at the crab fest, her hands shook as she served us platters of steaming crab. She didn't look hot with her eyes red and puffy, mascara leaking down her face. When she left our table, Dive Dog leaned in and whispered, "I heard her in the hall crying to the captain. She wanted to get off the boat."

"Her kids are in Belize City at her mom's. She's scared for them." i grabbed a big crab claw. "Give her a break."

Dad gave me a sympathetic look, had spied me chatting her up earlier.

"Poor thing." Mom watched the girl spill beer at the next table.

Dad and i descended into the pile of steaming legs, cracking the claws, ripping the joints, breaking the long sections in two, sliding fat chunks from the shell, swirling the sweet meat in butter. Inhaling the whole platter. We both went for the last leg. With a quick jerk, i tore it out of his hands. He shook his head and smiled at Mom. "When are you going to teach this boy respect?"

i laughed—we all did. i squirted Mom when i broke the leg open. She frowned, wiped her face, leaned forward. "Hold still." She reached to wipe the butter dripping down my chin.

i pulled back, wiped it with my own napkin, still steaming over her new free-dive rules.

The *Festiva* jerked against her moorings, and the waitress stumbled, spilling a platter of crab legs. The captain scowled at her while she scooped them back on the platter and hurried out of the salon to get a fresh tray. i wondered if he'd let her call home. She looked so scared. He should have let her leave. i should have said something. Told the jerk off. But we had a platter of crab to deal with, and everything would be fine, right?

Wrong.

She's dead now. So is Mom, Dad, Dive Dog. Everybody in that dining salon except me and the stupid, imbecile captain, who should have let her go, is dead.

That's consequences for you. Party on, friends. You're invincible.

But now you're dead.

chapter 7

TRIPPING

MICHAEL'S DIVE LOG—VOLUME #8

DIVE BUDDY: **Staring Chick**

DATE: **10/2**	DIVE #: **1 with her**
LOCATION: **Washington**	DIVE SITE: **Grand Coulee Dam**
WEATHER CONDITION: **sunny**	WATER CONDITION: **cascading**
DEPTH: **wish I knew**	VISIBILITY: **looks murky**
WATER TEMP.: **probably 50°F, less**	BOTTOM TIME: **24 minutes**

COMMENTS:

Stuck on a stupid field trip. i wanted to ditch it, but i was dumb and slept last night. i woke up at 2 a.m., covered in a layer of cold sweat, twisted in the pants quilt, shaking from a nightmare. Mom was in it, sinking, breathing in water, screaming my name as she drowned. That didn't happen. It couldn't. There was nothing i could do.

i had to get away from that bed, Dad's old room, Gram, that hideous crack in the wall, the *why*s and *what*s that ricochet in my head. Two hours on a school bus that smells of baked dust watching DeeDee make out with half the football team brings me to Grand Coulee Dam.

The pound of falling water, the sweet liquid scent pours through me as soon as i get off the bus. i didn't think about hearing it, seeing it, smelling it again. i probably wouldn't have come.

The dam itself is worth seeing. Massive. The old guy who guides our tour says his father helped build it.

"We were starving to death down in a California Hooverville. I can remember picking fruit for ten cents a day. Ten lousy cents. We come up here. Dad got a job pouring. Big man, my father. Strong as an ox. Had to be. Still, it took him and a couple of others to tip those buckets. They come out swinging on a gondola. Timing had to be just right or you'd have a whale of a time. My dad was the best."

Big man. The best. Can't this guy talk about something else? Not dads. Especially big ones. Best ones. Dead ones.

Stan called again last night. Recovery divers got Dad's body out of the wreck. i'm supposed to be relieved, but why? What are we going to do with a toxic, waterlogged body? Seemed to make a difference to Gram. i didn't get a chance to talk to Stan about a coffin and bringing the body back before she took the phone. She shut herself in her room and talked a long time.

"This dam saved our lives." The wiry old man reels off some facts about its size, something about three times bigger than the Great Pyramid.

Why didn't someone, something save our lives? Why didn't we just get off that stupid boat and find someplace like this? Isadore's surge was just thirty feet high. Grand Coulee Dam is a thousand feet high, a mile across the river, concrete, reinforced with steel. A safe place to be in a storm.

The jerk teacher, Taylor, makes us watch *A Century of Water for the West* in the visitors' center. Then we eat lunch in a grassy picnic area that overlooks the dam. Benches, seagulls, bored kids sprawling all over the place. What a treat.

The river cascades down the dam's concrete face, churning into white foam at the bottom. i don't freak. Crap. Maybe i'm as numb to water as i was to DeeDee. No. There it is. i feel the pull. The rushing wet of it. i need to get closer.

i walk to the edge of the overlook where seagulls squawk on black stone lumps and scan, searching for a way down. i break off a chunk of sandwich and chuck it. Gram packed me tuna. Mom would faint. The birds scream and fight, flapping around the spot where it lands. A couple of greedy gulls about take my hand off vying for more. i throw the whole smelly thing at them.

"Aren't you hungry?" intrudes from behind me.

i turn around. Staring Chick is sitting cross-legged on a bench a few feet behind me with a vintage suede jacket draped on her shoulders. She's never actually said anything to me before. At school she just rants in class and sits on the stage reading or scribbling in a notebook. Her hair is long again today.

"i don't eat tuna." i turn back to face the river.

Staring Chick joins me, dumps potato chip crumbs on the rocks for the gulls to fight over. "I boycott my mom's tuna casserole every week." She pulls a Save the Dolphins necklace from under her T-shirt and jingles it—half smiles.

i start to tell her to get lost and, by the way, quit staring at me all the time, but she smells nice. Tropical hair stuff. Baby powder. Old suede leather. Freaks me that i can stand here with the scent of water all around me for the first time since Belize and breathe in this girl. Maybe i'm not completely wrecked.

She shakes her hair back, nervous, releasing more intoxicating tropical vapor and a full-blown smile that really does make her beautiful.

"Do you think anybody dives down there?" i nod toward the river far below.

"You mean right off this cliff? That'd be crazy."

"Scuba." i know this is just a river. Lousy conditions. Currents. No vis. But it's wetter than a wheat field.

i can tell she's reading the back of my jacket—*Eagle Ray Dive Club, Marathon, FL.* Everyone knows i came from Phoenix. She'll want to know why my jacket says *Florida.* As if you can dive in Phoenix.

Up close, her eyes have a blue ring around the iris that turns green in the middle. Those eyes drift from my face to the river and back.

My gut muscles tense.

She bites her lower lip and draws her eyebrows together. "Wouldn't you get sucked into the hydroelectric turbines? Didn't you watch the film?"

My stomach relaxes. "The current probably goes downstream."

"Good thing." She laughs at herself. "Those turbines looked pretty mean."

i don't answer. The water rolling by beneath us has claimed me again. i want to feel it on my skin, sink under it, and swim to a coral head. i need to know if it will welcome me or churn me up and spit me out. Again.

"Washington's crazy." Leesie folds up her lunch bag and jams it in her pocket. "We make a shrine out of that ugly concrete ruining this mythical river."

i give her a confused look. "What?"

"Sad, isn't it? The Columbia was this wild raging thing—a god to the Native Americans. Look what we've done to it." She nods toward the wall of concrete that rises above the water. Her face is serious again like in class. "There used to be cool falls just north of here. Not Niagara—but the Native Americans who live over there"—she points at the pines across the river—"held a massive jamboree at them every year when the salmon ran. Now it's buried under Lake Roosevelt. The Salmon People held one last festival before the reservoir wiped out their villages and the sacred fishing grounds. They called it the Ceremony of Tears. Poetic, huh? Can you imagine it? Their lives were washed clean away because of some idiot's idea of progress."

Washed clean away? i can relate.

"And then it got worse. Get this. You're stuck on that reservation, smashed together with a bunch of other tribes, but it's okay because you've still got the salmon. You've always lived off the salmon. You worship them. Then every single fish that tries to get back home to spawn dies. No locks. Seventy-five species extinct. They say it only took four years. Can you imagine all those dead fish? Pretty gross."

"That wasn't in the film."

The smile is bigger this time. "Makes the whole dolphin/ tuna boat thing look small, doesn't it?"

"Unless you know dolphins."

That shuts her up. Maybe she'll leave. No.

"Hey, I'm being rude. I'm Aleesa, from physics and English." And all the rest of my classes. "Friends call me Leesie."

Whoa. "*The* Leesie? From the wall in the guys' john?" i take a step back so i can evaluate her award-winning feature. "This is what the fuss is all about?"

She whirls around, hiding the asset in question. "That's not fair." She blushes pinker than the stuff she has on her cheeks.

"You're above the urinal i always use. It says—"

"I have a brother." The pink heats to deep red. "I know what it says."

i never would have guessed Staring Chick is Leesie, Queen of the Urinals. She's too farm fresh. Tight enough jeans stretched across her nice butt. Incredible hair. Not too much crap on her eyes. Nothing much under that jacket, though. Not the type to inspire graffiti.

"So what's with all the names and checkmarks?" It can't be what i thought. Not this girl.

"I can't believe you're asking me this."

Neither can i, but i want to know before i tell her to get lost.

"They pinch me, okay?" She studies the rocks.

i glance over where DeeDee and her friends loll on the grass. Since the bus, Troy and his drones ignored her. "You even beat out DeeDee."

"I'm not like that." Leesie pushes a loose wisp of hair away from her face, tucks it behind her ear. Even her neck glows scarlet.

"Obviously." i take one last deep breath, hold her tropical-fruit-and-leather elixir in my head, and get ready to shamble away.

"You know"—Leesie looks up—"you could use another urinal."

i exhale. "There's only two. The other one's DeeDee's." i shake my head. "Way more than i want to know there."

That gets her to smile again. i decide not to shamble yet. This is my spot, isn't it? My attention drifts back to the river.

i close my eyes and listen to the falling water. "i like the sound of this. Haven't heard anything wet since—" Belize. Isadore. My mom screaming. My dad trapped in the dining room, drowning with everyone else. Me helpless to do anything but save my own butt.

She shifts closer to me, softens her tone. "Since what?"

My eyes drift open. i can't go there. Not after bathroom graffiti.

She senses my tension, takes a step back. The look on her face makes me hurt. "i'm sorry," she whispers. She barely says it—i've heard it a thousand times—but the breath of her words feel fresh and soothing as a cool compress held to my fore-head.

Then the jerk teacher calls us back inside the visitors' center for another film.

Leesie turns to leave, stirring up her enticing hair, and walks off. i stare at her famous backside and decide it *is* worth the fuss. i have a crazy urge to creep after her, sneak into the theater, find a place behind her, and bury myself in that hair. It smells tropical, but not coconut. Coconut would kill me right now. i want a strand to take home. i could glue it on my wall next to the crack. i search the ground. Maybe she sheds.

i glance up, and the place is deserted. The thunder of wa-ter rolling off the dam overwhelms the scent she left behind. Could i go back there—in it, under it? Isadore dragged me down again last night. i hate her. What happened to the joy of coasting along a coral wall with a white-tipped reef shark, sur-prising schools of juvies hiding out in a swim through, fighting the currents to explore my favorite wreck? Is it lost forever? Stolen by a freaking hurricane.

chapter 8

GROPING

LEESIE'S MOST PRIVATE CHAPBOOK

POEM #27, BUS RIDE TEMPTATION

It gets mostly fringe and armpit—
Troy's hand as it snakes across the seat back
and slams into my chest,
searches, fumbles, finds—
sending the darers howling and me up the aisle, biting
back tears that signal another victory
for the dark side.

Laughter rolls forward, annihilating me,
as I crumple into Michael's
seat. He startles
awake, appraises with gray eyes
that turn silver in the afternoon rays.
His baseball cap tilts toward me—
You okay?

No big deal, I lie until the bus rolls to a stop
and the doors bang open.

I maintain glacial when Troy's leering face
blockades my escape and sprays,
Ooh, did I piss off the Mormon Ice Queen?
all over my vintage fringe.

I consider kneeing him hard,
but Michael, tall and solid, lanky
to the rescue, rises to steady my elbow.

Let her go.
Gonna make me?
Let her go.

I long to lean into his strength,
let him shelter me with the steel in his voice.
Kids push and holler from behind.

As I watch Troy swallowed in their midst,
I remember ninth grade, before the ice,
when his nasty hand dropped Hot Tamales into mine
and I strayed into spiced breath hot in my ear—
Lunch, downtown, lost in the bushes . . .
the words oozing down my neck,
making me as red as his candy-stained tongue.

Yes, I wanted to follow incredible blue eyes down the hill,
let that hand twine in mine, disappear into cinnamon lips—
But I had *Thou Shalt Not* ringing in my ears.
Thou Shalt Not be alone with a boy.
Thou Shalt Not date until you're sixteen.

Thou Shalt Not make out in the bushes
with Troy the boy toy Hot Tamale candy.
> Thou Shalt remember who you are and the promises you've
> made.
> Thou Shalt dream of your perfect prince,
> short hair and white pressed shirt,
> well-worn scriptures tucked under his arm,
> a scuffed CTR ring on his pinky,
> who will cup thy face in his hands,
> kiss thee softly,
> and adore thee for eternity.
> Thou shalt let the Spirit move through thee and say,
> *Gotta finish my algebra,*
> and walk away.

Hot Tamale temptation descended,
day after day, cruder and crueler,
until I stopped feeling *Yes,*
stopped perspiring, stopped blushing,
and all I could say or think or be was *No.*
Hard and cold and oh, so determined.

I polished my temple photo and planned my escape,
worked and saved and studied—
so close now to BYU's beacon
beaming from Provo.

But now,
here is an aching soul standing beside me,
brave and strong and noble—
and something sweet and warm and beautiful

makes me want to whisper a soft *yes* into his ear.
Where did he come from? Why is he here?
And what, Lord, am I supposed to do with this
temptation?

LEESIE HUNT / CHATSPOT LOG / 10/2 11:13 P.M.

Leesie327 says: Do you think it needs quotation marks?

Kimbo69 says: Leave it . . . best poem you've ever written . . . way better than all that Salmon People stuff you wrote last year for our workshop.

Leesie327 says: That's so depressing.

Kimbo69 says: Pain is what art is all about . . . I thought you were into the suffering scene.

Leesie327 says: I've had enough for a while.

Kimbo69 says: You okay?

Leesie327 says: It's still raw. The poem, I mean.

Kimbo69 says: Right . . . in the first stanza you need to change *searches* to *gropes*.

Leesie327 says: No way. I can't write that word.

Kimbo69 says: Well, you're going to have to write it or say it to somebody tomorrow when you report that jerk.

Leesie327 says: Report Troy? I'd be more likely to get away with flaying him alive.

Kimbo69 says: In the real world they call this harassment . . . at my school guys get busted big time for crap like this . . . you think the teacher saw?

Leesie327 says: Who knows.

Kimbo69 says: So Michael . . . finally . . .

Leesie327 says: Gosh, Kim, I got dizzy just sitting by him. He has these chocolate brown curls that stick out from under his baseball cap and tumble down the back of his neck. I really wanted to touch them ... It was so strange. I talked to him at the dam, though. Wasn't too stupid. Helped him for maybe a minute.

Kimbo69 says: Sounds more like he's scraping *you* off the side of the road ... better watch yourself ... even the noble ones will want to make you a real woman.

Leesie327 says: I've never had a guy defend me like that. I had to do something.

Kimbo69 says: Did you give him your number?

Leesie327 says: I'm saving my cell money for college, remember? I gave him my email ... told him I'm on ChatSpot.

Kimbo69 says: Did he give you his?

Leesie327 says: Nope.

Kimbo69 says: Too bad ... but now that you've, shall we say, broken the ice ...

Leesie327 says: Yeah. Maybe I can help him back. I kind of know what he's going through. You think it's weird, but my faith has a lot to offer someone who is grieving.

Kimbo69 says: You want to save his soul? Can you do that while you drool over his body?

Leesie327 says: Save his soul? Mormons convert. Evangelicals save. Well, the Lord does both, really, no matter who you are.

Kimbo69 says: Does He sanction the drooling?

Leesie327 says: My BYU interview is coming up. No drooling for me.

Kimbo69 says: You can't drool at BYU? I thought you were going there to drool.

Leesie327 says: I don't think you want a chastity lecture tonight. Part of my application is filled in by my branch president. He tells them if I'm worthy to go—morally clean.

Kimbo69 says: You mean a virgin?

Leesie327 says: Something like that. If he doesn't recommend me, I won't get in.

Kimbo69 says: How does he know?

Leesie327 says: He asks.

Kimbo69 says: So it's not that big a deal . . . you could lie.

Leesie327 says: Kind of impossible. Besides, if I sinned, I'd have to confess to him to repent.

Kimbo69 says: Repent? Jesus is supposed to save you from your sins, isn't he?

Leesie327 says: That depends on your definition of save.

Kimbo69 says: You're losing me fast . . . you really believe if you do it, you're damned . . . hanging in Hades . . . BBQ every night . . . pitchforks, horns, hot red cat suit?

Leesie327 says: It boils down to this: no hell. Everyone goes to heaven. But some heavens are better than others. If you promise Christ you'll keep the rules and then sin, you don't get to be in the same one as Him—unless you repent.

Kimbo69 says: That's not so bad.

Leesie327 says: Not be with the Savior? Are you kidding? It's failing.

Kimbo69 says: So you can do that repent thing.

Leesie327 says: Repentance requires deep, personal pain. No witch hunts or anything like that. Mostly between you and God. That's what makes it so hard.

Kimbo69 says: Why does it hurt?

Leesie327 says: Guilt, I guess. I go nuts if I keep an extra dime from the store . . . that kind of massive guilt for major sin would take divine intervention to get over. Crap, Kim. I just got a request.

Kimbo69 says: It's got to be him . . . get out your holy water.

Leesie327 says: What'll I say?

Kimbo69 says: Let me lurk . . . I'll help . . . I can always tell what a guy's after in about two minutes . . . you've got salvation at stake here.

Leesie327 says: Actually, exaltation, but sick—I can do this on my own. I'm much better online than in person.

LEESIE HUNT / CHATSPOT LOG / 10/2 11:39 P.M.

Leesie327 says: Is that Michael? Nice screen name.

liv2div says: works

Leesie327 says: I didn't say thanks on the bus.

liv2div says: that troy's a jerk

Leesie327 says: Creepiest creep. Wanna help strangle him? Drop him off the railway trestle?

liv2div says: you could get arrested talking like that online

Leesie327 says: Sorry. Not usually this sadistic.

liv2div says: and i thought you were a sweet country girl

Leesie327 says: Country girls sweet? Know anybody else who eats their pets?

liv2div says: now i won't sleep for sure

Leesie327 says: That's what happens when you take naps on the bus.

liv2div says: no, that's what happens when you lie awake every night staring at a crack in the wall, trying to figure out what it looks like and why you care

Leesie327 says: Doesn't sound fun.

liv2div says: just don't start in with the pity crap

Leesie327 says: Well, you were Mr. Cool today with Troy boy.

liv2div says: sometimes i think i'm mr. frozen

Leesie327 says: And I'm the Ice Queen.

liv2div says: no you're the butt queen

Leesie327 says: Low, really low.

liv2div says: actually yours is high that's why you won

Leesie327 says: Now I'm thinking maybe you're Mr. Creep.

liv2div says: sorry . . . are you okay? i thought phoenix was rough . . . this place is brutal.

Leesie327 says: I'm used to it. Not that, but some guy's always, you know.

liv2div says: the butt wall

Leesie327 says: Yeah. Hey, I don't usually do this, but—want to go for a drive with me tomorrow? We can drive up to the lake, maybe the sun will be out again and Mr. Frozen can thaw.

liv2div says: ice queen and thawing don't add up

Leesie327 says: Please. I owe you big time.

liv2div says: you don't owe me

Leesie327 says: It'll be nice. Peaceful. Windy Bay in October, yellow, gold, red. No annoying speedboats—just birds, trees, water. Maybe a sunset. Pity free guaranteed.

liv2div says: there's really a lake around here?

Leesie327 says: Big one. Better than hanging around here for the football game, isn't it?

liv2div says: i guess

Leesie327 says: You're Mr. Lukewarm already. Progressing.

liv2div says: hey what's defuddled?

Leesie327 says: Whoa. Where'd you get that?

liv2div says: back of the bag you gave me with your email

Leesie327 says: Kind of personal.

liv2div says: tell me what it means and you get it back

Leesie327 says: Deal. Pick you up about 3?

liv2div says: you know where i live?

Leesie327 says: Small town. Everybody knows.

LEESIE HUNT / CHATSPOT LOG / 10/3 12:16 A.M.

Leesie327 says: I'm going out with him. Well, not really—just a drive. I can't believe I asked him.

Kimbo69 says: Neither can I . . . you asked him out? What happened to all that poor me I can't like him because he's not a Mormon?

Leesie327 says: It just came out. I was amazing. Poetic. Inspired.

Kimbo69 says: What if he thinks you're into him?

Leesie327 says: It's just a drive to the lake. Friendly. The poor guy is so numb, I could be a post.

Kimbo69 says: Well, sorry to point this out, girlfriend . . . but you are kind of a post.

Leesie327 says: Hit me when I'm low.

Kimbo69 says: You sound anything but low . . . find out anything else about him?

Leesie327 says: I memorized the name of his scuba club on his jacket. I was just going to Google.

Kimbo69 says: Maybe you should wait and ask him.

Leesie327 says: This was your idea. Hey, his club has a site.

Kimbo69 says: Really?

Leesie327 says: Oh, wow.

Kimbo69 says: What is it?

Leesie327 says: Pages and pages of condolences. Oh my gosh, there he is. In his parents' obit. That's him. This is huge. Look at all these people who died. Divers, like him. They were all on some kind of scuba boat yacht thing. A hurricane hit them. Isadore— ever hear of that? Category four. That's pretty bad. The boat capsized. Everyone drowned but him. He's the only one left.

Kimbo69 says: How come he survived?

Leesie327 says: Doesn't say. No wonder he's so destroyed. And I'm flippantly joking about offing Troy. I've got the sickest feeling in the pit of my stomach. Stupid DeeDee and her sharks. What can I say to him?

Kimbo69 says: Nothing. If you bring it up, you're toast. Try to get him to talk, though. That's what my mom always does after she breaks up. Talks and talks and talks.

Leesie327 says: It's just this one drive. He'll probably never spend time with me after tomorrow. I just had to do something.

Kimbo69 says: A guy that hammered may want some comfort . . . if you know what I mean . . . better practice your self-defense.

Leesie327 says: He's not like that. I can tell.

Kimbo69 says: You got dizzy just sitting in the same seat with him when you should have been feeling crap because

that creep groped you . . . and now you're what
my boy Byron would call positively giddy . . . you
can't tell a thing.

Leesie327 says: *Each man's grief is my own.* My boy, Donne.

Kimbo69 says: Pack your can of mace. Kim 101.

chapter 9

MUCK

MICHAEL'S DIVE LOG—VOLUME #8

Dive Buddy: **Leesie, again**	
Date: **10/3**	Dive #: **2 with her**
Location: **Teacup**	Dive Site: **Leesie's lake**
Weather Condition: **got bad**	Water Condition: **flat calm**
Depth: **to my chest**	Visibility: **2 ft**
Water Temp.: **38°F**	Bottom Time: **117 minutes**

Comments:

i'm ready by 2:30, prowl through Gram's tiny house, check the clock—2:31. i ate today. Not a good idea. Hurling is a definite possibility. i stalk Gram's desk in the living room. The framed snapshots of me and my parents that litter the desk threaten to pounce. Puking in Gram's pink bathroom sounds better and better. There's some unopened mail—bills and crap. i shuffle through it looking for something interesting. Gram's junk mail is lame. Polident variety.

Something noisy pulls into the driveway. "That's her," Gram calls from the kitchen.

Great. i bolt into the bathroom. i look like i walked out

of a zombie flick. i turn on the water so Gram doesn't hear me puking.

She pounds on the door. "Michael, she's waiting."

Why am i doing this? Yesterday on the bus, i felt massively strong facing down Troy for this girl. i don't think that's what Stan meant with his pep talk, but it was a good change from massively destroyed. But whoa, do i want to spend time with her? It was easy online. No eyes. No faces. No feelings. i don't know. Maybe if she shows up in that jacket.

i turn my back on Gram's safe pink bathroom and follow her out the door.

Leesie jumps down from a white pickup. Loose hair, leather jacket. Good start.

"So what's *defuddled*? You promised." She's speeding her truck down a country highway, and i figure the awkward silence has gone on long enough. i take the crumpled lunch bag that she gave me with her e-mail written on it out of my pocket and hold it out to her. There's lists of words and short lines scribbled all over it.

"*Defuddled*? Opposite of *befuddled*." The corners of her mouth turn up a bit, but she doesn't look at me. "Isn't that obvious? I'm writing a poem—"

"Is there an assignment i missed?"

"No." Still eyes front.

"You write poems for fun?"

"I like words—trying to fit them to what I see and feel." Now the glance. "Weird, I know."

i stare out the window. "i've been writing a lot lately."

"I've seen you at school. I like your black binder. Nice size.

Eight by eleven is so bulky. And it even zips." Then she realizes she basically just fessed up to stalking me. Pink cheeks, eyes glued to the road.

"That's my dive log. Waterproof. Easy to pack."

"Cool." Her eyes dart in my direction again. "I'd like to read your stuff."

Dream on. "So your poem—"

"Right. One of the lines is *no longer befuddled.*" Her voice softens. "Don't you think just *defuddled* sounds better?"

"But it isn't a word."

She pulls a cute scowl. "Doesn't matter in a poem."

"So who's no longer unfuddled? You?"

"*De*-fuddled." Her eyes flick over my way again and then back to the road. "My grandmother." She swallows hard. "She died last spring."

"Hey, i'm sorry." i feel like a creep for prying and razzing.

"We nursed her at our house for three years. I watched her suffer, and all I could do was hold a straw to her lips and smooth Vaseline on them when they got dry. She passed away quietly one night while my mother and I held her hands. Peaceful. Beautiful. Not scary like I thought her death would be. I thought I loved my grandmother before she got sick, but now I love her more than ever. I know it was a release, but it didn't make letting her go any easier."

i stare out my window at cement grain elevator towers. The hilly fields behind them are bare. Dad always said he loved the ocean because he grew up here where the wind made waves with soil. Maybe when they are full of wheat, it's nice, but now? I don't see it. Can't dive in dirt. Even the blazing color of the leaves means they are all just dying.

The awkward silence replays. i set her old lunch bag on the seat.

Leesie clears her throat. "That heavy, sad feeling—"

i nod like she's got me in a trance.

"It's not as intense now, like—"

Me. She doesn't have to say it.

"It waxes and wanes. I don't think it will ever go away. I don't think I want it to."

What does she know about it? Her grandmother? Please. Take me home, chick, i don't care how damn good you smell, how great you look when you smile, how soft those lips might be, how those jeans make your butt amazing. i grunt, "What happened to pity free?"

"That was stupid." She keeps her eyes on the road. "Sorry to intrude." Her hand leaves the steering wheel. She reaches toward me like she's going to touch my arm, stops, lets her hand drop to the seat, keeps driving with her left hand at the top of the wheel.

i look back at her scribbles. "i don't get the line about silver eyes. Your grandmother's eyes were 'silver in the sunlight'?"

She flushes again, pushes her hair back out of her face with her free hand. "That line must be about the salmon."

"That's some freaky fish." My eyes are gray. Silver is pushing it.

She snatches the bag from the seat and stuffs it in her pocket.

Leesie drives through the Coeur d'Alene reservation past plywood shanties with *CIGS* painted in red across the front, empty fireworks stands, and stacks of dead trees at a sawmill. It gets warm in the cab of the pickup, and her leather and tropical fruit smell fills me up. i actually doze—the first *real* rest I've had in a while. i wake when the pickup bumps onto a dirt lane that switches back and forth, down through a forest to the lake. She rolls down her window.

"Smell the pines." She inhales, deep. Some of her pines are orange and dead looking. The pickup brushes by a fat green branch overhanging the road. i close my eyes and breathe. The fresh clean of it washes through me.

She parks the pickup on a strip of grass. "There's a toilet in the shed. You have to dump a bucket of water down it to make it flush." That reminds me of the heads on the first live-aboard we tried. Mom was ready to leave after day one. Dad and i teased her the whole week, but she stuck it out. Always did. No matter how hard we pushed her. That sad, paralyzing feeling engulfs me again.

"This way." Leesie scrambles down a bluff about six feet high to a narrow strip of sand fifty feet long. "How do you like our beach? This is the only stretch of sand on all of Windy Bay."

i mime impressed.

"It washes away in the winter, but Dad hauls up a fresh load every spring."

i stand on her sand and stare at her lake. Midnight blue. Calling me.

"Pretty, huh?"

i don't answer—can't answer. i bend down and touch the water. Maybe 40 degrees F. Way too cold—even with my seven mil.

Leesie leaves, returns with an armload of dry driftwood. "Still lukewarm? You—not the lake. Coeur d'Alene never warms up."

The wood clatters when she drops it. i don't look around. i'm entranced by the soft, pulsing water. "So what do you do here?"

She walks over to me. "You up for marshmallows?"

i shake my head.

She squats down and digs a flat rock out of the sand. "We used to have a sailboat, but Dad sold it a couple of years ago to fix the tractor."

"Swim much?"

"Not anymore. I used to be a fish." She brushes the sand off the rock and hands it to me. "My baby sister, Stephie, is like that now. Totally fearless. When I was eight, I got tangled up in a bunch of seaweed—"

"This is a lake."

"Lakeweed, then. I couldn't get free. Kicked. Thrashed. I swear something pulled me under. I couldn't get back to the surface. Dad got me out. I had this nasty rash on my legs. I canoe these days. Anything touches me in the water and I kind of lose it."

"That's too bad." i chuck the stone. It doesn't skip. "Anything to see down there? Wrecks? Cool fish?"

She laughs. "There's a healthy crop of lakeweed." She stands, walks to the end of their cement dock, and leans against a piling. Her hair catches the setting sun. "We lost some fishing poles last summer. It drops off just past the dock. Gets deep fast."

i join her, stare at the space between two log pilings where they used to tie up their sailboat. "How deep is it here?"

"Comes up to about—" She rotates to face me, draws a line across my chest with the side of her hand. She lets the edge of her hand rest on my chest a few seconds longer than she needs to make her point. i'm pretty sure she's making another point. Her head tips back, and she's staring again.

i try not to flinch.

The old me would have taken the invitation and stepped right into it, but i stand there with her hand light and small on my chest and all i can do is control the urge to flick it away. i can't follow up the touch, lean down and kiss her, or even take hold of her hand. Maybe that would be strong, but i just can't do it.

She pulls her hand away with a jerk. It's too awkward to keep looking at her and pretend that didn't just happen, so i focus on the far shore, clear my throat. "Can we take your canoe out?" If i can't get in the water, at least i can float on it, caress it with the paddle, force it to obey me.

"Sure." She sounds relieved. i thought she'd be mad. Did i misread the whole thing?

We paddle to the middle of the lake. Leesie steering, me in the front. i'm not so bad with the paddle. She's great. Stronger than she looks.

i'm loving it—could stay out here forever.

Leesie spots some dark clouds in the distance. "Shoot. We should head in."

"Not yet." i trail my fingers in the water. They're going numb. It feels so good to touch it that i don't even care. "How deep is it here?"

"Really deep." She turns away from the clouds and rests her paddle on her knees.

"Fifty feet? A hundred feet? What?"

She frowns and shrugs. "Who knows."

i unzip my club jacket and rip off my hoodie. "Want me to find out?" My T-shirt goes next.

"What are you doing?" She's freaked.

i'm fighting my belt buckle. Stupid numb fingers. "i free dive—like pearl divers."

"Don't be crazy." She holds her paddle in front of her like a weapon. "Stop it. Now!"

i kick my shoes off, finally get the belt, and slide my jeans off. Leesie's staring and red-faced. It's just boxers. She said she has a brother.

She's scowling for real now. "The water's freezing." She waves her paddle at me.

"i'll be right back." i roll over the side, gasp as needles of cold prick every pore, gulp air.

"Get in here," Leesie yells in my face, and grabs at me.

i push off and dive. i keep my eyes wide open, but all i can see is a blurry smudge. i don't have any fins and no weights so i have to fight to get down—only make it to about forty. No sign of the bottom. No sign of anything. It's creepy and black and oh, so empty. No coral. No fish. No sunshine. No parents. Only Isadore lurking deep beneath me. Brooding. Heavy. Crushing.

i tear to the surface with my lungs screaming for air. i break through twenty feet from the canoe. The sky looks darker already. My body's numb.

Leesie paddles over. i even let her help me in. "Thanks for scaring the life out of me." Her face looks as dark as the sky. She drives her oar blade into the water.

I'm dripping wet, shivering, and useless. Fresh freezing pain mounts in waves as the air warms me into sensation. i mumble a lame apology through chattering teeth.

"There're towels in the shed. I'll find you one in a minute." She kicks me a paddle. "So how deep is it?"

"Pretty deep. i couldn't see the bottom."

"The bottom's muck. You don't want to see it."

Muck.

Mangrove toes claw out of soft swamp mud and swirling salt water. i'm not at the lake with Leesie anymore. i stand in the swamp's silt, gulp air, up to my ankles in *muck*. The wind and water knock me flat, carry me farther downstream until i hook a mangrove root. i pull myself along the bottom, grasping the twisted toes, find a mature tree, and wrap my arms around her, shivering in the stagnant murk that slaps at my waist. The wind pulls. The water rips. i hold my mangrove buddy tight, start talking to her, willing her to stand against the storm. Dizziness washes over me. i start free-dive vent cycles to fight it off. My stomach churns into an anguished mass of seawater and crab. The pain in my gut is real. i double over, retch.

"You okay?" Leesie's quavering voice stops the scene. Her hand is on my shoulder, shaking me, touching me again.

i wipe my mouth, shrug away from her grasp. "i need to go home." i'm freaked, jittery, but not from the cold. i expect the nightmares by now, but this was vivid. There. For real. Totally transported.

Drops splatter fat on the windshield as Leesie drives up the rough track through the pines. She doesn't look over at me or try to make small talk. We make the highway before the full storm hits. She pumps the headlights up to bright and leans back into the seat, her arms straight out like a race car driver. Her foot presses heavy on the accelerator. She senses me staring at her. A glance. She's wearing her Ice Queen face. Our eyes lock and then hers go back to the road. "Feeling better?"

No, but at least i'm dry, and she's got the heater cranked.

The pickup roars down the highway. My fingers clutch the armrest beside me. Lightning flashes. Thunder rocks the truck, and Isadore starts to blow.

i sneak out of the *Dive Festiva*'s dining salon, where the captain tells everyone to be calm and my waitress cries. i race to our cabin, grab the camera and strobe. Then i'm out in the storm.

Darkness edged with a yellow-green glow envelopes the lagoon. Rain falls in sheets driven slantways by the wind. i shelter in the lee, filming chaos, drinking in the power. Palm fronds and broken boards shoot through the air. Sand and gravel pelt the deck, falling like hail. Isadore beats me flat against the bulkhead.

Mom calls from the stairs, "Michael! Get down here."

No way am i leaving. Mom yells something about taking cover. i inch around the bulkhead and get a face full of muddy grit.

"Michael!" Mom screams. "Michael!"

Isadore twists her voice and blows it away.

The *Festiva*'s engines roar. Isadore slams into the boat and keeps right on going. She takes me along for the ride. i figure Mom's safe back on the *Festiva* and the storm just got me. She drags me under, and i fight to breathe, get a mouthful of her, choke. My free-dive training takes over, and i hold my breath.

Then rain, cold and fresh, hits my face. i stand by a white pickup. Leesie holds an orange emergency blanket over my head. She hands me a half-full bottle of water. i gulp and spit. Gulp, swallow. "Did i hurl all over?"

She wrinkles up her nose. "You just made nasty sounds." She pushes me back into the pickup, fishes around under the seat, and finds a plastic grocery bag. "Just in case."

The engine revs, and we're hurtling down the country highway through the rain—again.

i think maybe i could tell Leesie about the hurricane dinner, the mounds of crab Dad and i downed, my crying waitress with three kids, tell her about Mom trying to wipe off the butter that dripped down my chin. Tell her how i pulled away. i'm so full of Isadore. The shrink said i should talk.

"So you're all right now?" Leesie steers the pickup around a wicked curve, one hand on the wheel, one small hand lightly touching my arm.

"Sure." i ease my arm away from her warm fingertips.

And i don't tell her a thing.

chapter 10

UNFUDDLED

Kimbo69 says: Spill it, girl.

Leesie327 says: You're home early for a Saturday.

Kimbo69 says: I would be if I were home. This club is wired.

Leesie327 says: You're dancing?

Kimbo69 says: Not this second . . . but Mark wants my body back out on the floor, so be quick.

Leesie327 says: I haven't been to a dance since Jared left last spring. We used to drive up to the big church dances in Spokane together. I hate driving up with only Phil the Pill for company.

Kimbo69 says: Who cares about your stupid brother? If you don't tell me about your charitable outing with Michael right now, I'll never critique another one of your poems.

Leesie327 says: It started awkward and got worse. He actually dove into the lake.

Kimbo69 says: Fully clothed?

Leesie327 says: No, he took them off.

Kimbo69 says:	Right in front of you? Whoa. Good body?
Leesie327 says:	I tried not to look, but yeah—made me weak. I was right about his legs. The muscles are so perfect. I was dying, but he barely noticed me. It was like I was his chauffeur or something.
Kimbo69 says:	He dove into Lake Coeur d'Alene in October? That's a little . . . yikes.
Leesie327 says:	I know. It scared the crap out of me. I didn't know if he was going to come back. Then he goes and has these weird fits. Not really a fit. Zoned completely.
Kimbo69 says:	My mom had flashbacks after her car accident . . . not pretty.
Leesie327 says:	He bolted when we got back to his grandmother's. I'm not surprised. I have that effect on guys.
Kimbo69 says:	It couldn't have been that bad.
Leesie327 says:	Even in the car I was dumb. I went on and on about my grandmother and that poem. Unfuddled, defuddled, befuddled. That's me.
Kimbo69 says:	Was he interested?
Leesie327 says:	Not really, but he says he writes, too. Hey, what if I send him my grandma poem?
Kimbo69 says:	You finished it?
Leesie327 says:	He kind of helped. A friend would do that, right?

TO: liv2div@chatspot.com
DATE: 10/04
FROM: leesie327@chatspot.com
TIME: 7:42 a.m.
SUBJECT: Unfuddling

Hey Michael,

You okay this morning? Sorry if I overreacted at the lake. I usually don't scare that easy. It started out nice. I hope you aren't sick. Thought you might like to read this—one writer to another. I like it better with your word. Thanks for the inspiration.

Later,

Leesie

SHE COMES TO ME
I lie in darkness,
spent of tears,
tired of sleep,
close to soft memories,
alive in her fuzzy sweater
draped on my chair.
I wrap my heart
in pastel patchwork
pieced by her hand,
my tired mind, empty,
open—

The night erupts into flowing
white glory:

She comes to me,
a pure and shining presence,
knocking on my soul,
defogged, unfuddled,
reveling in perfection,
spilling joy that
embraces my sorrow,
she smiles
and waves
farewell.

LEESIE HUNT / CHATSPOT LOG / 10/04 8:32 A.M.

liv2div says: read your poem . . . actually i read it a lot

Leesie327 says: You didn't have to. Really. Maybe you're a prose guy. I wanted to see what you thought about the unfuddled part.

liv2div says: kinda spooky

Leesie327 says: Spooky? Didn't see that coming. Does it feel spooky?

liv2div says: it's about a ghost . . . ghosts are spooky

Leesie327 says: Gosh, I gotta revise.

liv2div says: glowing grandma's not a ghost?

Leesie327 says: She's supposed to be more like an angel.

liv2div says: ghosts are out but angels are cool?

Leesie327 says: Mormons are big on angels. Real ones. None of that ditzy feathered stuff.

liv2div says: what else are Mormons big on?

Leesie327 says: That's a dangerous question, but I gotta go to church so you're safe for now.

liv2div says: church . . . didn't know you were THAT religious

Leesie327 says: It's not catching—unless you keep asking questions. I'm going to be late. Sorry.

liv2div says: wait . . . i need your help with something . . . want to go down to the town pool with me this afternoon?

Leesie327 says: Swimming season is over here. I thought your dip in the lake yesterday made that clear.

liv2div says: they're patching the pool so it's full again . . . i need to free dive some more . . . come with me . . . you're not afraid in a pool are you?

Leesie327 says: I can't go swimming on Sunday. Family rule.

liv2div says: just come watch me

Leesie327 says: It'll be way, way cold. Just like yesterday. Your Arizona boy toes will never unthaw.

liv2div says: i'm going to wear a heavy wet suit

Leesie327 says: Gosh, I'm not that kind of a girl. Now, DeeDee might appreciate this.

liv2div says: get real . . . will you do it or not . . . i can't go by myself

Leesie327 says: This is about safety?

liv2div says: my mom wouldn't ever let me dive by myself and now

Leesie327 says: When?

liv2div says: is it dark by six?

Leesie327 says: Better make it seven—still daylight savings.

liv2div says: good . . . gram will be sacked out with her hearing aid off

Leesie327 says: Then we better meet at the pool.

liv2div says: little miss holy's getting into this

Leesie327 says: Don't tell anyone. I'm supposed to be inhuman.

chapter 11

POOL DIVE

MICHAEL'S DIVE LOG—VOLUME #8

DIVE BUDDY: **Leesie**	
DATE: **10/4**	DIVE #: **3 with her**
LOCATION: **Teacup**	**749—guess this counts**
DIVE SITE: **town pool**	WEATHER CONDITION: **night**
WATER CONDITION: **flat**	DEPTH: **9ft**
VISIBILITY: **30 ft**	WATER TEMP.: **34°F**
BOTTOM TIME: **4 minutes FREE DIVE**	

COMMENTS:

i walk up to the pool from Gram's. Thinking about diving—really getting off somewhere, strapping on tanks, and sinking a hundred feet—makes my heart pump warm blood all through me. Lukewarm? For the first time in this dreary wasteland, i actually feel hot.

Tonight's a test. If this works, i'll cut school and take off for a week. It's still warm enough in the Keys. October diving is great there. The place is always next to empty. We loved that. But now—empty? i don't know. It's not just off-season. Maybe i could go, fool myself that the missing divers are all back home at work. But my mom and dad? Our condo sitting there full of all our best memories?

i better make it Cozumel, where i can lie back and drift on the currents, let them carry me back to the world Isadore stole. Silent Peaceful. Carefree as juvie fish flitting over the coral. Majestic as an eagle ray spreading its wings and flying through a canyon. Blue so true it sinks right through you. A load better than huddling under the pants quilt, holding my breath while Isadore shrieks at me. Freak—it'd even beat out my pills.

The lake yesterday. Huge mistake. I've never felt that freaked underwater. This time i'll be in a safe, controlled environment. i've even got a buddy. She's there already, pacing around her country girl white pickup that glows under a streetlamp.

Leesie meets me at the edge of the light. No smile. Arms folded. Hair pulled back. "You sure you want to do this?"

"Thanks for coming." i feel so dumb. "Sorry for yesterday." i kick a piece of gravel and then look back at her. Her eyes are blue tonight, fill her face. "Truce?"

She falls for that. An echo of her smile hints. With a little encouragement she'd fall for a lot more. She'd probably be better than diving in frozen lakes and swimming pools. But she'd have to be pretty good to top a week drift diving Cozumel.

i close in on her, whiff her trapped hair and hip suede, and almost ditch the dive test and go with the hormones she's sparking. Maybe i'm not completely numb to chicks. Thawing? In the Ice Queen's realm?

She backs off, turns toward the pool. "Let me show you the way in."

We climb over the counter and drop into a room full of chewed foam noodles, lifeguard rings, and broken kickboards.

A blow-up dolphin sags in the corner. i follow Leesie through an empty doorway out to the pool. i take off my jacket and slip off my track pants. i've already got my wet suit on.

She slaps her hand over her eyes. "I didn't realize you'd be stripping again."

"i'm not. Look, fully clothed."

She peeks through her fingers. "That'll keep you warm?"

i hold out my arm. "Warm enough."

She comes over to me and touches the neoprene sleeve. "Poor DeeDee." She tips her head back. Our eyes connect.

"What?"

"She's missing a show."

"Come off it." i look like a string bean in a wet suit.

She eases away and perches on a picnic table.

i turn and stare at the water. "This is my thickest suit. i lost my three mil in Belize or i'd double up."

"Belize?"

i ignore that. "Those are heaters, right?" Round plastic disks with black cords snaking out of them bob in the water. "They won't electrocute me, will they?"

Leesie shakes her head. "You're safe. They just keep the water from freezing—that's it. You ready for another swim in ice water?"

i whip my weight belt around my waist and buckle it. "Be back in a minute." i take two strides to the pool's edge and dive in. It's not painful like jumping into her lake. It's cold, even with the seven mil, but i can hack it.

"Be careful." Leesie's pacing the pool's edge. "What are you doing?"

i zone her out, kick my legs up, and fall through the water.

i relax on the bottom, facedown, eyes shut. Everything's sunlit blue. No black, dark lake. No quarry vis. i'm actually warm. My final dive with my parents, Mom in the lead, Dad and me lagging behind with the camera, replays in full color. We find a barrel sponge with a party of hermit crabs packed down its tube and shoot video of a pair of queen angelfish. Dad films Mom, and she pushes away the camera.

Lying on the bottom of that pool, i feel like i can open my eyes, and they will both be there, hovering inches above me. Just like Leesie's poem. i want my parents. Come to me. Now.

My eyes stay shut. i know there's only empty water and an ugly patch. My parents are gone. i hold my breath and swim with memories. The cold turns into a drowsy warmth, and my dream parents dissolve.

Then i'm trapped. Isadore has me. She sucks me deep. The pressure pains sharp in my ears. i manage to equalize before the drums rupture but use air. i slam into something hard, big rock, maybe a wreck, fight to the surface, think i've made it. Breathe and get seawater. Choke. i break the surface again and inhale through teeth clenched to keep the salt water out, packing like crazy. Isadore pulls me under again. i fight her, claw through the water trying to find the surface, holding my breath. i will myself to relax and float with the storm surge. The storm gets quieter and quieter, fades into shimmering Caribbean blue.

My parents are there—just through that canyon. i'm swimming as fast as i can, but i can't catch them. They're ahead of me. Caught in a current that won't take me. Please. Wait. i'm almost there—

Leesie's in the water, grabbing my weight belt, wrenching me away.

"What do you think you're doing?" i shout at the surface.

"S-s-saving your l-l-life!" i don't need her screaming in my face.

We swim to the edge of the pool. i climb out. She tries to pull herself up but can't, so i grab her arms and yank her onto the pool deck.

"You're saving me?" The cold air hits my wet suit, and i start to zip out of it. "Good one."

She drags herself upright. "You don't have to be a snot about it."

Goose bumps rise on my chest. "i didn't ask for a rescue."

The glow of the streetlamp makes her face look bluish white. She pulls off a dripping fleece. Her skin shows through her soaked T-shirt. Her bra keeps her decent, but it's made of thin stuff. As i peel my wet suit down to my waist, i can't help noticing she isn't totally flat-chested. Small, sure, but enough's happening there to make me stare.

She gives me a lesson in Disgust 101 and crosses her arms. "You were down there for like four minutes. What was i supposed to think?" Her teeth chatter as the night air super-chills her wet clothing.

i put my hands on my hips. "i told you i free dive."

"That means you don't have to breathe like normal people?" Hysteria plays at the edge of her voice. "We had a deal." She's screaming.

"Shut up." i glance around—expecting sirens or at least a night watchman. "You should have left me alone." i keep my voice low and cold.

Her face draws up tight. "If that's what you want." She takes off, manages to get over the counter despite her soaked jeans and wet tennis shoes.

i pick up my duffel bag and follow her to the pickup. "You better get out of that wet stuff." i hand her my towel. "You can use this."

Her mouth drops. "Here? No way." She pushes the towel back at me. Guess she doesn't change much on boats.

"At least get in the truck. You're going to freeze." i push her into the passenger's side, slam the door. i get dressed behind the truck, throw my bag in the back, and get into the driver's side. "Keys."

She points at the ignition where they swing, lets me try to start it a couple of times, then reaches over, slaps my hand out of the way, and turns the key. She jams her sopping shoe on my foot and pumps the gas pedal twice, holds it down halfway: the motor roars to life.

i back up, swing the truck around, and drive up the hill. Left, right, right and we're in Gram's driveway.

"Just leave it r-r-running."

"You can't go home like that." i'm steamed at her, but she's too cold. It could get serious if she doesn't change fast. "You looked after me yesterday. My turn. Come in and get dried off."

"Your grandmother will freak."

"Asleep, remember?" i try to add something calm and reassuring to my voice. "Come on. Let's get you into something dry."

"What do you mean *let's*?" The scowl isn't cute this time.

i crank the keys, and the pickup's engine dies. "Get inside before you're hypothermic." i open the driver's door and get out.

She slides into the driver's seat. "i'm already hypothermic."

"You're right." i grab her arm and tug. "Your lips are blue."

That scares her enough to let me pull her out of the truck. The wind hits, and as she stumbles against me, the shaking gets worse. i take her arm, support her to the door, open it, and flick on the light. Air, warm and yellow, flows out, embracing us in the dark.

She puts her hand against the doorjamb. "I can't go in there with you."

"What?"

"I can't go in there with you." She clenches her jaw but can't keep her teeth from chattering.

"What are you talking about?" i seize her wrist and push her inside, shut the door. "Go in the bathroom and take off that wet stuff before you get sick. i'll get you something to wear."

She turns to face me and takes a step back like i'm going to attack her. "I've got to go." She's dripping a puddle on Gram's worn linoleum floor. "I can't be in a house alone with a guy. Family rule." She's too cold to blush but would if she could.

She's more into me than i thought. "Gram's here." i keep my voice normal, matter-of-fact, consciously fight my reflex to drop into seduction mode.

"B-b-but—"

i push her down the hall. "Go get in the shower. Turn it on warm, not too hot."

chapter 12

THAWING

MICHAEL'S DIVE LOG—VOLUME #8

Dive Buddy: still Leesie		
Date: still 10/3	Dive #: still 3 with her	
Location: Teacup	Dive Site: Gram's	
Weather Condition: inside		
Water Condition: i don't know—she's the one in the shower		
Depth: coursing	Visibility: probably	
Water Temp.: too hot	Bottom Time: not long enough	

Comments:

When i come up from checking on Leesie's clothes, she's finally emerged from the bathroom. She sits on the couch, her mouth a straight line, her hair twisted up in a towel. She looks good in my sweatshirt, swims in the pants, but the pale gray around her face is nice.

"Your stuff will be dry in a half hour or so."

"Thanks." She leans forward and untwists the towel, rubs her hair.

Part of me wants to just get her out of here, but another part says, "Hey, go sit next to her." My shirt touching her body is getting to me. Her cheekbones seem higher. Her face looks smaller, delicate. Unearthly. i get this primal protective urge— like on the bus. But after the fit she threw at the door?

i take a chair on the far side of Gram's small living room. Be decent. That's all i have to do. "Are you warm enough?"

"Fine." She stands up and folds the towel.

i take it from her and hang it in the bathroom. She's sitting on the couch again when i get back.

"Do you want some cocoa or something?" i ask to ward off the evil eye she's drilling into me.

"What's going on with you? Why do you keep doing this to me?"

i stare at my hands.

"What were you thinking?"

None of your business. i glance at Gram's shrine of family pictures on the desk next to my chair. A copy of the one of Mom, Dad, and me sitting in a dive boat that disintegrated in my wallet is there. i pick it up. We all wear big smiles, lots of teeth. Mom has her arm around me, and my head is on her shoulder. She's sitting on Dad's lap. He's got his massive arms around us both, holding us together.

Leesie clears her throat.

After what she's put up with the past couple of days, guess i owe her something. "i needed to get back in the water. Back *under* water."

"So was it worth it?"

i set down the picture, look over at her. "You soaking wet? Yeah. Definitely."

She tries not to, but she smiles. She drops her eyes, fluffs her damp hair, twists it into a ponytail, realizes she doesn't have anything to hold it with, and lets it fall back down. She looks up and catches my eyes on her, but she holds my gaze. "I'm still waiting."

"i haven't been underwater since Belize." i stare at Gram's flowered rug.

"Belize is where—"

i nod. "Hurricane hit our boat. i was up on deck with the stupid camera when the storm surge hit. Isadore took me, but i held my breath. My dad. All my friends were trapped. My mom came on deck searching for me. But she—" i can't say it. Drowned. i see her sinking and choking, breathing in seawater. Dying. No. That didn't happen. She's a diver. Divers don't drown.

Leesie leans forward, her chin in her hands, elbows on knees, eyes soft now. "I'm so sorry."

"That lake of yours freaked me. i thought maybe the pool . . . i had to go there. See if i could."

She closes her eyes. "And i messed it up."

i get up, cross the room, sink beside her on the couch, not letting my thigh bump hers. "i was down there long enough. And"—a knot forms in my throat that i can barely speak around— "maybe it was good you were there."

She shifts toward me, relaxes enough for our shoulders to touch. "Don't do that again."

i stare across the room, trying to make out the details of that picture of my parents and me. It's fuzzy from here. Did i want to stay at the bottom of that pool? Never come up? Sitting in Gram's living room, that freaks me, but down there it all made sense. Diving is life to me. Isadore is death.

We sit quiet. Leesie's too smart or too scared to say anything.

i find myself longing for that shimmering blue place with my parents. It tasted so good.

Leesie whispers, "Do you mind?" She slides her hand under mine and lifts it to her knee like it's something frail she doesn't want to break. She weaves her fingers through mine, curls them up around my cold hand. She strokes the back of it. It feels good, safe, her hand smoothing over my hand.

i sink back into the soft cushions of Gram's fifties couch. "The shark story is a bunch of crap."

Leesie starts. "Somebody actually said that to your face?"

"DeeDee asked to see the scars."

"Kids here are dumb. Generations of pesticide use."

"We dove with sharks all the time." i remember a hammerhead slipping through the blue at the limit of my visibility on a Cayman wall dive, sharks whizzing around my head in the Bahamas, and the massive bull sharks at the Blue Hole in Belize. i feel myself getting emotional. i sit forward. "i'll go check—"

Leesie's knee presses into my thigh. "It's going to be all right."

No way. Never. Not for me.

Heat emanates from Leesie's leg, warm from the shower, and wriggles into the sadness, under the pain. i lean my head back, incline my face toward her hair, and breathe deep and slow, in and out, over and over. Training. Hanging on tight to her hand. With every vent, i suck in more and more Leesie. My grip on her hand tightens. Her fruity shampoo mixed with chlorine whirls around me. i cling to her hand like i held on to the mangrove tree that saved me in Belize. Isadore tugs, but i have Leesie's hand—don't want to let it go.

Her hand in mine writhes. My eyes stray down. My fingernails are digging dints into the soft flesh on the back of her hand. A tear makes a wet path down her cheek. i let go.

"Look what i did to you." i shift so a space opens between us.

"It's nothing." She buries her bleeding hand in my sweatshirt's pocket. "I'll be back." She slips away—just to the bathroom, though. She can't leave. i still have her clothes, drying.

i stretch out on the couch, listening to the water run in the bathroom sink, sorry that i hurt her.

She comes back and leans against the doorway. Her eyes travel over the pictures on the desk. "I should go."

"Not yet." Please, no. *She comes to me.* i need to ask her before she evaporates. "Was it real?"

She looks down at her hand.

"i know that's real. i'm sorry." Four red fingernail digs—i can see them from across the room. It's like i branded her. "i'm a freak these days."

She blows on the cuts, meets my eyes again. "It's nothing."

"That *'she comes to me'* stuff in your poem. Was it real?"

Her eyebrows draw together. "You want to talk poetry?"

"Did you make it up?"

"No."

My palms get sweaty, and my fingers tingle. My slow, freediver heart revs. "You saw your grandmother?" i need so bad to believe what she's going to say. Maybe she's a medium. Are Mormons into that? Fine by me. Pull out the crystal ball. Turn off the lights. If she can find me something other than two dead bodies in a morgue in Florida, i want to know.

Leesie breaks eye contact, stares down at Gram's flowered

rug. "It's not like she zapped into my room and flew around." Her voice is quiet. Calm but strong. "The whole thing happened in my head."

i roll on my back, stare at the ceiling, disappointed. "Like a dream."

"No. Not a dream. A few weeks after Grandma's funeral, my mom and I spent the evening crying together. I went to bed, said my prayers, and tried to sleep."

"You pray?" i sit up. She crosses the room, takes her old place on the couch next to me. i turn toward her.

She leans forward. Her hair hangs like a veil between us. "I think this was kind of a vision."

"Okay. A vision." Is that what happened to me at the lake? A vision? And in the pool tonight? What was that?

Leesie nods. "My mind raced. I couldn't sleep, and then my grandmother was there, inside my head, pulsing with light."

She shifts her hair so it falls down her back, almost dry. i touch it—just the ends with the back of my hand. She doesn't protest.

"You have amazing hair." i take a handful, let it glide through my fingers. She closes her eyes, tilts her head back. i take another handful.

She opens her eyes and stares into mine, doesn't blush or look away like she usually does. "Grandma wasn't like anything I'd ever seen before. So changed from the body we laid in her coffin. Not old. Not young. So beautiful I couldn't breathe."

Leesie's hair cascades through my hands again and again, the scent of it, the rhythm, hypnotizing me.

She comes to me.

She comes to me.

She comes to me.

Awed joy rustles in her voice. "Happiness flowed out of her, filled me up. Tangible—like you could pour it from a pitcher." She oozes with the power of what she tells me, what happened to her.

i drop her hair, break eye contact. "Couldn't you have just imagined it?"

"Overcome. That describes what I was like when she left." Leesie doesn't continue until i face her again. Her eyes are tender now, reach down to my soul. "I lay in bed, holding my pillow, totally embraced." She brings her hand to my face, pushes a stray lock from my eyes. "In the morning, putting the whole thing into words was impossible, like trying to capture a beam of light." She takes my hand again. "Could I make that up?"

i look down at our hands. "i don't believe there's anything after. More than this. It's over. You really think there's heaven?"

"It's real. I know it is. I've been told it all my life, but now I've seen it." She squeezes my hand. "It could be real for you, too."

"i don't think so." My eyes seek the snapshot across the room. "We always just dove."

"Life is so much more than that."

i drop her hand. "You don't know—you don't dive."

"I had to write this essay for, well, that doesn't matter, but it was about what has shaped my life the most." She captures my hand again. "These past few years with my grandmother made me stop taking things for granted." She strokes the back of my hand with her hurt one. "To see Grandma like that, healed and whole. I'll never be the same." She rests her head on my shoulder. "You've exhausted the diving opportunities around here. Maybe you'd like to try something new."

i shake my head again, but i let her keep hold of my hand. i lay my cheek on the top of her head and breathe her in deep.

She wants me to try her faith? Maybe i'll just try her.

i wake with the dusty gold afghan from the back of the couch tucked around me. i don't know when i fell asleep, when Leesie left. This morning the water is blue, clear, like in the pool, but i can't look. Please, give me quarry vis. Thawing stinks. Warm flesh hurts. That *be strong* crap is a joke. Walking? Talking? School?

No way.

chapter 13

INSPIRATION

LEESIE'S MOST PRIVATE CHAPBOOK

POEM #28, FAMILY PRAYER FOR MICHAEL

Stephie climbs on Dad's back while he kneels,
head bowed, half strangled
as she grasps him around the neck calling,
Pick me, pick me.

I hit my knees as she pipes,
Dear Heavenly Father,
shrill into the night air.

Thank thee for Mom and Dad and Leesie and Phil and me, too.
Bless us nothing bad will happen.

And bless Michael. About time
You blessed Michael.

Help the people who are hungry get something to eat.
Bless that Leesie and Phil will be nice.

Don't worry about Leesie.
She'll survive.
Bless Michael.

Help us not miss Grandma too much.
And bless the pigs, especially the mama ones with
new babies.

And Michael, please don't forget
my Michael.

In the name of Jesus Christ,
Amen.

LEESIE HUNT / CHATSPOT LOG / 10/5 12:13 P.M.

Kimbo69 says: The cafeteria reeks today. Hope the librarian doesn't see me in here. She doesn't like crumbs on the keyboards.

Leesie327 says: I can't eat. He's not at school. What if he went back to the pool after I left?

Kimbo69 says: Calm down . . . you're going to make yourself sick.

Leesie327 says: I can't stand school today. I want to scream at everyone. It must show. Nobody's even pinched me.

Kimbo69 says: I've never seen love make someone quite this rabid.

Leesie327 says: Stop it. I'm concerned. Anyone would be. I'm

like the only person he has to talk to. Shouldn't I
check on him?

Kimbo69 says: Give him some space . . . remember he's
grieving.

Leesie327 says: I can't imagine what he's going through. And I'm
so stupid. I almost started telling him about BYU
and filling out my application. Kind of crass when
the guy's whole life is destroyed.

Kimbo69 says: Did you tell him you found that website?

Leesie327 says: Are you crazy? I faked that I knew nothing.

Kimbo69 says: Kind of a lie.

Leesie327 says: Don't call it that. I never lie. At least I used to not.
I even tell my parents the truth.

Kimbo69 says: It'll be okay.

Leesie327 says: That hardly helps.

Kimbo69 says: How's your hand?

Leesie327 says: Inspiring.

LEESIE'S MOST PRIVATE CHAPBOOK

POEM #29, NAIL PRINTS

Four little marks, pink half-moons,
that record his grief on the back of my hand.
They sting when I touch them—
but how can I discover what he means
with my baby sister's Barbie Band-Aids
blurring my vision?

Strange how I hide his prints
from Mom's prying eyes,

how my throat closes when I glimpse them,
sore and puffy, as I walk through crowded hallways
empty without him, how my lips
ache to touch them
even though they are on the back of
my own hand.

Strange how I guard them
from ointments and aloes,
hoping the thin scabs
will scar me with his
nail prints.

LEESIE HUNT / CHATSPOT LOG / 10/6 11:39 P.M.

Leesie327 says: He wasn't at school again. What if he's sick?

Kimbo69 says: It's not your fault.

Leesie327 says: Well, it kind of is. If I'd said no, he would have stayed safe at Gram's.

Kimbo69 says: I doubt that . . . maybe he'd be dead.

Leesie327 says: Why did I think I could help him? He needs a professional.

Kimbo69 says: And a friend . . . hang in there . . . so what have you been writing?

Leesie327 says: Didn't I send you my grandma poem?

Kimbo69 says: It's good . . . what else?

Leesie327 says: Nothing.

Kimbo69 says: She lies again.

Leesie327 says: It's not finished.

Kimbo69 says: It's about him . . . let me read it.

Leesie327 says: Way too private.

Kimbo69 says: And I don't send you private stuff?

Leesie327 says: It's weird. You won't get it.

Kimbo69 says: It's just a poem . . . I read all your poems.

Leesie327 says: Not this one.

Kimbo69 says: Have you chatted?

Leesie327 says: He's not online. His grandmother answers the phone. Maybe I should go over there.

Kimbo69 says: That's kind of desperate.

Leesie327 says: What if I made him an apple pie?

Kimbo69 says: Pie?

Leesie327 says: My mom makes tuna casserole and takes it to people who are sick. I think he'd like pie better.

Kimbo69 says: Why don't you try taking him his homework?

Leesie327 says: But the apples in our orchard are ripe.

chapter 14

CONFESSIONS

liv2div says: there's this pie in the kitchen gram said you made it

Leesie327 says: Gram's cool. We talked. She said you weren't feeling well. Pie always makes me feel better.

liv2div says: wanna go back to the pool with me?

Leesie327 says: They drained it again.

liv2div says: how about your lake? i'll bring the seven mil.

Leesie327 says: The storm washed out the road.

liv2div says: but it's massive . . . i found some maps . . . looks like the highway goes right along it for a while

Leesie327 says: It's going to freeze soon.

liv2div says: Spokane . . . know any deep pools up there?

Leesie327 says: Did you like my pie?

liv2div says: sorry . . . not so hungry these days . . . why pie?

Leesie327 says: Kind of a Mormon thing. Most girls make chocolate chip cookies. Apple pie is so much more poetic. My church has a big university. I think they offer a degree in pie.

liv2div says:	brigham young? a girl i knew in phoenix went there. she was really smart. i don't think she's studying pie
Leesie327 says:	Yeah. It's kind of impossible to get in there. So, I'm not your first Mormon friend?
liv2div says:	i didn't know her that well . . . she was student body president . . . kind of visible
Leesie327 says:	She didn't introduce you to the missionaries and teach you the Gospel?
liv2div says:	you're not planning that, are you?
Leesie327 says:	We're it for Mormons in Tekoa. Nearest elders are in Spokane. No one will pounce. I promise.
liv2div says:	my soul's fine as is . . . slaughtered . . . but i don't think finding religion will fix it
Leesie327 says:	That all depends on the religion.
liv2div says:	is that what this is about? i thought maybe you liked hanging out with me . . . girls usually do
Leesie327 says:	I'm honored.
liv2div says:	can we get together again?
Leesie327 says:	Tomorrow at school?
liv2div says:	how about tonight? i'm freaking here waiting for Isadore to attack again
Leesie327 says:	Like at the lake?
liv2div says:	she's been relentless
Leesie327 says:	It's too late.
liv2div says:	early for me . . . i could come to your place . . . take gram's car
Leesie327 says:	You're really feeling well enough?
liv2div says:	i'm not sick . . . i've been waiting all night for you to sign on . . . where have you been?

Leesie327 says: I was at church. We have activities for youth on Wednesday nights.

liv2div says: and you go be a *youth*? don't you get enough do-gooder juice on sundays?

Leesie327 says: I need all I can get.

liv2div says: so can i come over?

Leesie327 says: You think you can drive this road?

liv2div says: does it require a special license?

Leesie327 says: Country hicks only.

liv2div says: maybe i can sneak in under the radar

LEESIE HUNT / CHATSPOT LOG / 10/07 9:56 P.M.

Leesie327 says: Kim. Where are you? This is getting intense.

Leesie327 says: Please, Kim, sign on.

Leesie327 says: He's on his way out here. I don't know what to do. Why aren't you online?

Kimbo69 says: Cool it. I'm here.

Leesie327 says: You should have heard him just now trying to find his way back underwater. It breaks my heart. So I let him come out where I can keep an eye on him.

Kimbo69 says: Don't tell him about your chat with his grandma. I can't believe you did that. Relationship rule #1: Don't tattle.

Leesie327 says: I already mentioned it, but I'm not that stupid. I didn't tell him what we talked about. He'd hate me. It's not like I planned it. She kind of unloaded, and I realized she had to know. She's his guardian. If he's suicidal, he needs real help. What if he did something? It would be my fault.

Kimbo69 says: I think you're taking this island thing too far. If the guy wants to kill himself, he'll kill himself. There's nothing you can do.

Leesie327 says: I convinced her to at least take him to her doctor. What if I'm not there to drag him out next time? I actually showed him Coeur d'Alene. He could go back without me.

Kimbo69 says: Relax . . . go make yourself beautiful . . . don't you dare tell me you're just friends . . . give the guy something to live for.

LEESIE'S MOST PRIVATE CHAPBOOK

POEM #30, WHO?

I stand in the bathroom and brush
my hair shiny.
I want it silk for him:
I want his hands in it
again,
his tan cheek nestling on it
again,
I want his arms to clutch me so close
I can feel him
inhale—
Who am I?

Who is this girl who commandeered
his hand? Who soothed him and testified?
Who aches to hold him?

Who is this girl who applies

watermelon lip gloss, wraps
in her accidentally sexy thrift store find,
and creeps down the stairs?
She hustles past my parents
nodding to the late news
into the safe basement
dark.

The stairs creak and I know
who she is: a criminal.
I flee into the cold
night, shivering, ashamed
that this all feels so
delicious.

I perch on the bottom step,
my top lip perspiring,
and await
my Michael,
gray hoodie, black jacket,
jeans that hold him too close,
biblical hair, the stubble hiding
his face—his warm mouth that betrays
him more than he knows—
a pain in his rich gray eyes
that starts me
praying he'll need me
again.

THERAPY

MICHAEL'S DIVE LOG—VOLUME #8

Dive Buddy: LEESIE	
Date: 10/7	Dive #: 4 with her
Location: Teacup	Dive Site: Leesie's farm
Weather Condition: night	Water Condition: none
Depth: perfect	Visibility: perfect
Water Temp.: perfect	Bottom Time: not long enough

Comments:

i launch into the night in Gram's old blue Chrysler wondering if Isadore can attack while i'm driving. Would i crash and burn? Am i that psycho?

i must be. If i'm sane, what am i doing driving out to see Leesie? i should be heading down the highway toward Lake Coeur d'Alene. When i couldn't get her online earlier, i tried to book a dive trip, but all i could think about while i surfed for deals was her hair. She thinks i'm a freak, or a patient, or her next convert. i don't want that.

What do i want? i want to feel like a normal guy out with a hot chick, but i couldn't even kiss her at the lake. i'm not even sure she wanted me to. Sunday night there was something precious and holy about her. Touching her, connecting, gave me the first moments of peace i've had since Isadore. i'm crazy to taste it again. Is that enough for her? Will she be okay if i just want to hold her hand, sink into her cool blue-green eyes, and breathe down her hair?

i take the first curve on the gravel road out to her farm too fast and spin out. Freaks me. i cut my speed and put on my high beams. The road twists again and then goes straight up and down steep hills, past empty fields, and, every mile or so, a house surrounded by low corrugated metal buildings, old wood barns, or a square grain elevator tower.

Leesie's old-fashioned farmhouse sits back from the road. She waits for me, wrapped in her fringy suede, sitting on the bottom step of a short flight of cement stairs that lead from the road up to the yard. i can see the front of the house from the car, wide steps and a big porch. The light shows pumpkins and cornstalks crowding around the door.

When i get out of the car, she greets me with, "You shaved."

"Sorry."

"No, you look—" She trails off.

i washed my hair, too, so i know that barnyard smell isn't me. i pull a face.

"Gross. I know." She stands up. i wish she'd smile. Her hair refracts the floodlight shining on the yard. "It doesn't always stink like this. The barnyard's still drying out from that thunderstorm."

"What *is* that?" i plug my nose.

"Hogs." She crinkles up her nose. "Just up the road." She

motions toward the curved outline of a huge barn, dark against the bright night sky.

i glance around. From what i can see, the place is full of neat gardens like Gram's used to be. The shape of a grain elevator hulks across the road from the house.

Leesie takes a step toward me. "You want a tour? Most of the plants came from your gram. Must be hard on her not being able to keep her garden up like she used to."

"Naw." i focus back on Leesie. "Maybe another time when we can see better."

"We could walk down to the sow barn. There's a new litter of piglets."

i can only imagine how that place stinks. "Can't we just go inside and talk?" i step closer to her.

"You want to meet my parents?" Leesie drifts over to the front fender. "I didn't tell them you were coming. Just slipped out."

"You don't have a 'family rule' about that?" i back up to the car, lean against it, close to her but not touching.

She finally lets loose a smile. "Not yet. I better not be out too long." She lifts her brows. "I don't usually—"

"Sneak around with a guy?"

"And you're not even a member."

"Of what? The butt-pinching club?"

She laughs. "My church." Her shoulder settles against my arm.

i lean into her. "Is that a prerequisite for sneaking?"

"Kind of." Her words come out sort of breathless.

Standing next to her, touching her again, makes me feel breathless, too. Maybe i can do more than hold her hand.

"i came all the way out here on your crazed road." i touch her hair. "What do you want to do?"

She starts away from me. "That gives me an idea." She walks around Gram's car, sizing it up. "You ever been hill jumping?"

i shake my head. i want to touch her hair again. Smother my face in it.

"Better give me the keys."

i hesitate. Gram loves her car. She's had it for decades.

"Don't worry. I've been driving this road since I was fourteen."

i drop the keys into her hand. i'm ready to agree to anything as long as she doesn't disappear into her house and leave me to pig stink and Isadore reruns, trying to find my way back to her lake alone.

"I like this." She holds up Gram's crocheted bunny. "Really you."

She starts the car up. i get into the passenger's side, fasten my seat belt. She flips a U-turn and drives, slow and stealthy, for about half a mile, then revs the engine. We squeal up the first hill, spraying gravel in our wake. Leesie guns it at the top.

i feel my face relaxing into an idiot grin as we speed down the other side. "Whoa, left my stomach back there." This is a feature of the Palouse hills Dad never shared. i can see him doing this—in this same old car.

Leesie keeps her face straight, glances over at me with one eyebrow raised. "Next one's steeper—you get more of a pop." Before i know it, Gram's ancient Chrysler roars up another hill.

"How fast are you going?" i yell over the straining engine.

"Just seventy. I don't want to push it."

We pop over the second hill. Leesie yells, "Yee ha!" like a bronco buster in an old western.

"Are all country girls like you?" i hang on to the dashboard.

She giggles and guns it over another hill. "Yee ha!" She fishtails it down the backside. "You want me to spin it? This is a good spot for a 360."

i shake my head and yell, "No!"

She barrels up the last hill, flips a U-turn in the loose gravel, and heads back through our dust cloud for another round, laughing and yelling, "Yee ha!" all the way.

i almost feel like i can laugh with her, yell like a cowboy, not care about anything except the next hilltop gut rush.

We get back to her house too soon. She parks by the steps.

"Are we done?" i don't want it to be over, don't want her to leave. "Can we go again?"

"I don't think we should put Gram's car through anymore." She cranks the gearshift into park, shuts off the engine.

"Do you think we left any of it back there?"

"Should I check the bumper?" She tries to look serious. "I think I heard something clank."

"Gram'll kill me."

"It's fine." She pats the dashboard. "Poor old thing needed a workout."

"What happens"—maybe i should have asked this sooner—"if you meet another car coming up the other side of the hill?"

"That's why I hang to the right at the top."

"No way."

"Way. There's room for two cars." She tips her head

sideways. "You just don't want to meet a grain truck or some doof in a tractor."

"i trusted you with my life?"

"And Gram's car."

i undo my seat belt, stretch. Gram's car predates bucket seats. i move along the bench a few inches closer to Leesie. The pig stink doesn't penetrate the car. i find the scent of her jacket, but i'm not close enough to whiff her hair. i stretch my arm across the back of the seat.

She tries to turn in her seat, can't because of her seat belt. She unlatches it, twists sideways with her right leg up on the bench, hooked under her left. Then she puts her foot back down. Her hand drifts toward the door handle—no—back to the steering wheel. Yes.

i need to feel that she's warm and real. Solid. My hand slides down the seat back and picks up her free hand, the one i hurt. The calm from Sunday night returns. i examine her cuts, curved to fit my fingernails. "How is it tonight?"

"Okay, I guess." Her clear eyes fill mine. "How are you?"

"Better." My voice sinks low. "Thanks for letting me come out."

"If you want to talk about it—"

"Naw." My voice is husky. i press her hand.

She draws it away. "I've got to go. I can't—" The other hand is back on the door handle.

No. Please. i edge closer to her. "What did you do at church tonight?" i whiff her hair. "Burn incense? Talk to more angels?"

"Incense?" She leans toward me. "Mormons don't do incense."

"Not even the hippie kind?" i flip the fringe on her jacket, keep a couple pieces to play with. "No angels, either?"

"If you have to know"—she watches me twist her jacket fringe together—"they just showed the Sex Lady video again."

"At church?" Maybe Mormons are hipper than i thought.

"It's about abstinence. Very churchy."

i drop the fringe. "So you're totally brainwashed?"

"Taught the truth." She untangles the suede strips, combs the rest flat with her fingers.

"That's why you have that rule?"

"You mean: 'do not go into a house alone with a member of the opposite sex'? That's only the beginning. My whole life is a list of rules." She pulls a card out of her pocket and hands it to me. i can't read it in the dark.

She sits forward, stares out the front window. "Keep both feet on the floor. Never go into a guy's bedroom. No parking. No necking. No petting. No fornication. No tongue."

"No tongue?"

She drums the steering wheel with her fingers.

"Seriously, you can't even French-kiss?"

"It's not like I can't. I have a tongue." She licks her lips. "I just choose not to use it."

"Fornication?"

She nods, won't face me. "That's the biggie."

"Lightning bolts fall from the sky?"

"Something like that. Painful confession, eternal salvation put on hold, and it would break my dad's heart. My mom would strangle me."

"You'd tell your parents? That's sick."

"I wouldn't tell them, but when you're guilty of major sin—"

"Guilt? Sin? Are you for real? How can you love someone without actually loving them?"

"With your heart."

"It doesn't work that way."

"You're an expert?"

"Just been there."

She doesn't reply.

It's too dark to see if her face is red again, if her cheeks are hot. Mine are. In the cold car, in this cold country, i feel hot all over. "So, you're, um, saving yourself?"

She nods. "This is where you shake my hand and drive off into the sunset." She's the Ice Queen again. Guarded. Distant. i don't want her like that. i want her to melt. Maybe we can thaw together.

"What about regular kissing?" spills out of me in that husky voice.

Leesie takes a deep breath and reels off another perfect answer. "The problem with kissing is it builds desire but doesn't satiate it."

i slide close to her. "Are you quoting the Sex Lady?"

"No. A prophet said that." She studies the steering wheel. "Kissing leads to frustration or sin—"

"i can live with frustration."

She finally turns to face me. "Michael—you shouldn't—"

i stroke her cheek. It is warm.

i can do this, want to do this, need to try. i'm not sure if it's wrong or strong. i just want my arms around her slim body, her heart making mine beat, her full lips pressed to mine.

"If i kissed you"—i put my hand under her chin, tip her face to meet my mouth—"would it be okay?"

chapter 16

SAVE ME

LEESIE'S MOST PRIVATE CHAPBOOK

POEM #31, SAMARITANS

I'm supposed to save *him*,
soothe his hurts, cheer his heart, enlighten his soul,
but with salt-soft lips, skilled but gentle,
suspecting mine don't do this often or ever,
in the front seat of his gram's rusty blue Chrysler,
he wants to save me.

I panic at the glory of his mouth
caressing mine, pry open the car,
and Cinderella up the porch steps,
away from his arms cradling my body,
his hands harbored in my hair,
his lips lingering at my speed.

He races me to the door, presses me to it,

I can't . . .

You're not . . .
We shouldn't . . .

He obliterates my protests with hot resuscitation.
My cheek melds to his shoulder,
and we savor not alone
until he steals my hand to his lips,
kisses the places he hurt.
I'm lost to his firm chest,
his slender fingertips, his long wavy hair,
his mouth sucking my bottom lip—
The world spins, the stars shift,
and I can't see anything except his smoky
gray eyes gazing into mine.

You scare me, whispers
from my mouth across his.

Good, he breathes into me.
I need you to save me.

I will save him.
I can't let it be.
Please, Lord,
save
me.

LEESIE HUNT / CHATSPOT LOG / 10/08 1:17 A.M.

Kimbo69 says: Wow, girl.

Leesie327 says: What am I doing? I was going to be the one who never fell for a non-member like all those miserable women at church who gave up and married outside it.

Kimbo69 says: Slow down . . . you just kissed him . . . no one is marrying you off.

Leesie327 says: That isn't me. I'm going to BYU.

Kimbo69 says: Of course you are.

Leesie327 says: Those women end up dragging their kids to church alone every Sunday or they leave. They all get divorced. I'm not getting divorced.

Kimbo69 says: No one wants you to.

Leesie327 says: And I'm not leaving the church. I'm just—what?

Kimbo69 says: Falling in love . . . no one can deny you that.

Leesie327 says: Maybe I should stay away from him. I'm going away next year. Is that fair?

Kimbo69 says: That's a long way off. He's leaving, too. We all are. Besides . . . can you . . . stay away?

Leesie327 says: No. He needs me. I'm all he has.

Kimbo69 says: And you want him.

Leesie327 says: Don't put it like that. I care about him.

Kimbo69 says: What are you thinking about right now . . . honest answer.

Leesie327 says: Him crushing me to his chest and kissing me breathless.

Kimbo69 says: You want him . . . what are you going to do when he goes for more than a pristine kiss?

Leesie327 says: Tonight we went as far as I can go.

Kimbo69 says: He's just getting started.

Leesie327 says: That's not what he said.

Kimbo69 says: You really don't know guys . . . they'll say anything.

Leesie327 says: He's different.

Kimbo69 says: Is he?

Leesie327 says: He has to be.

chapter 17

LIGHT OF DAY

LEESIE HUNT / CHATSPOT LOG / 10/08 12:06 P.M.

liv2div says: i've been thinking about last night

Leesie327 says: Me too. I can't stop thinking about last night. You coming to school this afternoon?

liv2div says: do you think it's sick that my parents are dead . . . i can't eat . . . i lie in bed staring at a crack in the wall too tired to sleep, too tired to get up . . . i can't even concentrate on diving again . . . all i want to do is make out with you

Leesie327 says: I'm not sure I follow.

liv2div says: you are the only thing i've really *wanted* since isadore . . . is there something wrong with that? do you think it's . . . disrespectful?

Leesie327 says: You make it sound nasty.

liv2div says: i don't know . . . maybe it is

Leesie327 says: I get the hint. Light of day. Second thoughts. You pressed me, you know.

liv2div says: that's not . . . .try to understand

Leesie327 says: I do. Bye.

MICHAEL'S DIVE LOG—VOLUME #8

DIVE BUDDY: **Leesie**

DATE: **10/8**   DIVE #: **5 with her**

LOCATION: **Teacup**   DIVE SITE: **Gram's**

WEATHER CONDITION: **partly cloudy**   Water Condition: **dry**

DEPTH: **shifting**   VISIBILITY: **murky**

WATER TEMP.: **warm**   BOTTOM TIME: **didn't look at my watch**

COMMENTS:

i'm the infidel. Forbidden. She needed an out.

She took it way too fast. Freak. The afternoon hours stretch ahead of me and all i have to fill them with is the plate of burnt French toast Gram just gave me. Or i can fill it with Leesie.

i stuff my mouth full, wave at Gram, grab my jacket, and head up the hill to the school.

When i walk through the double glass doors, Leesie's sitting on the stage scribbling in her notebook. Her nose looks red. Are her eyes wet? Did i do that?

The other kids leave a space around her like she has a disease. Except Troy. He stands in front of her, puts his hands on her knees. She bats them away. He says something. She turns pink.

DeeDee and her clones sitting on the radiator sneak into the corner of my eye. i think DeeDee yells something at me. i ignore her, cross the room, and boost myself onto the stage beside Leesie. i put my arm around her waist and dredge up a nasty look for Troy. "Leave her alone."

"Who died and made you king?"

Dumb but still cruel. The guy's gifted. i slide off the stage, bringing Leesie with me, landing face-to-face, and say, "Out of the way. We don't want to foul ourselves in your filth."

Troy doesn't budge. "You're wasting your time, Scuba Boy."

i let go of Leesie and grab the front of Troy's shirt. "Shut up." i push the jerk out of the way. Massively strong. Hero strong.

i steer Leesie for the front door. "Let's get out of here." i want to cut class, make out with her all afternoon.

"The bell's going to ring."

My hand slips down to her hip—i hope Troy is still watching. "You want to go to class?"

Leesie nudges my hand back to her waist and makes me walk toward her locker. She's blinking a lot. "Good thing you showed." She sniffs. "I was getting ready to knee him hard."

"Right."

She elbows me. "We had self-defense in PE. That's my best move." She stops and gets a drink at the fountain.

i bend over her. "When are you going to report that jerk?"

She stands up. Her face is in control again. "Don't go there. I'd end up getting suspended."

i wipe a drip from the side of her mouth. "i'd like to rip him apart."

"Then you'd get suspended, too." She's walking. "Don't worry. It's all going to be over soon."

"You still planning to hang him off the trestle?"

"No. We're seniors."

"Oh, right." i hadn't thought of that.

We arrive at her locker. She opens it, turns to face me. "If I'm just a diversion, that's fine." She touches my lips with her fingertips. "Maybe it's better."

"What do you mean?"

"The religion thing." She chews on the lip i sucked on last night, want to suck on right now. "I can't get serious with you."

Serious? My life is nothing but serious. i nod anyway. "Right."

"And I don't think it's sick."

i nod again.

"I think it's natural." Her forehead wrinkles. "Comfort. Affection. You need that now worse than ever." She turns around and rummages through her junk, picks up her physics text.

"It's trig next." i lean over her shoulder, inhale her hair, and take the book from her.

She turns her back on her trashed locker and puts her hand on my chest. "For me it means something."

i pull her math text off the top shelf and replace it with the physics book. "Got it."

She takes it without looking. "I wouldn't kiss you"—her voice drops to a whisper—"if I didn't care." The stillness in her face seeps into me.

i put my hands on her shoulders. "You really okay with this? With me? If you're going to get zapped by a vengeful god—"

"Last night I decided"—her eyes close—"I want to care more."

i take her face in my hands, kiss her eyelids and then her mouth, long and slow right there in the hall behind her locker door with her trig book smashed between us. i hope Troy is watching and gets the message. DeeDee, too. i hope the whole freaking world is watching.

Leesie's god.

My Isadore.

Take that.

HOMEWORK

MICHAEL'S DIVE LOG—VOLUME #8

DIVE BUDDY: **Leesie**	
DATE: **10/8**	DIVE #: **6 with her**
LOCATION: **Teacup**	DIVE SITE: **Gram's couch**
WEATHER CONDITION: **good**	WATER CONDITION: **may rain later**
DEPTH: **kind of shallow**	VISIBILITY: **3 ft**
WATER TEMP.: **comfortable**	BOTTOM TIME: **107 minutes**

COMMENTS:

Leesie follows me home after school. i bring the laptop out of the bedroom, set it up on Gram's coffee table. Leesie spreads out my books and hers, coaxes me through a bunch of overdue assignments. i struggle with dumb stuff, can't concentrate long, get really stuck on English. Nothing to write. i sit on the couch, holding my laptop, staring at a blank white page in a sea of blue. Leesie works beside me, her pen scratching away.

i give it up and Google *Cozumel Diving Deals*. It's taking forever. i lean over and kiss Leesie's cheek.

She elbows me away. "I'm working here."

"Sorry, i was just checking." i inhale. She's got her hair trapped again.

She stops writing, squirms. "What?"

i put my hand on her rib cage. "i just wanted to make sure you're real."

She sighs, leans back, and lets me kiss her. "Real enough?" She strokes my face.

"You're not going to dump me tomorrow?"

"Dump you?" She picks up her pen and bends over her notebook. "You've never been dumped."

"Are you always like this? So committed?"

She stops writing and swallows. "I'm never like this."

i put down my laptop, pick up my dive log, flip it open, get lost between the pen and the page, studying Leesie's smooth, pink lips. "Am i your first? Kiss?"

She turns red. "Am I that bad?"

"Let me check." i kiss her—lose my writing stuff in the cushions between us. "Fast learner."

She pulls away. Finds my dive log. "What does a diver write about in Washington?" She looks hopeful. Wants me to share.

i tuck the log away safe, reach for her again, but she fends me off.

She winks at me. "You're not my first."

i can't see her with any of the guys at school, especially Troy. "Who?"

"You are nosy."

"And you're not? Come on, you know everything about me."

"I know nothing about you."

"Everything worth knowing."

"Not all the girls you've kissed."

"You want names?" i pick up the laptop. The screen shows a page of promising hits. "i don't think i know them all."

"That's comforting."

"Your turn." i lean against her arm, trying to mess up the rhythm of that perfect pen scratching. "i'm waiting—" i put the laptop down and cross my arms.

She keeps scribbling. "Just a guy in our branch."

"Your branch?" i snatch the pen out of her hand.

She pulls another one out of her bag. "Branches are tiny LDS congregations. We meet in Rockford, a couple of towns up the highway."

"And LDS is?"

"Latter-day Saints. Official nickname for Mormons." She starts writing again.

i steal her second pen. "You have an old boyfriend at church?"

"No." She sits up and puts her hand out for her pens.

i shake my head.

"Okay. This guy, Jaron, and I grew up together. He's kind of like a big brother—gave me rides to regional church stuff in Spokane. Dances mostly. He's in Brazil on a mission teaching people the Gospel."

"You dated big brother?" i put her pens on the coffee table next to my laptop.

"He always had girlfriends in the wards, big LDS congregations, up in Spokane. We went out once before he left. Just for fun." Her creamy cheeks turn their pink. "He kissed me goodbye and asked me to write." She grabs for her pens.

i catch her hand and won't let her go back to work. "Do you write to him?"

"Some." She slumps back into the couch cushions. "We're friends."

i play with her hand. "You're blushing about it. i'm not sure if i'm cool with that. What other secrets have you got lurking behind that pure facade?"

"Secrets? Me?" She frowns and sits up, reaches for her pens on the table. "Jaron and I are real friends."

"i guess i believe you." Why does it bug me that some Mormon nerd kissed her? "So what was it like? The kiss. Was it any good?" i lean over and nuzzle her neck. "If it was just a peck, it doesn't count. i'm the first."

She slips the band off her hair. "Better than a peck"—fruity hair scent flows into me—"but not like you."

i think about Mandy—at least she trained me well. "i had a good teacher."

Leesie covers my mouth with her fingertips. "I don't want to hear."

So i show her. The no-tongue thing makes for a creative challenge. i suck softly on her cheek and kiss her jawline. My lips explore her neck, careful not to leave a mark that will get her in trouble. i lift her hair and tunnel under it, kissing the soft back of her neck, rubbing her leg with my other hand.

Leesie arches her back and shifts her body so her lips get the action. She digs her hands into my hair and draws me in. i kiss her closed eyelids and then press hard on her mouth again, pushing my body into hers, forcing her prone on the couch.

She immediately twists out from under me. "Are my feet on the floor?"

i roll onto my side and look down. "One is. Almost."

She sits up and puts both feet firmly on the floor.

i ease myself behind her. "Lesson over?" i drip the words into her ear.

She kisses my temple. "Recess."

* * *

Later, i drive her home, kiss her good night at the front door, take my time about it, afraid of what will happen when the door closes and i'm alone. i want to let my hands slip north so she'll know i appreciate her As, but i don't want her to freak and think i'm a creep like Troy, so i control myself, keep her rule.

My toes are numb by the time i catch sight of a pixie peeking at us. "There's a little face at the window."

"You better go."

"The fish?"

"My mom's miracle baby." Leesie kisses me one last time and opens the door.

"Kissing, kissing, kissing," swirls singsong into the night.

Leesie scoops up the kid and twirls her around. "Be quiet, Stephie." She stops twirling long enough to say, "Good night," and kick the door shut.

i watch them through the narrow window that flanks the door. Leesie throws the kid on the sofa and tickles her. She looks beautiful, laughing and happy, playing with her sister. i stand there like a creep peeping Tom, can't tear myself from the scene. i never wanted a sister or brother. Only child was cool— Mom and Dad and me. Easy to travel with just three. Stephie runs up the stairs, probably still singing her kissing song. Leesie chases after her.

i stare at the empty room, hoping she'll come back.

chapter 19

PIECES

Leesie327 says: I think I lied to him this afternoon.

Kimbo69 says: Relationships thrive on honesty . . . unless you detest his mom.

Leesie327 says: Obviously, that's not going to be my problem.

Kimbo69 says: And that is such a waste . . . you are the perfect girl to take home to mom.

Leesie327 says: Gram likes me.

Kimbo69 says: You call her "Gram"?

Leesie327 says: She asked me to. We had a secret conference today. She got him an appointment with her doctor. It's almost three weeks away, though.

Kimbo69 says: You're going to have to keep lying about that one.

Leesie327 says: That wasn't the lie. Michael asked me about Jaron.

Kimbo69 says: What does he have to do with it . . . he's in Brazil . . . and you say there's nothing to that.

Leesie327 says: There isn't. Honest. I was upfront about him, but

then Michael asked me if I had any more secrets.
I knew I should say something about applying to
BYU, nonchalant, ask him where he's going next
fall, but the words stuck in my throat.

Kimbo69 says: That's not really lying.

Leesie327 says: Maybe it was inspiration. The scholarship essay
questions will be online next week. I can bring it
up then.

Kimbo69 says: Don't . . . there's no rush . . . in a few weeks ask him
what his plans are for next year.

Leesie327 says: His whole world just drowned. I doubt—oh, it's
him—just seeing his screen name makes me quiv-
er and feel like I'm going to throw up. Got to go.

LEESIE HUNT / CHATSPOT LOG / 10/8 11:22 P.M.

liv2div says: you waiting for me?

Leesie327 says: Chatting with a friend. Just told her I had to
split.

liv2div says: who are you bragging about me to

Leesie327 says: Poet pal. She's way better than me.

liv2div says: i don't know . . . you're pretty good

Leesie327 says: Michael!

liv2div says: are you blushing? i really dig your blush

Leesie327 says: When you say stuff like that, it's simply delicious.

liv2div says: weird . . . that makes me hungry . . . i haven't been
hungry since belize

Leesie327 says: You studied hard today.

liv2div says: don't think that's what gave me an appetite

Leesie327 says: Don't say that. I've had too many Sunday school
lessons about appetites. After you dropped me

off, Stephie's singing woke up the whole house.
My dad came in and told me to be careful.

liv2div says: did he blacklist me?

Leesie327 says: No. He was cool. Just told me to remember the
rules, remember who I am. He and Mom want to
meet you.

liv2div says: he didn't put his foot down about the insane scuba-diving infidel?

Leesie327 says: He figured out pretty fast that would be point-
less. Everybody outside Utah dates nonmem-
bers. It's one of those rules that are a good idea
but kind of impossible.

liv2div says: listen, babe, all your rules are kind of impossible

Leesie327 says: Babe? That's delicious, too. You think I'm a
babe?

liv2div says: so, babe, it's no big deal? he's not going to come
after me with a pitchfork?

Leesie327 says: Huge deal. He laid down a new rule: no more
sneaking out. Warned me not to let it develop
into a problem.

liv2div says: i'm a problem?

Leesie327 says: Gigantic delicious problem.

liv2div says: you got to stop that . . . my stomach actually
growled

Leesie327 says: You eat my pie yet?

liv2div says: good idea . . . 2 seconds

liv2div says: this is amazing . . . babe actually made this? even
peeled the apples?

Leesie327 says: Picked them off the tree at midnight.

liv2div says:	so it's babe's magic pie
Leesie327 says:	Blessed. I don't believe in magic.
liv2div says:	no incantations from leesie, the babe of apple pie goddesses?
Leesie327 says:	That sounds like blasphemy.
liv2div says:	did you really pray over it?
Leesie327 says:	No. I could send one—start a trend in e-prayers.
liv2div says:	don't strain yourself
Leesie327 says:	It's no trouble, really.
liv2div says:	i'm not on speaking terms with your god guy these days
Leesie327 says:	Come on, now. You could definitely use divine intervention.
liv2div says:	had enough of that
Leesie327 says:	Are you serious? You shouldn't joke about God.
liv2div says:	i'm not
Leesie327 says:	You think God killed your parents?
liv2div says:	i don't think god can do anything
Leesie327 says:	That's so sad. Times like this . . .
liv2div says:	yeah, yeah . . . this god guy you believe in . . . isn't he supposed to be all-powerful . . . control the universe? if there's a god like that, didn't he control that hurricane? send it right at us?
Leesie327 says:	That's not fair.
liv2div says:	your parents are asleep in the next room . . . don't talk to me about fair
Leesie327 says:	But Heavenly Father doesn't work like that. He sent us here so we can learn and grow. Hurricanes are a natural phenomenon that occur in the

world, following natural laws. He doesn't sit up in heaven planning how He can torture us.

liv2div says: zactly what he did to me

Leesie327 says: No. You can't blame Him.

liv2div says: you're saying there's a god but he's not responsible for any of the crap that happens to people?

Leesie327 says: He doesn't cause it.

liv2div says: that's convenient . . . what about miracles?

Leesie327 says: You're the miracle.

liv2div says: i held my breath . . . i thought god was supposed to be able to calm the storm . . . what about my dad? what about my mom?

Leesie327 says: He can do anything, but He's more likely to tell us to get out of the way.

liv2div says: didn't tell us

Leesie327 says: Are you sure about that?

liv2div says: what do you mean?

Leesie327 says: Nothing. Listen, maybe you should try praying on your own. You don't need incantations. Just talk to God.

liv2div says: get real

Leesie327 says: Trust me. It's so real. No matter what happens, for whatever reason, He's there waiting to help you pick up the pieces.

liv2div says: great . . . call me next time he stops by

Leesie327 says: Ouch!

liv2div says: what do you expect? pieces . . . only piece left is me . . . what's the point of that miracle? unless your ultimate god-man zaps my parents kicking and breathing into gram's living room he's no use to me . . . i gotta get some milk to wash this pie down . . . it's sticking in my throat

Leesie327 says: Are you back? I didn't mean to go preachy on you. I'm sorry.

liv2div says: gross . . . gram's milk is sour

Leesie327 says: You sound mad.

liv2div says: you've got beliefs . . . fine . . . just don't expect them to make sense to me

Leesie327 says: This is going to get so complicated.

liv2div says: keep your religion out of it

Leesie327 says: It's who I am.

liv2div says: you made that pretty clear

Leesie327 says: So where does that leave us?

liv2div says: i don't know

Leesie327 says: I was trying to help.

liv2div says: i don't want help . . . i just want . . .

Leesie327 says: Anything.

liv2div says: you . . . tonight . . . can i come back out there?

Leesie327 says: That probably wouldn't go over too well.

liv2div says: come here, then, leese . . . please . . . i can't take isadore again . . . not if i could have you lying beside me glowing like an angel . . . what better talisman could there be?

Leesie327 says: I'm sorry. I'm so, so sorry.

liv2div says: i just want to hold you . . . that's all

Leesie327 says: I'll leave my computer signed on. If you need me, I'm here.

liv2div says: you want me to sleep with a laptop?

Leesie327 says: better than my old desktop

liv2div says: that won't slow isadore down . . . you would . . . i know it

Leesie327 says: Don't do this to me, please. Just sign on. Anytime. I'm here.

liv2div says: at 4 in the morning? you're up then?

Leesie327 says: Sure, that's when I write my best poetry.

liv2div says: you are a babe . . . kind of a big liar . . . but still a babe

chapter 20

ADDICTION

LEESIE HUNT / CHATSPOT LOG / 10/27 10:15 P.M.

Kimbo69 says:	You dropped off the planet.
Leesie327 says:	Sorry. Michael's all-absorbing.
Kimbo69 says:	Don't forget the little people who made you great . . . college plans come up yet?
Leesie327 says:	He's so glued to me. I can't ever tell him I'm leaving—even ten months from now. Maybe I won't get in. Maybe the scholarship won't happen.
Kimbo69 says:	Is that what you want?
Leesie327 says:	I don't know. There's hardly any of me left to want anything.
Kimbo69 says:	Intense . . . write anything good lately?
Leesie327 says:	Just something insane.
Kimbo69 says:	You need to keep writing . . . no guy is worth giving that up.
Leesie327 says:	He takes all my time, and I want him to. I'm like addicted to his lips.
Kimbo69 says:	Now that's worthy of your muse . . . get to work.
Leesie327 says:	I'm feeling—this sounds so stupid—but I've got all

these new sensations bouncing about in me. I'm like a different person, but I'm so tired. I'm even falling asleep during seminary.

Kimbo69 says: You mean that churchy class you have in the morning?

Leesie327 says: My poor dad gets up early every morning to teach me and Phil. I feel so bad when I'm too tired to pay attention, but Michael—how can I miss even a minute of him?

Kimbo69 says: Be strong . . . tear yourself away from Mr. Magnificent a little earlier.

Leesie327 says: It's so hard to stop kissing him, and even when I do get in early, I can't sleep because I feel so guilty about what I've just done.

Kimbo69 says: You doing more than making out?

Leesie327 says: Necking? Parking? How many more rules am I going to break?

Kimbo69 says: That's what rules are for.

Leesie327 says: God's rules aren't. What's going to happen to me?

Kimbo69 says: You're honestly scared?

Leesie327 says: When I finally fall asleep, I have these crazy dreams that I should not be having. I think I'm going to swear off sleep altogether. Nights are a big waste of time.

Kimbo69 says: Not if you share them with someone.

Leesie327 says: Thanks, Kim. That really helps. He needs me the worst at night, and I'm useless. He should dump me and find someone who can give him what he needs.

Kimbo69 says: You are what he needs . . . relax and enjoy this . . . it only happens for the first time once . . . I think you really love him.

Leesie327 says: Or I'm a nympho. I really care about him, but the physical stuff is so much louder. Does that make sense? It drowns out the sweetness that sweeps through me when I see him waiting for me every morning. By nighttime, it's screaming. That's lust, isn't it? I am definitely in lust. You know how wrong that is?

Kimbo69 says: It's normal, girl . . . calm down . . . do you think he loves you?

Leesie327 says: I know he needs me. He acts like I mean something. He's so tender and patient. It's getting more and more difficult to keep my feet on the floor.

Kimbo69 says: Maybe you should get over yourself and sleep with him. If you're this wired, you can bet he's half crazy.

Leesie327 says: I can't.

Kimbo69 says: That's convenient . . . not particularly fair to him.

Leesie327 says: It is what it is. There's nothing I can do about it.

Kimbo69 says: Cop-out.

Leesie327 says: Haven't I told you this a million times? My entire EXISTENCE would be over. BYU. Everything.

Kimbo69 says: I never took you for a drama queen . . . I thought he needed you?

Leesie327 says: What about me, Kim? What about my life? My beliefs?

Kimbo69 says: If you love him, nothing else matters.

Leesie327 says: What's killing me is when I'm brave enough to be totally honest, I love that he sees me that way. Me? A babe? It's such a joke.

Kimbo69 says: I don't think he's joking. The guy's grieving, girl. Be kind.

Leesie327 says: He's got this obsession with scuba diving. He keeps planning crazy trips. Yesterday he was wild to go back to Belize and dive the wreck where his parents drowned. I'm afraid he'll just take off one of these days and we'll never see him again. He'll be dead on the ocean floor, and I'll never even know. He found a dive shop in Spokane. That's all Gram and I need. At least his doctor's appointment is tomorrow. I'm going along to make sure he goes. He wants to take me gear shopping afterward.

Kimbo69 says: Gosh, girl . . . you need to give him something to take his mind off all that.

Leesie327 says: Give it a rest, Kim. I CAN'T. He doesn't really sleep, either—wakes up in the middle of the night freaked and needs to chat. Did you know that's a symptom of grief?

Kimbo69 says: 2 a.m. chatting?

Leesie327 says: Sleep problems. Going to sleep, staying asleep, lack of appetite. Thank the Lord, he's eating more these days.

Kimbo69 says: You've been studying up.

Leesie327 says: Every site says something different. My mom just has Mormon books on grief. Inspiration but not a lot of practical stuff. Did your mom see someone after her accident?

Kimbo69 says:	She just bought a stack of books.
Leesie327 says:	Really? Can you look up post-traumatic stress syndrome?
Kimbo69 says:	Now?
Leesie327 says:	Please. I can't find anything about treatments. His flashbacks scare me. He'll just drift off. I have to wake him up, and he's not asleep. His eyes are open. Then he gets distant and doesn't talk. He has this bruised look to his face that breaks me. 2 a.m. chats don't help all that much.
Kimbo69 says:	Okay, okay, okay . . . just a minute.
Leesie327 says:	Thanks, really, thanks. I can't talk to Gram. I scared her enough already, and my mom would have him on a stretcher rushing him to Spokane with the sirens wailing, but it's too hard. I can't do this by myself. I'm counting on Gram's doctor.
Kimbo69 says:	This doesn't sound good . . . he could be really sick . . . it says medication sometimes works . . . getting the patient to talk a lot is the only proven treatment . . . this says it goes away on its own . . . or it never goes away . . . it's definitely serious . . . he should see a specialist.
Leesie327 says:	Tomorrow.
Kimbo69 says:	Is the guy a psychiatrist?
Leesie327 says:	A family doctor. But it's a start.
Kimbo69 says:	Is Michael talking to you about it?
Leesie327 says:	He won't even let me see what he writes. Whenever I drop hints about talking it out, he distracts me. He's so good at distracting me.
Kimbo69 says:	Make him spill it . . . his lips must be getting tired by now.

Leesie327 says: Don't say that. *I'll* need a shrink if that happens.
Gosh, I'm sick.
Kimbo69 says: Addicted.
Leesie327 says: Totally.

LEESIE'S MOST PRIVATE CHAPBOOK
POEM #32, AN ADDICT'S CONFESSION
Gray eyes silver steam
Sunday afternoon dream black lashes
crowding me, crowding me off the page.
My page-plotted perfect possibility before
gray eyes silver steam my nights
into jimble, jangle, jazzed desire
descending, bending, sending me
scattered, shattered, smattered,
flattened, rolled, bent,
sent, spent, meant,
mean to, seem to,
dream to,
scream.

NEW PRESCRIPTION

MICHAEL'S DIVE LOG—VOLUME #8

Dive Buddy: Dr. Drab	
Date: 10/28	Dive #: NOT
Location: another punk town up the road	
Dive Site: Drab's office	
Weather Condition: cold	Water Condition: not snowing yet
Depth: ZERO	Visibility: too clear
Water Temp.: frigid	Bottom Time: 20 minutes too long

Comments:

The nurse calls, "Michael Walden?"

Leesie squeezes my hand. i leave her to the dingy green waiting room sitting on an orange vinyl couch with a duct-taped slit that stretches clear across the back cushion. This guy is the only doctor for about six tiny towns. He's only in on Wednesdays.

The nurse gives me a gown. "You can leave your underwear on."

Nice. "i'm just here for a prescription refill."

She glances at her clipboard. "You're down for a physical." She takes my blood pressure and temperature and leaves me to undress. i don't bother with the gown.

The doctor comes in. He's tall and has a greasy comb-over. He listens to my heart and lungs, pokes and prods, and makes me cough.

Thanks, Gram. i really needed this.

The guy examines my foot. "This has healed nicely. Any tenderness?" He presses on the raw red scar.

"No."

"Good."

The nurse steps back in with a clear plastic bottle in her hand. "We'll need a urine sample." She writes my name on the bottle and leaves.

Dr. Drab sits on a low rolling stool and leans back with his hands locked behind his head. "You seem healthy enough. You want medication?"

"The doctor who treated me in Belize gave me these." i hand him my empty prescription bottle. "i've got symptoms. Sleeplessness, nightmares, and i've started having flashbacks."

"If you're sleepless, how can you have nightmares? Get your story straight, kid."

My fists ball up. "i'm not making this up. i really wish i was."

"I don't believe in over-medicating young people." He leans forward and pats my knee. "You're a strong boy. Get through this on your own steam. I prescribe time, a dose of fresh air, and regular exercise. You look a little pale."

"i dive. Scuba. Free diving." Sun, water, sea breeze. Just what he says i need.

Dr. Drab frowns. "Most kids around here play basketball. I'm sure Coach could use your height."

i shake my head. "i dive."

"No diving." He scribbles away on my chart.

"What?" i couldn't have heard him right.

He shakes his pen to get it to write. "After consulting with your grandmother"—he rolls his stool over to a small desk and searches in the drawer—"I've decided you should not dive until you're more stable."

"Stable? i'm perfectly stable."

He whips around with a fresh pen in his hand. "You just admitted to nightmares and flashbacks."

"This is just wrong."

"Your grandmother has had reports of dangerous, erratic behavior."

"This is insane." i'm talking too loud. "Diving is perfectly safe. i know what i'm doing."

"I've done some reading." He's right in my face now. "Nitrogen narcosis makes you feel drunk, doesn't it? If your judgment is already impaired—"

i take a deep breath and let it out, force myself to speak calmly, reasonably. "i've done hundreds of deep dives. i never get narc'ed. My judgment is FINE."

"No diving. Period." He scribbles, then looks back up. "I'll reassess in six months."

"Six months?" i'm shouting again. "i'm not doing that. You're freaking—"

Dr. Drab stands up, towers over me sitting there in my boxers. "It's my job to keep your grandmother alive. Don't you go making it any harder than it already is. Understand? Don't make the same fatal errors your father did. He was always so reckless."

"Sitting on a boat is reckless?"

"In a hurricane? I'll say it is."

"That's out of line." i'm on my feet now. Back in his face, anger bubbling through my pained-hazed psyche.

"Control yourself, young man."

i step back. Freaked. What the hell is going on here?

"You will not dive, understand?"

"No way." i slide on my jeans and grab my T-shirt and shoes. "No freaking way."

"Just let me say this. You are all Mrs. Walden has. And you've stressed her enough already. No diving."

"No way." i bang out of examination room and burst into the waiting room, still carrying my shirt and shoes. A kid snickers.

Leesie jumps up. Her face clouds when she sees mine. "What's wrong?"

i grab my coat and slam outside. i make Leesie drive Gram's car home. There are tiny snowflakes in the air. i don't drive in snow.

"Michael, talk to me. We're not going to Spokane?"

i pull my T-shirt over my head. The dive shop. That's ruined. "Turn up the heat. i'm freezing to death."

She cranks the heat, doesn't talk while i put on my shoes. i'm sucking air in free-dive cycles to calm myself down. She's learned not to interrupt that.

"He says i can't dive. He called me unstable. Gram fed him a bunch of crap."

"Don't get mad at her. She's concerned." Leesie bites that lower lip of hers i practically own now. "Slow down and think about it. She's lost a lot, too. You're not the only one hurting here." She passes a slow car and keeps accelerating—despite the snow. "What actually did he say?" She shoots me a worried glance.

"He got nasty about my dad." My voice breaks. "Seemed to think he drowned on purpose."

She hisses something under her breath. She must be livid. She never swears. "That's the problem with small towns. Everybody has known everybody for generations. Your dad probably beat him at football or something." She shakes her head. "Stupid man."

"So you think it's dumb, too?"

She doesn't respond.

"He wouldn't give me any pills, either. He suggested i go shoot hoops and get some fresh air."

"Did he refer you to a psychiatrist?"

"Maybe i can get the shrink from Belize to write him and tell him he's cracked. i can't not dive."

"What shrink from Belize?" She touches my knee. "You never told me about him."

"Do i have to tell you everything?"

The color drains out of her face, and her hand goes back to the steering wheel.

"i'm sorry, Leese." i stroke her suede jacket sleeve. She's my only ally. Last thing i want is to turn her against me. "i don't know how to explain it, but i know. i need to dive. i'll crack up if i don't."

"You tried that."

"Not really." i stare out the window at the endless hills of brown rolling wheat fields. "i need to get back into the ocean. Feel salt water on my skin again. Taste it. Breathe it. i miss it, babe. i really miss it."

She glances over at me. "Maybe in the spring you'll be up to it."

"i'm up to it now. You've got to help me."

"How can I help?" She frowns. "If you're not supposed to, you're not supposed to."

i smack my fist into my palm. "Turn the car around. Let's go to the dive shop after all. To hell with Dr. Drab."

She doesn't slam on the brakes and flip a U-turn. "Listen, I've got a youth activity again tonight. If we skip Spokane, we can go to that." She fakes excited. "We're cleaning out an old lady's barn."

i slump in my seat. "Sounds like something i'd like to miss."

"Please, Michael." Her hand slips off the steering wheel and connects with mine. "It would be good for you to get out."

"i want to go to the dive shop. i'm not interested in going to church with you." To her church is the answer for everything. "When are you going to stop asking me?"

"When you say yes." She squeezes my hand.

"i'll say yes when you do."

"What do you mean?"

i bring her hand to my mouth and suck on her knuckle.

"Oh." She scowls so i can't see how much she likes what i'm doing. "That."

"You're driving me insane."

"Not Isadore?"

"You and Isadore."

"And Dr. Drab."

"Everyone. Everything. Something's got to give."

"I'm sorry. You know—"

"i'm not going to say it's okay." i've said that a thousand times. "i can't today."

"Let's make a deal, then."

i stop chewing on her hand. "Really?"

She draws it away. "If you promise to take me to the big regional church dance Thanksgiving weekend up in Spokane, I'll quit bugging you about going to the branch."

"That's hardly what i wanted to hear." Her face goes rosy, which makes me want her even more. i try not to get angry, remind myself how hard this is for her, how scared she is. "You think i'm a creep. Just like Troy."

"i think you're human. How can you help wanting this?" She frowns down at her flat chest.

"You're a lot sexier than you think you are." i reach across the seat. Her jacket's undone. i find the edge of her safe zone, stroke the bottom of her bra through her sweater.

She goes scarlet. "I'm going to crash if you don't move your hand."

"Pull over."

We're driving through the tiny town just before Teacup. She turns left at a bank and parks under a big tree. She takes my offending hand, turns it over, and kisses the palm.

"Come here, babe."

She slides across the seat, and i roll her into an embrace.

She keeps one toe pressed to the floor mat. "Isn't this better than a dive shop?" she whispers before she plants her lips on me.

i kiss her back. "Nothing's better than a dive shop."

"Thanks a lot." Her next kiss is more urgent.

"Okay, this comes close." i suck on her lips one at a time. "Why can't i have both? The doctor's an idiot. i'm not doing it."

She sits up, both feet on the floor now, combs my hair out of my face. "Don't rattle poor Gram. You've got me. Do you really need to scuba?"

"But i don't really have you."

She frowns. "Be nice. The time you can't dive will fly by, and you'll be better."

"i'm not sick. i'm totally healthy." i lay some major lip action on her.

She breathes, "Maybe a little too healthy," back at me.

"Are you sure i can't have more of you?"

She pulls back. "Let's start with the dance."

"We're way past dancing." i slip my lips down her throat, but she's wearing a turtleneck. "i hate this sweater."

"Oh. Sorry." She dumps her suede jacket and rips off the sweater. She's got a tank on under it.

"Whoa, babe." My heart is still revving. "i thought my fantasies were about to come true."

She slips her jacket back on. "Not a thrill. Trust me."

"i wish you'd let me be the judge of that."

"Behave or I'm starting the car back up."

"Only if you take your jacket back off."

She shakes her head, but the jacket slides off. Arms, shoulders, bare neck and chest. Even a strip of stomach.

"Is all the skin you're showing safe?"

She nods slowly. "I guess so. What do you want to do with it?"

i start with her fingertips, run my lips up her arm, rest them awhile on her shoulder. She tastes amazing. Oceanic. Then i explore her clavicle. i rest my face on her chest, just north of the forbidden zone. Her heart beats hard and fast against my cheek. i leave a mark where no one will see it but her.

"Michael." She takes my face in her hands, tips my head back.

"i'm here, babe." i smother her mouth like she wants. She

shivers, but i know she's not cold. i pick up her jacket and drape it over us. My hands explore her back, coast around, find the bare strip of smooth flat stomach.

She stops me there. "We better go." She kisses me one last time.

i let go of her. Recess again.

She squirms into her jacket and starts the car.

"You really want to go to that dance?" i pick up her sweater lying on the seat.

"Please take me." She pulls a three-pointer and heads toward Teacup. "My birthday's a few days later. Let's celebrate."

After what just happened, i'm not sure what she means by "celebrate." Her rules keep shifting on me. i know what i want for her eighteenth birthday. One night with her beside me. Would i still be happy to just hold her? i don't know. i'm definitely not broken anymore. And her Ice Queen crown steamed right off her head. "Give it to me straight, Leese. What are you saying?"

"That I want to dance with you."

"And?"

"Just dance."

"How do Mormons dance?"

"You'll see."

chapter 22

SERIOUS

LEESIE'S MOST PRIVATE CHAPBOOK

POEM # 33, SOME GOOD ADVICE

She knows I'm lying,
my mother balancing on the edge of my bed,
her hands clasped around her knee, worrying
about me, *dating a nonmember,* like he's
a diseased criminal rapist.

I just kissed him good night—
with Stephie spying and my nosy mother
watching the clock.

This is what I get for bringing him home
after Halloween at Gram's
and letting Mom pump his hand and say
how sorry she is until he
turned green.

Five minutes—must have been some kiss.

Five minutes is nothing, Mom.
She knows that, too.

You're spending way too much time with him—

We just study.
And make out. And make out some more—
with my feet forever planted on the floor.
I can't say good night to his lips,
close the door on his shattered eyes, and leave
his hands empty.

He doesn't share your standards—

He's cool with it.

Watch it, Miss Aleesa.
Mom's eyes drill right through me.
Guys that age run hot all the time.

I can't look at her and admit neither of us
is cool. I don't ask her advice because
I know too much of the answer
and don't want to hear it.
We've got bigger things to worry about:
grief, death, fear, pain.
A monster that tried to steal him
and haunts him still.
Cold, deep water

that calls his name.
We're dealing here—
you should just shut up and trust me.
I'm keeping the rules—
the big ones.
I don't need to repent—
that much.
The Spirit is not gone—

completely.

I still have glimmers,
not the blazing clarity of before,
when it was the only voice in my heart,
but if I focus, if I try, if I need Him—
that still, small voice will whisper
again.
It has to.

I inspect the broken threads
in the quilt Grandma made me
when I turned twelve, fiddle
with a loose one, trying to tie
it off so the rip doesn't get worse
until,

He needs me,

trembles from my lips,
a pleading prayer, and now

my mother's forehead lines
deepen.

She shakes her head, sighs.
Amazing, isn't it?
The corners of her mouth ease upward.
She recalls my dad's green suit, brown tie,
his Idaho farm boy fresh fascination.
Intoxicating. She winks. *Still is.*

I pretend to gag, but in my heart I agree.
Intoxicating, captivating, exhilarating,
mesmerizing, enticing, enthralling,
alluring, absorbing—so utterly amazing.
How could I ever go back to living without
him?

Mom lets go her knee, leans forward, ties
the broken threads with practiced ease.
Do you love him?
She's concerned, scared
as I am.

Don't be sappy, we don't think happily ever after,
get a grip—
The protests rise too quickly to my lips,
and I'm lying to myself now,
denying my dreams of him and me in white
standing in the Spokane temple,
photo hanging over my bed.

Even though I know God is, at best,
his enemy, at worst,
my myth.

Mom stands up, and I pray she's leaving
convinced, calmed, pacified—
but the worry lines are back:

I was just nineteen when I met your dad—
Try not to get too attached.

I laugh and nod, let her think she's
handled this one. She leaves,
but now my eyes fill at the barest
thought of unattached, any hint
that he no longer needs me,
that he doesn't love me as much
as I sappy, happy ever after, please
hold me longer, kiss me again,
let me fill the hollows in your soul
love him.

> *Do I have to choose? Why can't*
> *I have two suns in my sky?*

chapter 23

SEASHELLS

LEESIE HUNT / CHATSPOT LOG / 11/05 3:17 A.M.

liv2div says: need to talk . . . are you there?

liv2div says: please Leese wake up

liv2div says: Leesie

liv2div says: hello

liv2div says: please

Leesie327 says: What's up?

liv2div says: did i wake you

Leesie327 says: Sorry it took me so long. What's going on?

liv2div says: that freaking doctor's dive ban is making me crazy

Leesie327 says: What happened? Are you all right?

liv2div says: you were in my nightmare

Leesie327 says: I'm a nightmare?

liv2div says: i get this dream about dead bodies . . . all the people i knew . . . floating underwater . . . i'm always in there with them . . . my tank goes dry, but you arrive with your leather jacket fringe floating freaky and your hair wrapping around me . . . we never make it out, though

Leesie327 says: I'm here. You're fine. It's just a dream.

liv2div says: this time the bodies all floated away before you got there . . . then a herd of gigantic salmon with your crazy silver eyes swam toward me . . . Native Americans riding them like horses . . . and you led the whole thing . . . you had a mermaid tail and major seashells

Leesie327 says: Me in seashells?

liv2div says: you were all going off to those drowned falls for a cry fest . . . you spotted me . . . swam over . . . tried to get me to come with you

Leesie327 says: And the seashells.

liv2div says: when i refused . . . you kissed me . . . sucked all the air out of my lungs . . . and took off with the salmon dudes . . . i kicked like mad for the surface . . . lungs burning . . . but it just got deeper and deeper

Leesie327 says: That's awful. I'm sorry.

liv2div says: you didn't really do it . . . it's not your fault, but it pumped me full of adrenaline worse than isadore . . . my heart's thumping crazy time like i'm going to have an attack . . . what do you think it means?

Leesie327 say: Nothing. Just a scary, scary dream.

liv2div says: you won't do that, will you?

Leesie327 says: Suck out your breath and leave you to drown?

liv2div says: swim away

Leesie327 says: Not planning that either.

liv2div says: i can take cold showers for the rest of my life . . . just don't get sick of me and dump me . . . please . . . i need you . . . every day of my life

Leesie327 says: I'm here until you get sick of me. I'm sorry I can't give you what you want.

liv2div says: i wish you could be here ... now ... we could love each other back to sleep

Leesie327 says: That makes me cry.

liv2div says: don't, babe ... i don't want to hurt you ... honest

Leesie327 says: I don't want to hurt you, either, but getting hurt is always part of loving someone.

liv2div says: who are you quoting now?

Leesie327 says: Listen, go back to bed. I'll see you at my locker. Why don't you dream about that?

liv2div says: been there, done that ... more than you know

Leesie327 says: Better not tell me. I'll have to repent. Try something new. Dream about the dance. They're doing a Winter Wonderland theme.

liv2div says: sounds more like Christmas than Thanksgiving

Leesie327 says: We'll have snow by then. Maybe a lot. The dance committee is just getting warmed up for Christmas. That dance will be spectacular. Last year they decorated fifteen live trees. I'm going to want to go to that, too.

liv2div says: are you trying to give me another nightmare?

Leesie327 says: You haven't seen me dance.

MICHAEL'S DIVE LOG—VOLUME #8

DIVE BUDDY: Solo

DATE: 11/05 ~~Dive #:~~

LOCATION: Teacup

DIVE SITE: Gram's

WEATHER CONDITION: cold out, warm inside

WATER CONDITION: maybe more snow

DEPTH: ½ inch   VISIBILITY: 0, dark but clear

WATER TEMP.: who can tell   BOTTOM TIME: 38 minutes

COMMENTS:

Leesie signed off, but i don't want to close the screen. i need to hang on to her until my heart rate slows. i inhale with my gut, hold it a beat, exhale. Inhale again. Study Leesie's words.

She wrote *love*. i guess i started it, but we're not talking about the same thing. She usually says nice, safe *care*. Love? She doesn't even know what love is. What real love can be.

i blow out my air, force myself to fill my lungs again. Fill up my gut, chest—tilt my head back and pack my throat and nasal passages. O_2 flows into my brain, but everything is still murky. Especially when i think about Leesie.

Maybe in some innocent, pure, angelic way, Leesie loves me. Can i find that kind of love? Or do i just hang on and hope she lets me show her the truth someday?

If i could love anything these days, i'd want it to be Leesie. i can't imagine a day without her. Not a day i want to live through. i want to be with her 24/7. Can't breathe if i go too long without a whiff of her. Just walking behind her to class turns me on. Making out with her is like a magic elixir. And a night with her. Even just holding her like i wanted at the beginning would be better than thousands of little blue pills.

But where love should be, there's this bottomless canyon of need only she can touch. Could that be her kind of love?

It's not the type of love i want with her. No matter what she says, what she believes, you have to give it all to get there. Intimate. Attuned. Living like you're one person. Carolina and i got close. It could be even better with Leesie, but every time she calls recess, i have to go back to the beginning. Her rules make love impossible.

LEESIE'S MOST PRIVATE CHAPBOOK
POEM #34, THE WHOLE TRUTH

Online application blank,
essay questions unanswered,
interviews unscheduled.
Two months to the deadline,
but early acceptance is now:
I could know my future
tomorrow.

The clock ticks.
My dream slips, but
how can I push
send
with his bruised heart beating
in my hands?

Please tell us what strengths you will bring to our academic community:
Three hundred painful words,
each one a lie—

not to them—
to him.
Will I swim away?
Not until next August.
Isn't that as far as
never?

chapter 24

CERTIFIABLE

MICHAEL'S DIVE LOG—VOLUME #8

DIVE BUDDY: Leesie	
DATE: 11/12	DIVE #: 40 with her
LOCATION: Leesie's farm	DIVE SITE: sow barn
WEATHER CONDITION: sunny	WATER CONDITION: none
DEPTH: 0 inch	VISIBILITY: murky
WATER TEMP.: NA	BOTTOM TIME: 15 minutes

COMMENTS:

Leesie's dad's pig has a bunch of new babies. Or a bunch of pigs have a new baby. Something like that. She's psyched over piglets down at the sow barn. When i take her home, instead of making out in Gram's car like we usually do, we leave it parked by the front steps, and she drags me down the gravel road.

Leesie slips her hand in mine. "Only two weeks to the dance." She flashes her smile. "It's going to be so great to go with you."

"i don't think i can." We're walking past their big barn. The pigs huddle together in a perfect circle. "That flyer you gave me says semiformal. i just have jeans."

"Nice try." She hangs on to my arm now, too. "In LDS-speak that means Dockers, cords, anything like that, and a dress shirt. Let's go shopping next Saturday. You need a winter coat, too."

"You're getting way too bossy."

She stops walking, steps in front of me so she can kiss me. "Please," she whispers, "it'll be fun."

"Only if we can buy some slinky tops that show you off better." i reach under her jacket and caress her back.

"Like that even exists." We kiss until it gets too cold standing in the road. Maybe i do need a warmer coat.

Leesie pulls her leather jacket tight around her slender body. "Hey, what happened to my turtleneck?"

i put my arm around her. "i burned it."

She scowls and leads me to the barn. It's about half a mile from the house, a long metal building shaped like those houses you learn to draw in grade school. Low and ugly, nothing like the soaring wooden barn close to her house. It sits next to a tiny, murky pond.

Leesie sees me eyeing the pond. "Don't get any ideas."

"Gross, Leese. i'm not a sewer rat."

"That pond is totally clean. The ducks love it."

The pond's surface is barren. "What ducks?"

"The ones flying south."

We linger at the edge of the pond waiting for ducks. i stand behind her with my arms around her middle, my face in her hair. "Speaking of diving—"

"We weren't—"

"i called the dive shop in Spokane. They run trips over to the wrecks near Vancouver. Advanced heart-pumping stuff." i hug her. "How far is Vancouver?"

She tenses up. "How can you want to dive a wreck?"

"Probably too rough this time of year. Summertime, though. We should check it out."

"You've totally lost me. What am I supposed to do? Paddle around in my canoe?"

"Learn to dive. Scuba is so easy, babe." i nuzzle her neck to get her to relax. "Your fear of the water will disappear after the first day." She's still uptight. i try rubbing her shoulders, but she shrugs away. "i know there's still a fish swimming around inside you."

"Did the doctor change his mind?" Why does she go there?

"i need to dive." That comes out too harsh. "i never realized how hard it would be." i try to keep my voice in coax mode. "If you go with me, it makes it all easy."

"But I can't keep you safe."

i'm hanging on to playing nice by a strand of her gorgeous hair. "i'll keep you safe."

She shakes her head. "The doctor said—"

"Come on, babe." i lean over and kiss her temple. "Dive with me," i breathe into her ear. "i need *something* from you."

She twists in my arms so she can scold me eye to eye. Her face drifts deep into frown territory. "I'm doing my best."

"Shopping trips and dances? i'm not a chick." i capture her lower lip and suck on it. "Learn to dive." i kiss her again and whisper, "Be my buddy."

She settles her face on my neck. "You've got yourself convinced diving will make your parents' deaths go away."

Now i tense up.

She strokes my face. "It won't. Nothing will. You need to open up. Talk to me. Cry."

i push back from her. "Like i really need a snivel fest. i'm trying to be strong." i pull her close against me, kiss her hard and urgent. "i need to dive."

She hides her face in my chest, breathless, clinging to me. "It's not safe."

"How about this"—i tangle both hands in her hair—"you do one pool dive, just easy resort course stuff to try it out, and i'll cry on your shoulder the whole next day."

She tilts her head back and glares. "That's so sincere."

"It's just a pool." i glare right back. "We'll have a dive instructor with us. What more could you ask for?"

Her eyebrows draw together. "What does Gram say?"

i stroke Leesie's cheek. "She doesn't need to know."

She pulls back. "I draw the line there."

"Crap, Leese." i lean over her. "Why do you have this compulsion to make everything difficult?"

"I'm just trying to do what's right."

She squirms, but i don't let her loose. "One day you're going to wake up and realize it's all wrong."

She stops twisting. "Where will you be on that day?" Her voice is so sad it makes me hurt. "Cheering as I crash and burn?"

i rest my forehead against hers. "How can you say that, babe?" i swallow hard. "i'll be waiting to catch you." i try to convince her with my lips, but she breaks it off.

She leads me to the barn and opens the door. i balk at the smell.

"Don't be a wimp." She pushes me inside the hot barn.

The place reeks like a giant outhouse. A pig snorts.

Leesie gives me a smile to brave me up. "Heat lamps and mama pigs."

My eyes water. "This better be good."

"Relax." Her voice has that authoritative tone she uses when she's on a rant at school. "You won't smell it after a minute." She drags me down the aisle to where a big, fat mama pig, basking in the glow of a heat lamp, stretches on her side and feeds a bunch of squirming, pink, rat-like babies.

Leesie grins and leans over the pen. "There's eight. Good litter. Shoot, Dad's cut their tails already."

A bucket at my feet holds a razor knife and a pile of tiny tails.

My stomach foams into the back of my throat. "This is making me sick."

"I thought you'd like to see them. The piglets. I didn't know about the tails."

i rush outside. Inhale. Blow it out. Inhale again.

Leesie follows. "You're just a squeamish city boy, aren't you?" She fakes a laugh. "Guess I better not tell you what else Dad cuts."

"Should i be afraid?"

Her grin evaporates.

"Is this some kind of a twisted warning?" i kick a mound of clean pine shavings.

"Of course not."

"i've heard about shotguns, but a farm dad with a razor knife? i don't need that."

"We're not hillbillies. My dad doesn't want to hurt you."

"Right." The guy tosses around fat mama pigs all day. Compact but powerful. He could break me like a toothpick. "He looks at me like i'm Jack swiping his favorite goose."

"Golden eggs? That would come in handy. Maybe he could get a new combine. Too bad you are totally delusional."

"He scares the crap out of me."

"My dad is the sweetest man on earth. You'll see when you and Gram come out next week for Thanksgiving."

"Can't we just eat at Gram's?"

"You want to make Gram cook? She's psyched. I promise you all the pie you can eat."

"Freak, Leese, pie isn't the answer for everything."

She reaches for my hand. "Don't get upset."

"Why shouldn't i be upset?"

"You're right." She lets go and steps back. "Throw a fit. It'll be good for you."

Instead i lunge up to her, pull her tight to my body, kiss her until we're both hotter than is good for us. She calls it quits when i shove my tongue into her open, trusting mouth.

We walk back to her house in silence. i drive home to Gram's, steaming. Then i start freaking. i've blown it. She'll dump me for sure.

But that night when Isadore blows and my mother screams and my dad pounds on the door trying to get in and i wake up breathing like a new diver in panic mode, Leesie's there, waiting online, spouting something about Job, ready to tell me it's going to be okay.

Someday.

chapter 25

DANCING

LEESIE'S MOST PRIVATE CHAPBOOK

POEM #35, PERFECTION

Each crazy ice crystal melting
in his chocolate brown hair.

Snowboarder jacket
and black wool dress pants
I convinced him to buy.

Gray shirt compromise
that sets off his eyes—I

wanted white, he went for black—

Tawny yellow Valentino
eBay'd tie—more
money than I've ever spent.
(Maybe I won't eat at BYU.)

The Winchester knot
I practiced all week
and tie on his surprised
neck. The taste
of his lips when I

smother
his protests.

My rose-colored hip-hugging
swishy skirt, the clingy
V-neck top showing off my
clavicle.

Him and me in the privacy
of Gram's Chrysler
not riding up with my
parent chaperones
and Phil the Pill.

A fluttering white snowfall
purifies the night.

Should I drive?

*I can do it. Time
I learned to in the
snow.*

Perfect.

We make it for the opening
prayer—I can tell he's scared.

You pray at dances?

Refreshment tables ooze
brownies on doilies.
A chocolate fountain gurgles.
The girls are all beautiful,
wearing colorful dresses—no
cleavage, shoulders, barely a knee;
fresh, pure faces.
The boys, even the skinny
ones who still look twelve,
shooting hoops at the far
end of the gym in their white
Sunday shirts and ties, wear
unique power I want to clothe
Michael in.

The gym's overhead fluorescents drop.
A hundred strands of icicle lights
set on twinkle transform
the b-ball court. The first cut:
salsa. His face gets tight.

It's easy. I'll teach you.
I pull him into the mass
of kids showing off all those
Wednesday night lessons.

He breaks my grip.
Stalks the brownies.
I trail in his wake before
the tide of female eyes following
his perfection devour him
like the gooey rich brownie
he's choking on.

The next cut is slow, about loving
a disaster, theme song
for my life. I get him on the floor,
absolutely dying to sway close to him.
I assume waltz position.

Mormon dance rules.
I clasp his right hand.

His thumb caresses the marks he made.
I place his left hand on my back.
It slips to my waist and tickles the sliver
of skin that isn't supposed to be showing.
He settles my hand on his shoulder, kisses
my thumb, and pulls me into full body contact.
I tingle at how perfect that feels but ease back.

Rule number two:
We have to keep the width
of the Book of Mormon
between us.

He laughs low, a hint of mock.
But I don't let it mar moving
as one to the beat of the haunting
melody. He bends and whispers,

You're perfect tonight.

Our faces melt together.
I ache to whisper back
how much I love him,
and want to love him
forever, and just what
that would take.
I bite it back and dance
on a prayer the Lord will
convince him
he wants perfect,
too.

MICHAEL'S DIVE LOG—VOLUME #8

DIVE BUDDY: Leesie		
DATE: 11/28		DIVE #: 56 with her
LOCATION: Spokane		
DIVE SITE: big Mormon church—Leesie calls it a "stake center"		
WEATHER CONDITION: snow		WATER CONDITION: frozen
DEPTH: 2 inches		VISIBILITY: dark
WATER TEMP.: frozen		BOTTOM TIME: too long
COMMENTS:		

The tunes suck. The clothes are stiff. The tie she bought
is choking me. And her parents are here. They even dance.

Her dad twirls her mom, catches her, whispers, and they both laugh. Freak.

"Chaperones? Are they staying all night?"

"Mormon dance rule number three."

"That's a drag."

The slow song fades, and a fast one starts. A few guys stay out on the floor with the girls. Leesie doesn't let go of my hand. She steps back and gets pretty slinky. She's not pole dancing, but she can work her assets. She spins up my arm, and i catch her around her waist. She keeps up her rhythmic writhing.

"Do i have to dance the fast ones?"

"Yeah. It's for my birthday." She pushes off, lets go of my hand, and gets crazy.

Leesie keeps me out there even when it's mostly chicks. On the next slow song, she fudges the book rule. There's only a breath between us. "Your dad is watching." i pull back.

Her head whips around. "Don't scare me like that."

Her mom is deep in discussion with another set of chaperones. Her dad, who really did give me his injured-giant look before going back to the discussion, rests his hand in the middle of her mom's back. Her mom keeps yakking. She must be saying something brilliant because Leesie's dad gets this amazed junior high crush expression on his face like he still can't believe she chose him.

i'm drowning in this place. "Want to go outside?" Please, i can't breathe. We get refreshments and sit down instead.

A couple of girls in tight short skirts, boots, and bare legs take over center floor. The rest of the chicks keep their distance. They both get a good grind going. i nudge Leesie. "Can you dance like that?"

She purses her lips and shakes her head. "I'm not a stripper."

"Aren't they Mormons, too?"

"They're messing up everything."

"They're just dancing."

Leesie's mom goes up to them and says something. The chicks look dirty at her and stomp out.

Leesie swallows and frowns. "That kind of dancing isn't allowed, and they know it."

"So your mom bounced them?"

"They came to make their nasty, in-your-face, I'm-too-good-for-the-Gospel statement."

"Your mom kicked them out, though." i watch her mom walk back to her dad. "That's cold." Leesie's dad pats her back.

"I'm sure she just told them to cool it off." Leesie leans back away from the table and crosses her arms. "Those two snots always make trouble. We're going to lose them. Their parents don't know what to do."

Her mom puts her head on her dad's shoulder. His arm goes around her. My eyes go back to Leesie. "You're all freaked just because they act like normal chicks?"

"Hardly normal. They're into everything. They'll ruin their lives. It's really sad."

"Are all these people looking at you with me and thinking it's sad?" i glance around the room.

"No. The girls can't take their eyes off you." A smile creeps up on her. "They hope I'll convert you and then you dump me and date them."

"And the guys hate me?"

"Naw." She stabs a strawberry but doesn't eat it. "They're writing me off, though. They think I'm going to fall."

i lean over and whisper, "Why does that turn me on?"

"I am not going to fall."

"Should i take that as a personal challenge?"

She stands up. "Let's go outside and cool off."

We grab our jackets, and i hold the door open for her. Snow swirls in with a gust of wind. She walks out into parking lot lights and thickly falling snowflakes. i put my arm around her and guide her toward Gram's car. Her birthday present is in the trunk. i can't wait another three days.

She nudges me in another direction. "Can I show you something?" She grabs my hand and walks backward, pulling me along, deeper into the snowy night.

"Won't the snow wreck your suede?"

"It's tough."

Behind the modern sprawling church the dance is in, there's another building, all white and lit up. It's got a soaring steeple with a gold guy on the top.

"Isn't it wonderful with the snow falling around it? Don't you think it looks like a tiered wedding cake? Iced smooth and perfect."

"Why do you have two churches side by side?"

"This is the temple. Churches like that"—she points to the big building behind us—"are everywhere. There are only a hundred and thirty temples around the world. We're building more all the time. This one's mine."

"i still don't get it. You already have a church here." i circle my arms around her waist and cuddle her close.

"Temples are for special stuff. Weddings, for one."

We stand there a few minutes watching the snow sift down around the glowing building. White on white on white. A surreal, otherworldly feeling comes over me. i let go of Leesie and step away from her. She turns around, gives me a gentle smile.

With the pure white snow falling around her and the light of the beautiful building bathing her in blue, she's as ethereal as everything else.

Untouched.

Untouchable.

She wears the joy this brings her like a transparent cloak that shimmers as she holds out her hands to catch snowflakes.

My chest gets tight. Am i breathing? i don't think so. i float on the verge of shallow water blackout. If i pause here too long, what will happen to the me that's struggling to survive? i exhale, inhale, struggle to take a simple breath. Suck more air and grab Leesie's arm to break her free from the scene.

She's startled, pained, reads my panic, and relents. "I'm sorry. I thought you would like it."

i hurry her away from her temple, and it's strange power. "My turn. i have a surprise for your birthday." i guide her to Gram's car.

She eyes the front seat. "Let's go back to the dance for a while."

"In a minute." i stop at the trunk, pull out the bunny and her keys, scrape the snow off the lock.

"What's going on?"

i grin and open the trunk. "Happy birthday."

Two brand-new scuba bags full of the best gear i could buy bulge side by side, filling the trunk.

"This is for me?"

"The pink stuff." i pull her gear bag toward her and unzip it. Hoses and fins spill out. The sweet scent of neoprene tinges the air.

She steps back. "But you're not supposed to dive. Did you tell Gram?"

"i promise i will if you say yes."

"My parents won't let me."

"You'll be eighteen. You won't need their permission. Look where we're going for your open-water dives." i hand her a brochure for Cozumel's Intercontinental. "i booked two rooms. But mine has a king-size bed if you get lonely."

She doesn't jump on me and thank me like i dreamed she would. Her voice is colder than the winter night. "I hope you can get your money back."

"The tickets are nonrefundable. It's Christmas week. They cost a fortune."

She stares at the gear like it's going to bite. "How could you possibly think I'd agree to this?"

"Just consider it."

"You know me better than that, don't you?" Now she's looking at me like she glared at the gear. "Are you trying to ruin my life?"

"i'm just trying to survive."

"There's no way Gram will go for this. Her doctor said six months. You're still having flashbacks." Her face droops into an ugly frown. "Don't deny it. Diving is way too dangerous."

"i dove before i could walk. Gram's quack is not my doctor, and neither are you."

"I can't go along with this." She steps away from the trunk so the gear i painstakingly chose won't contaminate the air she breathes.

"Just try one day of cert dives, then." i gently tuck the gear back in its bag and zip it up. "Your first one is scheduled for next Saturday."

"That will only encourage you."

"Don't i need encouragement?" i slam the trunk. "You're wrong about this, babe. You're wrong about a lot of things."

"A king-size bed, Michael?" She shoves the brochure in my face. "Am I wrong about that?"

i take it from her, shake the snowflakes off the front, and open it. "i wanted it to be special for you. First time. Look, the room is gorgeous." The four-poster bed is soft cream flowing with pillows and a fat feather duvet. A sheer drape adds the fairy-tale-romance element that i know she digs.

But Leesie turns her head away. "The first time I sleep in a gorgeous king-size bed in a hotel room will be on my wedding night."

"But you'll be eighteen."

"That doesn't change the Lord's commandments."

"Okay. Forget the bed." i smash the slick paper into my pocket. "That was stupid. We don't even have to take the trip. Just dive with me. Please? i'm drowning without it."

She shakes her head, still freaked over the hotel room. "No. Not after this. You killed the whole evening." She gets into Gram's Chrysler and slams the door.

i get in the driver's side and start the car. Leesie doesn't slide to the middle beside me where she always rides. She's quiet. i'm silent, too.

At the first red light, i want to say something. Sorry? But i'm not. *She* should say it. Not me. i've said it way too much. Way too often. *She* killed the night, making me buy these clothes, dressing me up like her prepped-out Ken doll, gagging me with a stupid tie. i fix that. i loosen it and rip it off my head. Toss it in the back.

She catches her breath.

The light turns green, and i press on the gas. Gram's car lurches forward into the white night. Snow swirling in the streetlights disappears, and we're out into the countryside with only the headlights for company.

It could have been so sweet. i dreamed of Leesie getting certified and taking her to Cayman. We'd dive Bloody Bay Wall like my parents and i used to. We'd descend, and a spotted eagle ray would fly below us, daring us to follow. We'd chase it through a canyon, hit a hundred feet depth, and still be able to see rays of sunshine refracted from the surface. i'd teach her how to fly over the deep blue where the wall drops sheer for thousands of feet. i have a hard time seeing that now. i could go back to Cayman alone. Sink down the wall deeper and deeper. Stay down there forever. Then Leesie would wish she'd come.

The car grows thick with sadness as we drive through the snow. Diving again, diving with her, and everything else i hoped for when i booked that trip to Cozumel dissolves as the snow turns to gray angry sleet.

A blast of wind rocks the car. The road is getting slick, and it's hard to see where it goes.

"Do you want me to drive?"

i can freaking drive a car.

"Just don't hit your brakes, or we'll end up in the ditch."

Brakes? Not me. That's you, babe.

chapter 26

FRUSTRATION

LEESIE'S MOST PRIVATE CHAPBOOK

POEM #36, YES?

His knuckles line the steering wheel,
white as the ice pellets pinging the windshield.
Wipers whisk clear a path revealing
the grim tunnel we're crawling down,
heading off to nowhere.
Blackness edges closer and threatens
to overtake us.

Am I as cruel as I feel?
Is there any sense in denying him the ocean
he craves?
If I can't give him my body,
why can't I sacrifice my terror—
sink under the water,
let it close over my head,
encase me,
entomb me,

tangle me in its depths?
(A faint whisper tickles my ears with *yes*.)
But panic seeps in through my fingertips
and up to my heart that thunders
so loud I can't hear the whoosh of the wind.
What if I lost him to the water? What if I
lose him anyway?
Ice was so much simpler
than this premature snowmelt
that threatens to swirl me downstream
in a torrent I can't
hold back.

Dear Heavenly Father,
Is there something of me I can offer
to the disappointment glaring
from his granite eyes?

I strain to hear as the cold car
creeps slow down the white storm's trail.
No answer. Nothing.
What—it's just there—
No. It's not.

I am naked, unarmored.
Between the absolutes,
in the world of gray where I've strayed,
is there any *yes* I can give him?
An elbow? My shoulder?
An ankle? A toe?

Pathetic fare for a hungry boy.
Can I let him—no.
I know he loves—no.
What about...
    Maybe.

MICHAEL'S DIVE LOG—VOLUME #8

DIVE BUDDY: Leesie	
DATE: 11/28 still	DIVE #: 56 still
LOCATION: Leesie's farm	DIVE SITE: Gram's car
WEATHER CONDITION: sleet	WATER CONDITION: frozen
DEPTH: 3 inches	VISIBILITY: getting dark
WATER TEMP.: frozen	BOTTOM TIME: not long enough

COMMENTS:

i keep up the hurt silent act until we're close to her house. The sleet falls so thick i almost miss the turn onto her gravel road. We slide crazy around the corner. Leesie gives the wheel an expert crank that keeps us from crashing.

"You know, babe." i look sideways at her, playing cool even though my hands are adrenaline slick. "Your road used to scare me." The car slides again. i correct it this time. "But i'm driving it. Even in the snow."

"Ice. That's even harder than snow."

When we get to the farm, Leesie tells me to park down by the sow barn where no one can see us. If she thinks more piglets or even another frustrating make-out session will solve everything, she's wrong. "The storm is getting worse. i should get home."

"Please, give me a chance."

i drive to the barn, park the car. She undoes her seat belt, slides across the bench seat, and eases herself onto my lap, leaning across me so i have to hold her.

She nuzzles my neck, letting me drown in her loose hair. "I'm sorry I reacted like that to your present. The whole thing was really sweet. I know you're trying. So should I." She presses her lips on me, trembling.

At first i'm mechanical. Same old stuff. i'm angry and bored. Cold. i chew the corner of her lower lip like she wants. She kisses me back, mouth open, soft, trusting. i'm tired of soft, tired of holding back. i thrust my tongue deep into her mouth thinking she'll freak again, but she likes it this time, arches into me, won't give it back.

Why is she doing this? blinks on in my brain for an instant, and then i get too caught up to care. The only thing i can think about is where my hands will go next, where my lips will go next. i suck on her collarbone, run my tongue along it, and kiss the point of her top's V-neckline.

The hard thump of her heart pounds into my lips.

She forces my mouth back to hers, plays her tongue over mine, then shifts and sucks on my neck. i massage her stomach, pressing harder and harder. i gotta get my mouth on that, so i shift her from one arm to the other and lay her down on the seat. i shuck out of my jacket, break out of the shirt, then bend over and press my mouth onto the silky pale skin just beneath her navel. She gasps. Her skin, saltier tonight, takes me back to the ocean.

The steering wheel jams into my hip. i ignore it. i have my mouth on her flat, sexy stomach, my arms around her, pressing her body to my face. i feel her quiver. i sip her again and again, marking my territory. She caresses my naked back, writhes, lets out a little moan.

i readjust my position, whack my hip on that damn steering wheel. "Let's get in the back."

"What?" She raises up on an elbow.

"There's more room."

"What do you want to do?"

"Same thing you want to do."

"No, we've got to—"

i ignore that, stretch out on her, get into her mouth again. No recess tonight.

She spits me out. "I can't do this."

"That's not what your body's saying, babe." i commandeer her mouth—don't let her speak again until she's breathing hard.

"We've got to stop."

"No." i won't let go of her.

She pushes me off, holds me away. "Unless you've got a condom in your wallet"—she sounds relieved, like she found an out—"it's kind of a moot point, right?"

i roll onto my side, balancing on the edge of the bench seat, ease my wallet out of my back pocket, slip out my condom, and press it into her hand.

She drops it into the dirty snow on the floor mats, shakes her hand like it stung. "I can't believe you had that." She fights her way out from under me.

i sit up. "Why wouldn't i?"

"I didn't think you were—"

"Responsible?"

"The type of guy that carries around a condom." She opens the Chrysler's door, a rush of wind and sleet invades the heated car.

"They're your rules, babe. Not mine." i reach for her, but

she ditches, leaves me sweating in Gram's car. i retrieve the condom and crawl out after her.

"Come back, Leese. This isn't fair."

"You're going to freeze."

"Impossible." Ice pellets sting my bare upper body. "i've had enough frustration." i reach to kiss her, to get her hot again, maneuver her into the backseat.

She dodges me. i lunge and get ahold of her, lock her in my arms. i slip on the ice underfoot, and we both hit up against the front fender. The cold metal grazes my side. "Okay. If you don't want to tonight, that's cool." i bite her ear. "There's lots of ways of doing it without really doing it."

She's shocked, screams at me over the wind. "I'm not doing THAT."

"That's not what i meant." i let her up. "Please, babe, i need you." i hold out my arms to her. "You'll still be a virgin when we're done. i promise."

She backs away, into the driving sleet that's destroying her jacket. "I can't believe you're doing this."

"You did it." A flicker of anger sparks in my gut.

"You ruined the whole night." There are tears in her eyes and ice in her hair. "It started out so perfect." She bends against the wind, licks snow from her kissed pink lips.

"Give me a break, Leese." i take her arm and maneuver her into her freaking pig barn. "It was a bunch of lame kids dancing badly."

"It was perfect." She sniffs and shakes her head. "We should have gone back into the dance." The barn door slams shut and it's pitch dark.

The anger in my gut starts to smolder. "And have your parents in my face all night?"

"They like you." She flicks on the lights. "Give them a chance."

"You don't get it, Leese." i look down at the barn floor covered with soggy pine shavings. "I couldn't stand it. Watching them. Together. It's not fair."

That knocks her. She doesn't know what to say. Why would she? What has she *ever* given up?

A mama pig snorts. Babies squeal.

"And then you go and act like tonight's the night. i'm thinking, whoa, she doesn't want the Intercontinental, fine. Let's go for the backseat."

"Don't be so crass." She wraps up in her jacket like i'm going to attack her.

i grab her shoulders and shake her. "i'm a freak orphan! Creepy, just like your Troy." My voice is hard. "i want to love you, Leesie. If that's crass—fine."

"You just want to sleep with me." Even in this sweaty barn, she's turning back to ice. "You don't care about love."

"It's the same thing." My hands sting where i touch her. "One comes from the other."

"Not for me." Her head drops. She whispers, "I really love you." Her hands curl into fists on my chest.

"And my kind of love isn't real?" i shove her off me. "It's more real than all your religious fantasies." The anger pulses in my veins, pounds in my fingertips, turns my brain crystal clear. "More real than a bunch of stupid lies some guy made up because you can't face reality. Grow up and get over it."

"That's a lie," she shouts smack in my face.

"No, babe, you're a lie," i snarl. The anger in me sizzles, leaps, mounts. "If a list of dumb rules is more important to you than us—than really loving each other—you're a huge lie."

"Don't be like this, Michael, please."

"It's the only way i know. Truth."

"I never lied to you. Except—" She swallows hard, won't look me in the eye. "I've wanted to tell you a couple of things for a long time. First"—she comes close again, hangs on to my arms, trembling—"I told Gram about the lake and your pool dive."

"You *what*!?" i shove clear of her. The fury is burning.

Leesie stumbles but doesn't go down. i advance on her. "You put Gram up to Dr. Drab? What the hell, Leesie? What am i supposed to say to that?" The anger surges in me, molten and dangerous.

"I was scared, barely knew you." She backs away, terrified. "She's your guardian. She deserved to know. There's one more thing I need to say. I'm applying—"

"You interfering little bi—"

"Don't, Michael."

The rage is a river now, coursing all through me. "i thought you were my ally—but come to find out you're the puppet master. No wonder you dissed my trip." My efficient free-dive-trained heart races out of control. i gasp, can't get enough air. "i planned it special for you." i'm panting, too fast. Can't breathe in this putrid barn. Can't see. "And you wouldn't even stick your big toe in the water."

i want to hurt her. i reach out, ready to—i don't know what.

My mom's voice rings in my head. My hand drops.

Leesie rushes me, plants a desperate kiss on my mouth. So fake.

i wipe her off. "Don't touch me." i stumble out of the barn into the freezing snow, sleet scalding my face. "Don't touch me ever again."

chapter 27

GUILT RIDE

LEESIE'S MOST PRIVATE CHAPBOOK

POEM #37, SCUM

I tremble on my knees, praying he'll be back.
The barn door bangs in the wind,
slamming a shot of pain to my stomach.
He's gone.
      Slam.
He's gone.
      Slam.
He's gone.

My chic suede jacket
is a soaking wreck of dripping fringe.
My hair reeks like pig manure.
I wander outside, follow the dizzy icefall
into a world I don't want to know.
It's cold, getting colder, and the lights of the house
are so far tonight.
His tracks mar the snow black.

How many times have I walked this road
in the dark? There's the grain elevator,
lurking silent fortress,
Grandpa's barn, broad and solid,
unchanged by storms.
My feet climb slippery cement steps.
My hands open and close the solid pine door
that blocks out the howling night.
I flee to the bathroom, afraid the empty house
will see me. I stare in the mirror
while hot water thaws
my icicle hands, draw back confused.
All I see is scum.
Milk scum, pond scum, scrub bucket scum
that hides under pure white soap bubbles.

I cocoon myself and soak my pillow,
fake sleep when my family returns, kneels,
murmurs *amens* and *good nights*.

Scum can't pray.
Scum can't crack her scrips
and read at the ribbon,

Though He slay me, yet will I trust Him.

The taste of his tongue lingers in her mouth.
His raspberry kiss stains descend her stomach.
Her betrayal floats before her eyes—
fresh grief suffuses his face.

Scum broke him in the frozen night,
and all she can think of is
what it would have felt
like, what will happen next
time, if he's still awake, if he'd
let her in.

Please, Lord, don't slay me.

Are all her years of *No*
a joke? Cover for a weak sinner
who can't stay temple chaste,
who almost breaks the big one
the first chance she gets?

Scum can't sleep, for fear of his body
haunting her dreams.

In morning's light, scum can't face
shiny silver sacrament trays piled with purity,
can't drink cleansing from a miniature plastic cup
knowing Christ suffered for what she did,
what she wanted to do,
what, even now, she aches for
with every breath
she takes.

LEESIE HUNT / CHATSPOT LOG / 11/29 7:12 A.M.

Leesie327 says: Michael, are you there? We need to talk . . . please . . . I'm sorry.

Leesie327 says: Are you okay? I'm not. Really, really not. I feel horrible.

Leesie327 says: How come you don't answer? You're online. I can see it. Please talk to me.

Leesie327 says: That was me on the phone with Gram. She says you made it home. She thinks you're still asleep. Are you okay? I'm not. I'm really not.

Leesie327 says: Do I still get my birthday present? Please? Can we take Gram with us to Mexico? That would work.

Leesie327 says: I'm not going to church. Can I come over?

Leesie327 says: Michael? I'm here, okay? When you need me again, I'm here.

Leesie327 says: Michael?

Leesie327 says: Please answer. Don't hate me. Love me. I need you to.

Leesie327 says: I don't care if you love me or just want me. I love you.

chapter 28

GETTING BACK

MICHAEL'S DIVE LOG—VOLUME #8

DIVE BUDDY: **The Ice Queen**

DATE: 11/30   ~~DIVE #:~~

LOCATION: **Teacup**   DIVE SITE: **school**

WEATHER CONDITION: **still snowing**   WATER CONDITION: **frozen**

DEPTH: **5 inches**   VISIBILITY: **100 ft+**

WATER TEMP.: **20°F**   BOTTOM TIME: **all day long**

COMMENTS:

School is the last place i want to be, but i won't let Leesie think i need her to come down to Gram's and be my nurse-maid. i storm around glum and fierce. She looks way too good. Her hair, long and full and gorgeous, tortures me with its scent when she walks by. She's got on more makeup than usual. Bright glossy lips. Pouting. Mocking. Soft pink cheeks. Heavy eye gunk. i don't like it—makes her look plastic. Tight jeans and a pretty face. Fake. She should be upset, destroyed, red nose, swollen eyes, dirty, stringy hair. Tomorrow's her birthday. Guess she got what she wanted—me off her case.

That jerk Troy hangs out at her locker, biceps bulging,

giving her Hot Tamales candy. Creeps me out. Guy always has a red tongue. i was just a project, right? Her soul to save for the month. Maybe Troy's her next challenge. She'll turn him into a monk or something. i watch him whisper something to her. She slams her locker and stalks away. All hail. The Ice Queen cometh.

Between classes, she walks toward me down the hall. Her eyes latch onto me like she wants to talk. i don't. My head hurts from my mom screaming all night, and it's all Leesie's fault. She should have let me dive. What business did she have messing with that? What does she deserve today? Dirty look? Naw. Cold's better than nasty—give her back ice.

i stare beyond her and notice a guy creeping up behind, his hand poised to grab her butt. i give the freak a total hands-off-or-i'll-kill-you look. He hurries by, hands to himself. i can't help it, glance her way. Red face, eyes on the floor. She caught the look, thought it was for her. Part of me says stop and explain. The angry me knows better. i keep walking.

MICHAEL'S DIVE LOG—VOLUME #8

DIVE BUDDY: DeeDee

DATE: 12/11	~~Dive #:~~
LOCATION: Teacup	DIVE SITE: DeeDee's
WEATHER CONDITION: snowing	WATER CONDITION: frozen
DEPTH: 5 inches	VISIBILITY: smoky
WATER TEMP.: 20°F	BOTTOM TIME: don't care

COMMENTS:

DeeDee's coming in handy. i let her flirt all she wants. i'm starting to enjoy being around a stacked girl in a clingy, low-cut tank. After tiptoeing around in Leesie's rarified presence, i'm coming back to earth, happy to relax and be a guy and let DeeDee's jiggling flesh rev up my animal instincts.

i want old Troy boy to be ticked. DeeDee's his territory, right? But he's too busy going after Leesie to pay any attention.

DeeDee invites me to a party at her house. i go hoping Leesie hears. No way she'll actually be there. She has a Thou shalt not party rule, too. Nobody even invites her.

i arrive about eleven. Loud music. The place reeks of beer. i stand in the open door and remember the last party i went to in Phoenix. August. One last hot night in the desert before school started. Better tunes than this. A kidney-shaped play pool. Volleyball in the water. Chicks in wet swimsuits. Making out with one. Casual. Missing Carolina. Belize was only a couple weeks after that. It seems like years instead of months. Some guy dared me to hold my breath underwater for four minutes. i did five—easy.

DeeDee spies me at the door, grabs my arm, and reels me inside. "I thought you weren't going to show."

i shrug.

"Hey," she yells at a couple of guys in the kitchen, "you can't light that up in the house." She turns to me. "Want a beer?"

i shake my head no. Reflex. Alcohol and free diving don't mix. Not that i'll need to hold my breath for five minutes here. i should pour a few cans down my throat. i can use some artificial numbing. Maybe i'll head outside and ask the guys puffing away if they have any extra.

DeeDee has other plans. She knocks back the rest of her

beer and pitches the can. She herds me down to a crowded games room in the basement. The stereo blasts. A bunch of girls gyrate in the dark. DeeDee grinds on me until the song fades, then shoves over a couple sprawled on a couch and yanks me down beside her.

Kissing her is nothing like kissing Leesie. She tastes like beer and cigarettes, smells of BO and heavy perfume. After a few minutes choking on her, i thrust her off me.

"My bedroom's down here." She pulls me back and bites hard enough to stain my neck. "I think it's free."

Why does that make me feel sick to my stomach? Freak. Am i broken again? Damn Leesie. It's her fault.

i leave DeeDee pouting on the couch.

"Fine," she yells after me. "Go on back to that stuck-up Mormon slut."

Never.

i slink out of there, humiliated. Anger sizzles in my finger-tips, stings my nose. *Defogged. / Unfuddled.* Isn't that Leesie's poem? i want that to be me. No longer haunted by *her*—those hands, that hair, fruity shampoo, and old leather. Deep eyes and a smile that brewed hope. A hundred thousand virgin kisses.

MICHAEL'S DIVE LOG—VOLUME #8

DIVE BUDDY: Leesie

DATE: 12/14	DIVE #: doesn't count
LOCATION: Teacup	DIVE SITE: school
WEATHER CONDITION: overcast	WATER CONDITION: frozen
DEPTH: 5 inches	VISIBILITY: 20 ft
WATER TEMP.: 18°F	BOTTOM TIME: 3 minutes, 47 seconds

COMMENTS:

Monday morning a couple of DeeDee's friends station themselves close to Leesie's locker. i get busy at mine, within easy earshot, keep my back to them, pretend to hunt for an assignment in my binder.

"Did you see DeeDee with Michael?"

"Not for long. They disappeared somewhere in the basement."

"She said he was really good."

"How good?"

i turn my head to watch the full performance.

DeeDette #1 bends over and whispers in DeeDette #2's ear.

"You're kidding!" she says, nice and loud. They both whip their heads around and stare at Leesie.

She slams her locker door and stalks off to class. My first reflex is to pant after her, tell her it's a lie, tell her i can't stop thinking about her, that after her, DeeDee was repulsive. But my legs don't move. Leesie doesn't care. Her plastic face reveals that much. Let her think what she wants. If she doesn't know me better than that, fine.

i lose it with the Troy thing on my way to lunch. Easy to see by the way he hangs on her locker door, pulsing his pecs, that he's coming on to her again. i turn around, march back to them, hook Leesie by the arm, and hustle her across the hall into the teachers' bathroom. Shut the door. Lock it.

She jerks her arm away from me. "What are you doing?"

"What are *you* doing?" i stick my angry face into hers. "i thought you couldn't stand that guy!"

She backs away. "You think I have a choice?" She turns her face away. "He hasn't been this persistent for a long time. Guess he thinks I'm easy now."

i crowd her against the tile wall. "Want me to set him straight? Resurrect the Ice Queen?"

When she looks back at me, her eyes are full. "I'm sorry, Michael. Really, really sorry."

The dam i built with my anger cracks, threatens to collapse.

She slides past me, puts her hand on the doorknob. i see the four faint scars i left on it. i jam my shoulder against the door, won't let her open it. "Wait."

The air crackles between us. We haven't been alone since that night. Passion envelops me in a hot surge.

"Listen, Leese." i touch her hair. "Nothing happened with DeeDee."

She steps back. i ache to touch her hair again.

"That's not what I hear."

The dam goes back up. Floodgates close. My heart starts pumping rage. "Believe what you want." i leave.

Leesie doesn't follow me out.

chapter 21

HANDS

LEESIE'S MOST PRIVATE CHAPBOOK

POEM #38, NAIL PRINTS, PART 2

I can't hide here forever,
scrubbing my hands of him,
frantic to erase the scars that fit his fingernails
imprinted soft white on me.

I'm desperate to go back to unscarred hands
the faith of eight on baptism day—
a white dress and warm water running into the font,
Dad up to his waist, me floating on tiptoe,
Dad's hand on my back,
the other raised square over my head,
the whoosh of immersion
and washed-clean perfection.
Please, let me return to my father's blessed hands
heavy on my pure head, gifting me
with guidance, protection, calm assurance—
God's breath on my soul.

The Spirit can't abide me.
I am unclean. I can't wash away
the prints of his lips, his hands—
A sharp knock. Mrs. D's concerned voice.
I shut off the water. The scars glow in the
fluorescent bathroom light.
I can't hide here
forever.

LEESIE'S MOST PRIVATE CHAPBOOK

POEM #39, MUCK OUT

I ditch—first time
in my life—find
my dad in the sow barn,
where Michael left me.
Hurts to walk through
that door.

Dad's up to his ankles in muck.
He hands me a shovel. I scoop
reeking shavings into the battered
green cart I used as a kid,
trundle behind Dad's big silver wheelbarrow,
scraping the barn floor clean,
dumping the offal into a steaming
pile by the door.

Together, we fill our carts with pine
curls, fresh and fragrant, blanketing
the pens and pathways with clean,
new scent.

Dad leaves, but I linger—fall
to my knees again, at last,
scrape my soul raw,
plead for redemption,
loving and longing for His
sweet touch again,
needing Him like I never
have before.

chapter 30

PROTECTION

MICHAEL'S DIVE LOG—VOLUME #8

DIVE BUDDY: Sweet Banana Mango

DATE: 12/16   ~~DIVE #:~~

LOCATION: Teacup   DIVE SITE: downtown

WEATHER CONDITION: still winter   WATER CONDITION: still frozen

DEPTH: ??   VISIBILITY: getting dark

WATER TEMP.: frozen   BOTTOM TIME: 37 minutes

COMMENTS:

DeeDee keeps after me. Tenacious, that girl. i decide to like the taste of her cigarettes. Why not? What else have i got to do? i spend lunch making out on the stage with her. Easier to keep going if i know Leesie's getting an eyeful.

"Want another chance?" DeeDee's drooling in my ear. "To-night?"

"Sure, Dee." Leesie's already condemned me for it. It's about time i got some.

She giggles triumph. "Back door. Eleven. I'll be waiting."

i get away from her after school, walk downtown. It's a joke to call it that. One street with most of the storefronts boarded up. But there's a drugstore and Gram's favorite, the Variety

Store. Leesie and i bought Halloween candy in there. Can't go in that place. i cross the street deciding i'm more likely to find condoms in the drugstore. Freak. i've never had to actually buy them before. But the stash my dad conveniently left in the bottom bathroom drawer is back home in Phoenix. Teacup High doesn't have a bin of freebies in the nurse's office. Does it even have a nurse's office? If i'm going to DeeDee's, i need to buy some myself. Leesie touched the one in my wallet. No way can i use that.

i push through the door to the drugstore. The place is dark and tiny. A woman almost as old as Gram stands at the counter—probably her best friend. i buy some gum and bolt, cross the street, and force myself through the Variety Store door. A pimply-faced guy from school stands at the cash register. A couple of women with little kids are in line. Some junior high girls mess around in the makeup aisle.

i wander up and down the aisles looking for the men's section. i find shaving cream and aftershave but no condoms. i hunt until i find a few boxes hanging on the end of the sanitation aisle, next to tubes of yeast medication and home-pregnancy kits. i pick up a box, think about using them with DeeDee.

My dad slept around plenty. Way more than i ever will. i remember a conversation i had with him after Mandy played house with me.

"Don't feel so glum. There's lots more where she came from." Dad glanced around. "Don't tell your mother I said that."

"How many did you . . . i mean, before Mom."

"Didn't count." Dad wiped his hand across his face. "Too many. I wouldn't recommend that. Tough on your mom. Tough on me, too. Made it hard to settle down to one woman."

"But you just said—"

"Don't think you need to break the old man's record. Sex didn't kill a guy back then."

i know what Mom would say if she was standing with me staring at a box of textured tubes in the Variety Store aisle. "Respect yourself more than that. Respect her more than that. Even if other boys don't."

Damn, i miss them. i wish i was so far away from here. i'd give anything to be standing on the dock at the condo waiting for the club boat to come pick me up. Us up. It'd be so much better if it could be us. Every breath that keeps me living aches for that.

i'm dying to go back to the condo, face it all, but maybe stupid Leesie is right. i'm not even up to buying a freaking box of condoms. What will happen when i plunge back into the ocean? i heard about a guy with cancer who went over the wall and just kept sinking. Would i do that? Could i? The ache to find out throbs out of control. Leesie's lake will be iced over by now. Gram's got an ax in the garage. i don't have enough weights. Rocks?

i turn around, and a wall of shampoo and conditioner surrounds me. i pick up an orange bottle, set down the box of condoms, flip the shampoo bottle's lid open, and sniff. No. i try a red one—have to peel off the shrink-wrap to open it. Not that one either. i open another bottle and another. Tropical Breeze. Coconut Aloe. Pineapple Splash. Raspberry Dream. No, no, no.

"Hey, man—what're you doing?" The zitty cashier stands in the aisle, staring at the mess i made. "Dude, these aren't testers."

i hold another bottle up to my nose. "i'm just trying to find it."

"You're going to have to pay for these."

i pop open one more: Sweet Banana Mango. Leesie flows out. i close my eyes and inhale, exhale, go into my breathe-down right there in the store with acne man scrambling around gathering up the bottles i opened.

"You want me to ring these up?"

i hold out Leesie. "Just this one."

"Sorry, man." The clerk carries all the bottles i opened to the register.

i buy eight shampoos, six conditioners, and some over-the-counter sleeping pills. No condoms.

When i get home, i set Leesie's shampoo on my desk, chuck the bag with the useless bottles into the back of the closet. i remember the pills, drag them out of the bag, and swallow a couple with the dregs from a bottle of warm cola sitting on my desk. i resist the urge to take more. Stupid way to do it.

"Michael, honey, let's get the tree started."

Gram hauled her artificial tree up from the basement one branch at a time. She carried up the box of decorations without my help, too. Did she ask me to do it this morning? Last night? She shouldn't be carrying boxes up and down those stairs.

Gram and i work on the fake tree, faking cheer. i can't help but think how much better it would be with Leesie there. i have to make myself stop that. Nothing changed just because i found her freak shampoo. She's still as fake as Gram's ugly Christmas tree.

"Don't you like real trees?" i take the top piece that Gram fluffed and jam it in place. Mom always insisted on a live one. Real pine with long fat needles.

"They make such a mess."

"But they smell good."

Gram sits down on the couch. "I do miss that."

i sit on the couch beside her. The sleeping pills make me dopey enough to say, "What happened to them?"

She looks at me like i finally cracked. "You know. You were there."

"After. What did you and Stan do with them? i need to know. i keep having nightmares."

"You poor child." She smoothes her hand over my hair. "They were cremated. Stan sent—"

My eyes close. Cremated. At least i know. i force my eyes back open. "Is that what you wanted?"

She shakes her head. "We could have bought a plot here. There's room by your grandfather." Tears creep down her face.

No way can i tell her what salt water does to a body. What sharks do to a body. i turn away from her. "i'm sorry i brought it up." i stand and open the decorations box, searching for Christmas tree lights.

The pills finally get to me. i wake up around midnight on the couch. Gram finished the tree by herself. Glass balls. Silver icicles. She left the lights plugged in. For me, i guess. Big colored bulbs send yellow, blue, red, and green playing over the white ceiling.

Mom's Christmas light dogma was tiny white lights only—like at Leesie's dance. Mom made Dad and me string them all over the front yard in Phoenix. i always had to climb the ladder to wind them around the big saguaro that towered over our desertscape. Dad would hold the ladder and laugh every time i pricked myself. Mom shouted directions until Dad's gut laugh infected her. They both ended up falling down laughing at me. i'd give up and join them. The lights always looked awful.

Weird to think Mom and Dad are just ash now. Not even the bloated floating bodies in my nightmares.

On my way to Dad's old bedroom, the phone rings.

"I'm waiting." DeeDee has her silky voice on again. "You should see what I'm wearing."

"i'm kind of down. Maybe another time."

"I can come to your place."

DeeDee at Gram's? DeeDee in my dad's old bed under the pants quilt? "No."

"Then you better get up here fast."

We can talk, right? Leesie always wanted me to talk more. Maybe i'll feel like something else after that. Why shouldn't i? "i'll be up in a minute."

DeeDee meets me at the back door, dressed black and slinky. She starts in on me before i can get my coat off. i resist the panic that hits, keep my tongue jammed down her throat as she rips off my sweatshirt and maneuvers me to her bedroom. She pulls me into her cig-scented lair and onto her unmade bed. She's just flesh, right? She's using me; i'm using her. No big deal. i did this a lot when i was messed up post-Mandy, before i found Carolina. Cheap girl. Cheap sex. Not like being with someone you love, but doing it is doing it. Better than swimming with Isadore.

When i'm done, i pull on my jeans, look down at the floor.

Freak. i used Leesie's condom. i pick up the torn package, fold it carefully, and slide it into my jeans' pocket.

"Stay." DeeDee pats the bed beside her. "I'll sneak you out in the morning."

i don't reply. i haven't actually said anything to her the entire time.

"Please? It'll be nice. You owe me now."

Hold her? Sleep with her? No way. i get out of there, find my sweatshirt, grab up my coat, and split before she comes after me. i almost puke walking home.

Sex didn't ever used to make me feel like this. Evil—like i cheated. Leesie's worse than real ghosts. Tendrils of her wind around my insides. Not guts. Deeper. No matter how hopeless it seems, how much i try to hate her, how angry i am, it's still all her. Messing with DeeDee isn't going to change that. Makes it worse. And my mom and her respect mantra—i betrayed that, too. She's dead, and i can't even be loyal to what she taught me.

Life's never this freaked underwater. You just breathe in and out. Watch the fish. Float. Kick into the clear Caribbean blue that's so full of sunshine it glows. Nothing like the stormy blue, dark and dangerous, that tugs at me tonight. i get kind of desperate. Try to make-believe i'm still broken like that first day DeeDee came on to me. Then i make-believe i liked it. Make-believe i want to do it again. Until i get home and find Leesie's shampoo sitting on the nightstand in my dad's old room.

i fish the mangled condom wrapper out of my pocket, flatten the foil the best i can, try to fit together the rips, and lay it gently beside the slender bottle of Leesie. Damn.

i descend into my bed, curl away from the wall and its comforting crack, stare at that empty wrapper. i lie there choked on the verge, dying for salt water even if it's my own tears, wanting to dissolve into nothing, disgusted with the disease i've become, hating myself, hating DeeDee, hating my parents for leaving me alone like this. Desperately needing Leesie. i don't believe in her heaven, but hell meets me smack in the face.

i get creeped out, can't stand myself or the stink of DeeDee clinging to me. No salt water comes to wash it away. i can't even cry. Leesie always said i needed to. i believe her now. Maybe i could with her hand back in mine. But she's gone. She'll never come back.

i pick up her shampoo, cradle it to my chest, ease open the lid, and hold it to my nose. Not enough. i pour a small puddle of pearly white liquid into my hand, rub it all over my face, my neck, my chest.

i rush to the shower, shrug off my clothes, turn the water on hot. i dump Sweet Banana Mango Leesie on my head, work it up into a huge lather that foams down my face and body. The aroma is strong in the steamy heat. i twist the water off and stand there dripping with Leesie-scented lather. i start venting. Inhale. Exhale. Gut. Chest. Throat. Head. Pack. i repeat the cycles until my fingers tingle, hold my breath. Two minutes. Three. Four.

Nobody comes to me. Not my mom. Not my dad. Not Leesie. Nothing.

The soap seeps into my closed eyes and stings. i fumble with the faucet, turn it on. Hot water swirls my last hope of Leesie down the drain. Isadore steps in, holds me tight. i ride her waves all night.

FEELINGS

MICHAEL'S DIVE LOG—VOLUME #8

DIVE BUDDY: DeeDee	
DATE: 12/17	DIVE #: last one w/her
LOCATION: Teacup	DIVE SITE: school
WEATHER CONDITION: winter	WATER CONDITION: frozen
DEPTH: over my head	VISIBILITY: 0
WATER TEMP.: −40°F	BOTTOM TIME: one freaking day too many

COMMENTS:

This morning i'm grogged out, moving slow. Last night, i finally swallowed another two sleeping pills to get Isadore off my case. They didn't knock me out, so i took two more.

My alarm goes off. Gram gets me out of bed, pushes me out the door to school, and before my brain checks in, i'm at my locker with my hands full of DeeDee.

i scrape her off me. "That's enough."

She puts her arms around my waist and slips her hands in my back pockets. "You were awesome."

"You know, DeeDee"—i peel her off me again—"last night was fun, but—"

"Tonight will be even better." She kisses me, and i almost gag.

i shove her away. "Back off." My head hurts, and my mouth tastes gross. i stare over DeeDee's head at the books on my locker shelf, trying to remember what class i have first.

"What's going on?" Her shrill voice drills into my aching brain.

"Can you keep it down? i'm not really awake yet." Before Isadore left, she hurled a chunk of driftwood right through my forehead, i keeled over off the *Festiva*'s deck, and then i was back in my scuba-diving dream with the dead bodies. Instead of Leesie pulling me out, the angry dudes in buckskin riding giant salmon chased me over the edge of Niagara Falls. i'm still falling.

"I wore you out? Thought you could take a lot more than that."

"Listen, DeeDee." i put up my hands to fend hers off. "We had a good time. Enough. Now leave me alone."

She almost sneers. "You're dumping me?"

"We weren't together. It was just one night. How can i be dumping you?"

"It's her, isn't it?" DeeDee pushes me hard in the chest.

i stumble back, bang my elbow on the locker next to mine.

"She got to you again."

i register something in DeeDee's over-mascaraed eyes, and somewhere in my hazed-up brain i figure i've been a major jerk. i need to be nicer to her. "It's me. i'm a mess. i'm sorry."

"I can help fix that." She squirms in between me and my open locker.

"No." i step away from her pawing hands. "It doesn't help."

"But she did? I actually sleep with you, but I'm not good enough?"

"Shhh. Please." i drop my head into my hands and press on my throbbing temples.

"Don't shush me. You creep." She shoves me again.

i take her wrist so she can't jab me. "Look, we both got some, right? No hurt feelings, okay?"

"Feelings?" She spits the word right in my face. "What would a guy like you know about feelings?" She rips her arm away from me. "There's always hurt feelings. What do you think I am?"

Even grogged out from sleeping pills, i know enough not to answer that one.

"Well, I'm not. I liked you a lot." She storms away. Wish i could get Isadore to do that.

i stare at the books in my locker, trying to get my eyes to focus, feeling like a mound of steaming crap. Had the chicks i messed with at parties and then didn't call feel like DeeDee? Did they all have feelings? They acted so cool. She'd acted so cool. Was it all a big lie? Did they feel just as whacked as i did when Carolina dumped me? How could DeeDee possibly think what we did last night was making love? It felt like love with Carolina—made her more and more precious, until i couldn't go a day without holding her. That's love. i hate to admit it, but Mandy made me feel like that, too. That's the oneness i wanted with Leesie. Does DeeDee feel like that about me now? Am i hurting her, just like Mandy hurt me?

After class, DeeDee shadows me back to my locker.

"Please, Michael. We make such a good couple. You owe me, Michael."

All day it's like that. i can't shake her. i stop caring if i hurt her or not. She asked for it, practically forced me into it. She can take what she gets. Besides, because of her, i have no hope of getting Leesie back. Ever. Last night didn't mean anything to me. Even though DeeDee's putting on a huge drama-queen-guilt–me-out-of-my-socks-make-me-feel-like-a-creep-so-i'll-be-her-steady stage show, it didn't mean anything to her, either. But to Leesie it'll mean loads. She'll detest me—already does, now more than ever. i can't even tell her it was a lie anymore. And here's DeeDee all over me all day—making it truer and truer. i don't look in Leesie's direction, can't take seeing how much she hates me staring straight in my face.

DeeDee even follows me down to Gram's. i let the door swing shut on her.

i collapse on dad's old bed, sleep off the pills. It's dark out when i wake up. i wander into the living room, sit on the couch, zone out the window at the snow. Thick. Cold. White. Reflecting Gram's colored Christmas lights. The sun comes up. Gram tries to get me to go to school—last day before break. No way. Another day with DeeDee in my face. Forget it. And Leesie, if i saw her right now, looking at me with plastic, made-up eyes, it'd kill me. So i spend the day with my old friend Isadore, clinging to my mangrove buddy, helpless to my mom screaming, "Michael, Michael, Michael."

chapter 32

MESSED UP

LEESIE'S MOST PRIVATE CHAPBOOK

POEM #40, PHONE CALL

I should not have picked
it up the third
time it rang,
should not have held it to my ear,
should not have listened as she bragged
how good he
is in her
bed
with her
body,
while I cry and pray and try to
repent,
sitting in the branch president's
red-floored furnace room office
confessing how badly I wanted to
sin,
listening to healing words speak
calm and love and forgiveness,

while I fight the desire his body seared onto mine
and make my promises anew with a tiny cup of
water
and a crumble of
bread,
while I strain to feel a tremble of the
Spirit...

My Michael, my boy, my
love
lay with her.

I hang up the phone, but it rings again.
I pick up the receiver
and slam it down over and over
and over, but it doesn't splinter,
so I search for something heavy to
smash it.
How many tons is the pickup?
Dad's grain truck?
The combine?
I'm panting wild to run over the
plastic box that houses her sultry voice,
splinter the wires and filaments
that carry her to my ear,
ram the poles, tear down the wires—
hijack the tractor and go digging for bundles
of white high-speed cables
that put her too real too solid
flesh in between him and me
forever.

LEESIE HUNT / CHATSPOT LOG / 12/22 11:41 P.M.

Kimbo69 says: I got to get to sleep . . . our flight takes off early . . . but I got your poem . . . wanted to check in.

Leesie327 says: Did you finally get packed?

Kimbo69 says: I couldn't decide which swimsuit I look hottest in, so I grabbed a bigger suitcase and threw them all in.

Leesie327 says: You look hot in anything.

Kimbo69 says: True . . . but hottest . . . this is important . . . I'll let Mark decide.

Leesie327 says: Where are you going again?

Kimbo69 says: Cozumel . . . too bad you can't come with . . . the place is supposed to be full of scuba divers.

Leesie327 says: For real? Cozumel? I'll pass. Don't go flirting around and get Mark jealous.

Kimbo69 says: You're just going to sit at home the whole break?

Leesie327 says: My scholarship essays are due January 15. I want them word perfect. Maybe I'll write them in iambic pentameter. So lay it on me. What did you think of that poem?

Kimbo69 says: I like the part where you go wild with massive farm machinery.

Leesie327 says: Writing that was good therapy.

Kimbo69 says: Now go write mission boy a long letter and forget Michael and DeeDee.

Leesie327 says: I tried that, and then DeeDee called.

Kimbo69 says: You think she's telling the truth?

Leesie327 says: Some of it has to be. I know I lost him, but does she have to wipe it in my face?

Kimbo69 says: You really told the preacher man everything?

Leesie327 says: He's called the branch president. We don't have priests or preachers.

Kimbo69 says: Right . . . mission boy's dad . . . whatever you want to call him . . . he was nice?

Leesie327 says: He was so relieved I hadn't fallen off the edge—that he cried. He gave me a box of tissues and told me everyone has desires. Even "old farts" like him.

Kimbo69 says: He called himself an old fart . . . the branch preacher man?

Leesie327 says: One minute I'm crying. He's crying. The next we're both laughing. He gave me a great recommendation to BYU.

Kimbo69 says: He still want you to marry his son?

Leesie327 says: We didn't go there.

Kimbo69 says: You going to be okay?

Leesie327 says: As long as DeeDee doesn't call back. I only had to fix my concealer twice today.

Kimbo69 says: That's a start.

Leesie327 says: I've just got one thing left to do. Reparation.

Kimbo69 says: What is that supposed to mean?

Leesie327 says: To repent, I have to do all in my power to repair the evil I've done—to Michael.

Kimbo69 says: That's just crazy . . . I know you're nuts over the guy, but NEWS FLASH, he's hurting you as much as he can . . . keep away from the jerk.

Leesie327 says: I have to do something or it will never get better. It scares me, though. He was so angry, so disgusted. He still is. I think I'd be afraid to be alone with him.

Kimbo69 says: You think he'd hurt you?

Leesie327 says: No. Don't say that. He's not like that. He can't be.

Kimbo69 says: So what could you ever possibly do?

Leesie327 says: Try a little faith for a change. I'm leaving this in the Lord's hands.

Kimbo69 says: He'll get sick of DeeDee . . . you'll get another chance.

Leesie327 says: I don't even know if I want another chance.

Kimbo69 says: But you love the guy . . . you still do . . . it's seeping through the broadband.

Leesie327 says: Does he really love me, though? For him love and making it are the same thing.

Kimbo69 says: That's how it's supposed to be.

Leesie327 says: Not for me. Now that he's lost, he means so much more than soft lips. Love is so much more than that.

chapter 33

MERRY CHRISTMAS

MICHAEL'S DIVE LOG—VOLUME #8

DIVE BUDDY: Her?	
DATE: 12/25	~~DIVE #:~~
LOCATION: Teacup	DIVE SITE: Gram's—where else
WEATHER CONDITION: blizzard	WATER CONDITION: swirling
DEPTH: drifts	VISIBILITY: quarry
WATER TEMP.: frozen	BOTTOM TIME: 3 minutes

COMMENTS:

Gram's moving around in the kitchen early. She promised fresh cinnamon rolls for Christmas breakfast. She's not doing much better than me—thinner than ever, so frail. Whenever i try to get her to rest, she shoos me away, cooks food i can't eat, doesn't eat hers. Listening to her working in the kitchen, knowing she'll be on her ancient feet for hours today trying to make me happy, makes me feel like a guilty creep.

i roll out from under the pants quilt. Maybe she'll let me punch the dough for her. Didn't i like squishing it between my fingers when i was a kid? i barely remember.

The phone rings. i pick it up thinking maybe it's Stan

calling from Florida, forgetting the time difference here. Who else would call us? One of Gram's old ladies? Me and my parents usually spent Thanksgiving and most of Christmas break at the condo, wearing our seven mils, diving deep wrecks and shallow reefs. It would be good to hear Stan's voice, get an up-to-date dive report. i crave something that proves my old life isn't just a dimming fantasy that crashed into Isadore. If Stan's still real, i can go back.

Gram answers, too. She says, "Hello," before i can.

"It's me, Gram. Leesie."

i grip the phone tighter—afraid she'll get away—and silently fill my chest and gut, blow it out in a steady whisper.

"Oh, honey, it's good to hear from you. Michael's still asleep."

i suck air again. Controlled. Silent. Don't let her hear.

Leesie's voice flows around me. "That's all right. He doesn't want to talk to me."

No, babe, i do. i so want to talk to you.

i miss Gram's comment. Leesie's talking again. "Are you guys okay today?"

"Well, my. Of course, we've got the tree up and all decorated." Gram's voice gets quivery. "We're fine."

Breathe in. Blow it out. Thin stream. Don't drop the stupid phone.

"I wanted to invite you out here. Like Thanksgiving. But—"

"I know. And it isn't your fault."

"It is." Now Leesie's voice quivers. "And I'm sorry."

i close my eyes, inhale through my nose, trying to get the scent of her hair through the phone.

"He's just going through a tough time."

"Are you guys going anywhere?"

That stings. Still, i strain to suck in every wisp of her.

"No. We'll be here."

"Right."

She sounds so right. Now everything's wrong. i drown in wrong—it clutches at me, and i can't get free of its muck. i long to let go, sink, be done.

Gram doesn't say anything. Maybe she can't. i tip my head back so air fills my throat, flows into my nasal passages.

"Guess I better go. I was just"—Leesie's voice breaks—"thinking about you." She pauses, then whispers, "And Michael." She sniffs. "Don't tell him I called."

"Goodbye, honey." Gram hangs up.

i stay on the line. So does Leesie. She sniffs again. "Is that you?" A soft whisper i can barely hear.

i hold my breath. One, two, three long minutes. Then nothing but dial tone.

chapter 34

HAPPY NEW YEAR

MICHAEL'S DIVE LOG—VOLUME #8

DIVE BUDDY: **Solo**	
DATE: **01/03**	~~DIVE #:~~
LOCATION: **Teacup**	DIVE SITE: **Gram's**
WEATHER CONDITION: **dark**	WATER CONDITION: **snowing**
DEPTH: **haven't been out**	VISIBILITY: **nil**
WATER TEMP.: **still frozen**	BOTTOM TIME: **at least a week**

COMMENTS:

Gram and i take the tree down. She bugs me all afternoon to carry the boxes to the basement. i stay hidden in Dad's room. Easier to just shut the door. Block her out. Don't think about her and her fake Christmas tree crammed into an ancient box that's held together with cracked, yellowed tape or the dusty box of ornaments and ugly colored lights. Don't think about anything. Not even the glossy brochure i found crumpled in my coat pocket yesterday. i ripped it to pieces. We should be there now. Leesie and me. No, just getting home. Freak. i didn't even cancel. The credit card Stan sent me got a useless workout last week. Weird to be so loaded it doesn't matter. i won't be for long if i keep blowing it like this. Stan will pitch a fit.

Damn her. i pick up that shampoo back in its spot on my nightstand. She's still stopping me. Why didn't i get on that plane? Use my ticket at least. i need to stop moaning around. Am i that whipped? No way. Not anymore. Not today. Diving with her would have been such a drag. A brand-new diver panicking at every blade of sea grass? Why would i waste my gas on that? i should just flush this crap shampoo down the john. i head for the bathroom.

Get stopped by my bedroom door.

Freak.

i put the bottle back in its place. i resist the urge to open the lid and inhale. Maybe tomorrow i can use it all up. Wouldn't want more waste.

i get to work planning trip after amazing dive trip. i research the Brac, Maui, Guam, even the Similans off the Burma Banks. i find a ten-day trip to Palau. The boat looks fantastic.

On her way to bed, Gram raps on my door. "I know you're not feeling well, but can you please take the Christmas tree down before you go to sleep? I can get the decorations box in the morning. I'm tired of the mess."

i don't answer, just lie on Dad's old bed, huddle cold under the pants quilt, and stare at the crack on my wall trying to imagine taking one of those trips by myself. The spidery branches of the crack turn into flashes of lightning. i hide my head under the pillow trying to muffle the thunder. Isadore takes her time. She knows i'm not going anywhere.

i wake crammed into the corner of the bed, hanging on to

my pillow, not knowing where i am. Moonlight filters through the curtains and illuminates the crack on the wall. Gram's. Dad's old room. i turn on the light. Maybe Gram's got some wall gunk downstairs.

On my way to the basement, i bang my shin on the big box with the Christmas tree in it. i grab the awkward box and drag it to the top of the basement steps. i tip the box on end, slip around behind it, and pick it up around the middle. i try to be stealthy carrying it down the creaking wood stairs. Stupid. Like Gram can hear me with her hearing aid out.

i stash the tree next to the shiny gear bags full of scuba equipment that i bought for me and Leesie. i pick hers up and pitch it into a dark corner. i carry mine upstairs. Maybe i'll dump it out on my bed and try it all on. i need some hooks for my new BC. Dad was a master at hooks. i could order some. i take the stairs two at a time with my gear bag bouncing against my leg.

The decorations box accuses me from the middle of the living room floor. Poor Gram. i'm such a beast. i wing the scuba bag on my bed and whip the box down the stairs.

The basement is fitted out with big wooden shelves that Gramps built for Gram. Home-canned peaches, pickles, and jam line up in rows on the middle shelves. Boxes fill the upper and lower shelves. i try to figure out where the decorations box goes. Is it the empty spot on the top shelf center or bottom right? i find a place big enough and shove it in.

Two white boxes catch my eye. They seem new. No dents or dust. i turn away and then rotate back, stare at them in the dim light of a dusty 40-watt bulb. Dad's name labels one. Mom's on the other. The return address is a mortuary. i can't touch them, can't move, just stand there, fixated.

My hand reaches out and drops, reaches again, just brushing the corner of Dad's box. i bring my other hand forward, force both to grasp a corner of the box. i close my eyes and ease it off the shelf. Heavy. Dense. i rest it on my chest, wrap my arms around it, and lean back. i can't leave him down there with the chokecherry jam and old peaches. i carry Dad upstairs, holding my breath, place him gently in the middle of the living room floor, and run back downstairs for Mom.

i want to pound on Gram's door, wake her up and demand an explanation. Why didn't she tell me they were there? Why did she stick my parents' ashes down in the basement? How long have they been down there? What do we do with them now? i picture Gram's white hair down around her face, her puckered toothless mouth, her dentures soaking on the nightstand, the blurry look in her eyes as she strains to understand me without her hearing aid. It'd give her a stroke.

i sit on the couch and stare at the boxes, move them up onto the coffee table, back to the floor, sit next to them. i want those boxes to talk, wonder if i could recognize anything inside. Is it all just gray powder? i have this sick urge to open them and plunge my hands into their ashes. i'm crazy to find something the furnace didn't incinerate. A filling. My dad's dive watch charred and black. Time spins away from me, sitting on the floor next to my parents, going from one extreme to another, unable to touch the boxes, wanting to open them. i keep going back to waking Gram but decide that'd just be two of us freaking. i remember how she said, "Cremation," back when we decorated the tree. No wonder she hid them.

i wander back to Dad's old room, search through the top drawer for my sleeping pills—freak, the bottle's gone. Gram? i stretch out on the bed, stare at the ceiling, flip onto my stomach, punch my pillow, roll onto my side, and find my crack in the wall. Tonight it glares, and i sure didn't find wall gunk in the basement.

i sit up before Mom's screams start, don't bother with a light, grab my laptop from the desk, and sign on. Please, please, please.

Maybe there is a god. She's there.

chapter 35

DUST TO DUST

LEESIE HUNT / CHATSPOT LOG / 01/03 3:12 A.M.

liv2div says:	hey
Leesie327 says:	Wow. Didn't expect *you*.
liv2div says:	i can't believe you're up
Leesie327 says:	My wall doesn't have any good cracks.
liv2div says:	can you come over?
Leesie327 says:	Me?
liv2div says:	yeah
Leesie327 says:	You think of more nasty things to say?
liv2div says:	i need somebody
Leesie327 says:	You've got a new somebody.
liv2div says:	please, don't be like that
Leesie327 says:	What should I be like?
liv2div says:	i'm falling apart here

LEESIE'S MOST PRIVATE CHAPBOOK

POEM # 41, FALLING APART

I fumble myself dressed,
wrap in the jacket he loved—
it isn't the same,
but the cleaners did their best.
I whisper my destination at
my parents' door, ignore
Mom's protest and Dad's offer
to help, promise I'll call,
and tear through the night, flying
over those hills that stand between
us—cursing the snow-packed slickness
that forces caution, slows my momentum, and
provides time to imagine him lying in
Gram's pink bathtub with weights
on his chest, holding the breath
that used to stir my hair, trickle
down my throat, and sigh life into me.
I pray the tub's not deep enough for
shallow water blackout
and Gram's knives are too dull to
open veins, that he never got more of those
pills and doesn't think of wrapping
scuba hoses around his neck.

I zoom through town,
thanking the Lord for this chance,
blow past three stop signs to pull
into Gram's driveway and race to the door—
falling apart.

MICHAEL'S DIVE LOG—VOLUME #8

DIVE BUDDY: Leesie

DATE: 01/03   ~~DIVE #:~~

LOCATION: Teacup   DIVE SITE: Gram's

WEATHER CONDITION: winter   WATER CONDITION: stopped snowing

DEPTH: she says it's not bad   VISIBILITY: about 3 ft

WATER TEMP.: frozen   BOTTOM TIME: the rest of the night

COMMENTS:

She doesn't reply or sign off—she's still online. i wait and wait for her to post, but there's no answer. Should i post again? Beg her to come hold my hand? Promise not to hurt her again? i type, *please, Leese,* and leave it at that.

Where is she? Sitting in her bedroom, staring at the screen, wondering who the hell i think i am bugging her again? *I need somebody.* No, Leese, i need you. *Falling apart.* At least that's accurate.

She isn't going to post. Stupid to hope. i go into the living room. Stare. Flip open my cell to call Leesie, snap it shut. i twist Gram's old reading lamp around so it shines on Mom and Dad, walk back and forth from the dark kitchen to the boxes. Desperation draws me back to Dad's old bedroom. i zone on the laptop screen. Still no message.

Maybe i should drive out to the farm, crawl through her window, and beg. i actually put my jacket on and am reaching for Gram's pink-bunnied key ring when headlights slice through the night. A white pickup, shining like a ghost-mobile, rolls down the hill and turns into Gram's driveway. i flick on the kitchen light and open the door to a slim shape wrapped in suede. i want to scoop her into a gigantic hug and not let her go.

Leesie draws her jacket close around her, narrows her eyes. "You look fine. What's going on?" She sounds disappointed.

i turn and lead the way to Gram's living room.

Leesie follows. "Was this just something to get back at me? If it was, you're brilliant, because it totally worked. Look how I'm shaking."

"Basement. i took some stuff down. For Gram." i point out the boxes. "i found these. i just . . . found them"

"This is the big deal?" Leesie folds her arms and glares at me. i expect her foot to start tapping.

i nod, unable to speak and make it true.

"Well, what's in them?"

"My mom and dad." i gasp, struggle to keep my face from dissolving.

Leesie stares at the boxes, then at me, glances toward Gram's room. "Ashes?" Her mouth forms the word, but she doesn't voice it out loud.

She reaches out and brushes my forearm with her fingertips, pulls her hand back, tucks it safe under her arm. "I'm so sorry."

"No one told me. They were just there. Downstairs. On a shelf with—" My voice breaks. i have to stop and vent.

"Why didn't she tell you your parents were cremated?"

"i knew that much." i sniff hard. "i haven't been the easiest person to talk to lately."

She bends her head. "Sorry for that, too."

i sit down by the boxes, caress the cardboard, wanting to lay my cheek on Mom's box and hug it.

Leesie kneels beside me, stops my hands. "Michael, this isn't them. It's just their bodies."

i pull my hands free. "This is all i have."

"Do something special, then." She folds her hands in her lap. "Remember the Salmon People and their Ceremony of

Tears? That's what you need. It's powerful stuff, Michael. Believe me."

i stroke my mom's box and examine the label. "You think i should buy them coffins, stick them in the ground?" i already bought Mom one coffin. Was the cherry and pink satin ashes now, too?

Leesie rests a hand lightly on my bowed back. "Gram would probably appreciate that. Isn't your grandfather buried in the Tekoa Cemetery?"

"But they were divers. i can't see sticking them in the dirt." The label on Dad's box catches my eye: MICHAEL WALDEN. Weird to see my name on a box of ashes. i need to change it to MIKE.

"You need to consider Gram's feelings." The weight of Leesie's hand evaporates.

Was it ever there? Did I imagine it? Is she really sitting beside me? i turn to face her, grab that elusive hand, hold on to it too tight. "What about my feelings? What about theirs?" i'm getting too worked up. My voice is high and cracks.

She strokes my hand. "Did you ever discuss it? Casual, just in passing?" She isn't saying anything that helps, but her voice is liquid calm pouring into the tense room.

"Nope." i take a deep breath, hold it, exhale. "Who does that? Death never had anything to do with us."

"What about the will?"

"i could ask Stan."

"Good idea." She gives my hand a squeeze. "He might have some thoughts about a memorial service for you."

"i don't want any service." i pull my hand away from hers, let it smooth over the boxes again, close my eyes.

She retreats to the couch. "Listen, it's Sunday tomorrow.

Come to church with me. My branch president is really easy to talk to. We could help you plan a simple service—something that would make you and Gram feel better."

Better? Is she joking? "If i want a minister, Gram's got one down the street."

Leesie clasps her hands tight in her lap. "Why'd you ask *me* tonight?"

i tear myself away from the boxes, sink on the couch beside Leesie, close enough to breathe her in, but i don't touch her. "i still need you, babe." i want to hang on to her, wrap up in her like i used to, but my arms don't move. She doesn't relax toward me, lean into my shoulder, rest her thigh against mine. The inch between us seems like a massive wall. "Thanks for coming."

"Sure."

i close my eyes, inhale long and slow, exhale, cycle after cycle, breathing in the essence of Leesie. The suede is damp and overpowers her Sweet Banana Mango hair. She didn't shower before she came. Even her sweat smells good.

She's studying me when i open my eyes. Our glances touch and hold. In the bright glare of the desk lamp's spotlight, i see the pain i caused etched on her face. The dark circles under her eyes that she hid with all that makeup, day after day. Her face is thinner. Her soft mouth closes in a pale line. No pleased pink eases the paleness of her cheeks. The summer sun has faded from her hair.

i take her hand again, gently this time—touch the scars one by one. "i'd like you to come back."

"Really back?"

i nod, holding her eyes with mine. "Nothing's right without you."

"I thought I wanted this—more than anything—but I—"
She shakes her head.

"This is about DeeDee." My eyes hit the floor. "i haven't
seen her since before Christmas break."

Leesie pulls her hand away. "She called me. Said you were
over every night. I hung up before she could get too graphic."

"She's lying."

Leesie touches my face. "So you didn't—"

"Not at the party. i gagged on her."

"I'm supposed to believe that?" She turns her back on me.
"I saw you."

"Well, it hurt, Leese, when you didn't believe me. i wanted
to hurt you back."

She sits back against the couch again. "It worked."

i lean my shoulder into hers. "That was the idea."

"But she was lying?" She turns her face close to mine, waits
until i meet her eyes. "You didn't sleep with her?"

i break off the gaze and whisper, "Not every night."

She stands up. "What are you saying?"

i can't answer—can't admit it. When i look up, she's gone.
No. No way. i catch her opening the kitchen door.

i press my back against it, trapping her. "i didn't mean
to—thought we could talk. i was really down." i look at Leesie
for a second and then away. "Isadore's been relentless and you
hated me—but you know what DeeDee's like." i turn toward
Leesie, put my hand over hers on the doorknob. "It freaked
me, really. i didn't go back. Promise. Told her to back off the
next day." i let the fingers of my free hand comb the hair back
from Leesie's forehead, lean closer to her face. "i missed you
so much."

"So it's my fault?" She slides down the door, sits on the floor. "I'm not taking the blame for that."

"No, no. i'm sorry." i squat down next to her. "You got to believe me. It meant nothing. Don't leave me again, please." i clutch both of her hands.

"We're too different, me and you." She focuses on her captured hands. "Our values. Our morals. I thought I loved you enough that it wouldn't matter—anything you did." She sniffs, and a tear threatens to spill out of her left eye. "This? I don't know. It makes me sick that you were with her . . . like that."

"But you and i weren't together. It wasn't cheating. Felt like it, though. You haunt me, babe."

Pleasure doesn't break out on her face like it used to when i called her that. It stays serious and sad.

"Forget it. Please, forgive me." i let go of her hands, cup her face instead. "i won't hurt you again. i so, so promise. i'm not angry anymore."

i bend to kiss her, but she turns her cheek to me.

"I don't think I can." Her voice is husky and low. "Let me go, please." She stands.

i stay on the floor like a beggar at her feet, trying to think of something that will change her mind. "Please, don't leave now, Leese. i don't know what i'll do."

She closes her eyes and bows her head. Her lips don't move, but she's got to be praying. Her eyes drift open and wrap mine in their trouble.

i bow my head, steel myself for the click of the latch, cool night air on my cheek, the soft pad of her feet leaving.

But it doesn't come.

She reaches down, takes back my hand. "How about friends?"

i let her pull me to my feet. "Yeah. Sure. Friends. Great."

"I just have one condition."

i hold my hands up and take a step back. "You got it, babe, i mean, Leese, i won't try anything."

"It's not that easy. I'll stay. We can be friends, but you have to come to church with me tomorrow."

i don't even hesitate. "Fine. Sure. You win."

"This isn't about me. I want you to win. It might help with"—she motions toward the living room, those twin boxes of parental ash—"all this."

CHURCHED

MICHAEL'S DIVE LOG—VOLUME #8

DIVE BUDDY: **Leesie**	
DATE: 01/04	DIVE #: **2 with her again**
LOCATION: **Rockford**	DIVE SITE: **Leesie's church**
WEATHER CONDITION: sunny	WATER CONDITION: clear
DEPTH: **2-ft snowbanks**	VISIBILITY: 100+
WATER TEMP.: frozen	BOTTOM TIME: **left Gram's at 8:15**

COMMENTS:

i wear the black pants and gray dress shirt we bought for the dance. Can't get the tie right. Freak. It's a Valentino. She doesn't even own a cell. Her computer is an ancient desktop. And she bought me a vintage designer tie. And i, creep freaking jerk, threw it all away.

i get to Leesie's late—park in the front, run up the steps, and ring the doorbell.

"Thought you'd chickened out," she calls from the driveway, where she stands by the pickup with a set of keys in her hand. She wears a denim skirt, brown leather boots—not cowboy—a top i bought, and her damaged suede jacket. She runs down their curved gravel driveway and grabs Gram's bunny key ring. "My family already left. Better let me drive."

Leesie's branch is in Rockford, the third dinky town up the highway toward Spokane. She whizzes along the road, doesn't slow to 25 mph for the towns. "Small-town cops all sleep in Sunday morning." She squeals off the highway, pulls up in front of a small white building.

"Stylish, huh." She gets out of the car. "There's not a lot of us out in the country, so we rent this Grange hall. It's an old army barrack they had moved here."

i don't know or care what "Grange" is. The place screams "dump." Nothing like the nice building her dance was in or her fancy wedding cake temple.

Leesie opens a heavy wood door, held together with repeated coats of blue paint. We pass through a foyer and into a room filled with rows of metal folding chairs, milling people, and loud, happy talking. A woman with gray hair plays hymns on a black upright piano. She pounds as hard as she can and keeps the pedal to the metal, trying to drown out the cheerful buzz.

"Thought we were late," i whisper, hoping my breath tickles Leesie's ear.

"We never start on time." The cement floor is painted bright red, the walls a dull green. Works for Christmas, but what do they do on the Fourth of July?

"Want me to hang up our coats?"

She shakes her head. "Furnace doesn't work too well." She holds my hand loosely to guide me through the buzzing Mormons, says hello, to people, doesn't mess around introducing me.

Her mom and Stephie have a row of chairs saved. "Those seats are for you." Stephie points to the places on the end. "These are for Dad and Phil." She braves the chill to show off her flowery dress with a red velvet collar and headband to match.

i sit down, tighten my fingers around Leesie's so she can't let go of my hand. There's maybe forty people total in the room, lots of them kids. i catch sight of Phil, wearing a navy suit, a white shirt, and a tie covered with leering Tasmanian devils. He's on his feet at the front of the room, placing rectangular trays full of tiny white cups on a table covered with a white tablecloth. Leesie's dad, wearing almost the exact same suit and white shirt—with a more cautious tie—helps him cover the trays with a white embroidered cloth. They both sit down behind the table.

i don't know what i'm doing here or how this can help me figure out what to do with my parents' ashes. The place is bedlam, but i'd agree to sit just about anywhere with Leesie's fingers wrapped around mine. Do friends hold hands?

The piano music stops. A big man in his fifties, red-faced and balding, stands up. "Brothers and sisters, can you take your seats."

The buzzing trails off. Everyone sits down. They sing a hymn. They all bow their heads. Leesie drops my hand to fold her arms. A woman prays, short and in her own words. Leesie's soft, "Amen," mingles with the others.

A pleasant feeling comes into the room. Surprises me. i don't feel condemned, sitting with the holies. They call themselves "saints," but they seem like everyday families, kids and parents and a handful of old ladies. i relax, leaning slightly against Leesie's shoulder.

The red-faced guy says some more stuff. Everyone raises his or her right hand and then puts it down. It looks like voting, but no one votes no. Then they sing again. i like listening to Leesie sing. She has a pretty voice, holds the book so i can follow the words. Not that i even consider joining in. During the song, Phil and Leesie's dad are up front, standing behind the table covered with white cloths, breaking bread into little pieces. A couple of pudgy junior-high-age boys wearing rumpled white shirts and baggy tan Docks stand in front of the table.

"This is the sacrament," Leesie whispers when the song is over.

Phil kneels down in front of the table, reads a prayer, more *amen*s, and then he and his dad give small trays full of the broken bread to the junior high boys and they pass it around. When it gets to us, Leesie breathes, "You don't take any," into my ear.

i wish she'd take my hand again. It's getting cold, but i don't shove it into my coat pocket. i let it hang down where she can find it.

A baby starts to cry. The mother hurries out with it. Then Leesie's dad kneels and prays, and the boys are at it again, this time with water. i touch Leesie's hand as i pass the tray to her. Each tiny cup rests in its own hole. Four long rows. Leesie drinks a cup, drops the empty into a hole in the tray. The bottom's enclosed, holds the used cups out of sight.

Leesie passes the tray on to her mom, then glances back at me. She closes her eyes, bows her head. i feel her warm fingers winding around my cold ones. i slip both our hands into my coat pocket. Church isn't all that bad. Leesie glances sideways at me and then bows her head again.

When the passing is over, Mr. Red Face stands up and tells the guys to go sit in the congregation with their families. Phil and Leesie's dad take their seats. Stephie slides over so she can sit between them. Leesie's dad glances at Leesie and me. He must see her hand disappearing into my pocket.

Red Face tells a story about answering his secretary's questions about "the Gospel." He says he knows this church is the only true church on earth and sits down.

Leesie leans over and whispers, "This is fast-and-testimony meeting. We normally have assigned speakers."

"Which one's the minister?" Red Face doesn't wear a collar. Two other guys sit next to him at the front, but they don't dress the part either—just suits and white shirts.

"Don't have one."

"Why is it 'fast'?"

"We fast. Don't eat. Give the money to the poor."

"I ate."

She smiles and squeezes my hand. "It's okay."

Three little girls rush the stand. Each one knows the church is true and loves her mom and dad. Two of them giggle. The last one cries. Then Stephie parades dramatically to the front. "I'm thankful for my kitty. And that Leesie's happy again."

She stares right at me. So does everyone else. Leesie goes crimson.

Let the flaying begin.

Stephie, pleased with the sensation she caused, finishes her speech and flounces back to her seat.

Leesie's dad gets up right away. He speaks about praying for his family and getting answers. His soft voice pulls the congregation's attention away from us. Her father's words fill the room, soothing and warm. He says he loves his righteous son and strong daughters. Leesie flicks a tear out of the corner of her eye. Her face stays flushed, but she doesn't let go of my hand.

i get emotional, too, missing my dad who loved me, righteous or not.

Leesie's mom reaches over and pats Leesie's shoulder. She smiles at me and winks. She's not so bad. Carolina's mom made her go on the pill at fourteen. She could have used a little of Leesie's mom and some rules. Leesie should give her own a break. i study my knees and wish it wasn't too late to give my mom a break.

People are still murmuring their final "amen" when Leesie whispers, "Let's get out of here."

These masochists have two more hours of meetings, but Leesie said we only have to go to this one. She's cutting the rest with me. She gets stopped on the way out. "I'll catch up." i make it out of there and sit in Gram's car trying to figure out why this church stuff is everything to Leesie.

When i see her coming, i open my door, stand so i'm halfway in, halfway out. "Hey."

She comes around to my side. "Hey."

We stand there stuck, until she sighs and drops her lips on mine. i pull her into the car, holding her on my lap, and return the kiss. It feels so right to have her back in my arms.

"i don't get it."

"Just friends is stupid."

"Not this." i kiss her, and she tastes better than any heaven could. "This i get." i nod toward the ugly hall they rent. "That. i don't get that."

"I'm going to kill Stephie."

"How could any of that help me? i just found out you're all kind of egocentric about truth."

"Didn't you feel anything at all?"

"Embarrassment?"

"How about when my dad spoke? I saw your face."

i have to be honest with her. "You're right. i felt—"

"That's the Spirit. I felt it, too. It's so amazing when it's strong."

"Bereft. My parents loved me like your dad loves you. He spoke, and i felt bereft."

Leesie strokes my cheek. "I'm sorry. The word 'memorial' kept floating through my head all through the meeting. Does that mean anything to you?"

"Nope."

"You didn't feel a tiny bit warm?"

"That wasn't from you holding my hand?" When i try to follow that up with more heat from my lips, she gets stiff and slides off my lap.

"What did i do now?"

She flushes. "When you kiss me like that"—her voice gets small and pained—"I see you with DeeDee." Her eyes fill up.

"Freak, Leese. i'm such a creep."

"I really want to forgive you, but—"

"Forget her."

"I'm trying."

"Come back. i'll kiss you differently."

"I can't."

"Please."

"I think it's going to take some time."

i hold my hand out to her. "Whatever you say." Just don't ditch me.

She places her hand in mine. "And we're going to need some new rules."

i swallow hard and whisper, "No pressure this time. i promise."

She squeezes. "Thanks. That means a lot to me."

"It means a lot to me." i weave my fingers through hers. "Just let me know if you change your mind."

She closes her eyes, thinking. "I've got one. No skin. No hands on my back or stomach or legs."

"Arms?"

"That's okay."

"Neck?"

"Maybe, but you can never take your shirt off in my presence again."

"You can, though. i'm cool with that." i rub her legal arm, trying to get her to smile.

She doesn't. i can tell she's thinking about DeeDee again. Her eyes grow serious. "We have to ban making out, too."

"What?" She loves making out. She breathes for making out.

"If we start making out all the time like we used to, all the rules in the world won't stand a chance."

"Jeez, babe. What are we going to do?"

"Talk. Study. Go out. Clean up Gram's garden. We can start as soon as the snow melts. That will keep us busy."

i don't bring up diving, but i mentally add it to the list. "Can i even kiss you?"

"I don't know—try it again."

234 / angela morrison

i lean over and kiss her softly, with all the tenderness, shame, and hope i can muster.

"Yeah." She sighs. "That works." She sits up and shakes her hair back. "Goodnight kiss only. On my porch. Not in here." A smile creeps up on her face. "But it can last as long as we want."

"Is this outlawed?" i lean over and suck on the corner of her plump lower lip.

"No way." She's breathless. "That you can do—anytime."

So i do it again.

chapter 37

EVER AFTER?

LEESIE'S MOST PRIVATE CHAPBOOK

POEM #42, NOT EASY

One visit to church fails
to convert.

One kiss does not erase
her.

One promise does not dissolve
my doubts.

But one hand, warm,
holding mine, makes
none of it matter—
DeeDee, diving, the unchancy distress
when his lips caress mine—
even my dreams of BYU—
until I let go
of his hand.

LEESIE HUNT / CHATSPOT LOG / 01/09 12:09 A.M.

liv2div says: just wanted to say good night

Leesie327 says: School was rough today.

liv2div says: you saw that . . . with deedee?

Leesie327 says: One more day, and then we have the weekend to ourselves. How are you holding up?

liv2div says: i wish you were here . . . i want to watch you breathe, wake up with your hair in my face

Leesie327 says: Please don't write stuff like that. It hurts too much.

liv2div says: i'm sorry . . . i just can't believe you're back . . . you have no idea where i was heading

Leesie327 says: My poor Michael. Now *I'm* wishing I was there.

liv2div says: i've corrupted you again already

Leesie327 says: Are you making any progress with the memorial for your parents?

liv2div says: *the spiegel grove.*

Leesie327 says: And that is . . .

liv2div says: giant wreck off key largo . . . Dad donated big bucks to help sink her there . . . it's the perfect place to sprinkle my parents

Leesie327 says: You want to dump them in the ocean? Are you sure you don't want something more permanent?

liv2div says: the *grove* is massive . . . pretty damn permanent . . . for a girl who thinks my parents are floating in heaven having cocktails, you put a lot of emphasis on graves

Leesie327 says: It doesn't feel right to me.

liv2div says: it doesn't have to feel right to you . . . they are my parents ... dad loved diving that wreck ... it feels right to me

Leesie327 says: I don't think you've thought enough about it.

liv2div says: i forgot how bossy you can be

Leesie327 says: Memorial. Where did I see that word?

liv2div says: in your twisted brain that won't leave well enough alone

Leesie327 says: You asked for my help.

liv2div says: not your interference

Leesie327 says: It's a package deal. Take it or leave it.

liv2div says: guess i'm stuck ... leaving it didn't work so well for me

Leesie327 says: I think you need something special that you can return to that will remind you of your parents. A place where you'll feel close to them. I know you don't want a traditional grave or a fancy urn on the mantel.

liv2div says: sprinkling them in the ocean is the only thing i can think of ... i'll take gram out to the condo ... we, i mean, i have a condo in the keys ... where the club is ... i'll get the club guys together and take mom and dad on one last dive ... it would be sweet if you could come

Leesie327 says: Are you up to going back to that condo? Lots of memories.

liv2div says: good memories

Leesie327 says: Still.

liv2div says: yeah

Leesie327 says: Look at this. I found it. Reef Memorial.

liv2div says: what are you talking about?

Leesie327 says: I'm not sure yet. I'm Googling it. It was in the obituary next to your parents' on the club's website.

liv2div says: you're on the club's site? you've been there before?

Leesie327 says: Yeah. There's that picture from Gram's of you with your parents. Your mom's beautiful. You all look so happy.

liv2div says: i'm in the obituary?

Leesie327 says: Divers from all over the world have posted condolences. You should read them. It's really touching.

liv2div says: why the hell would i want to do that? sick . . . strangers crying all over the screen over my parents . . . my friends . . . who do they think they are?

Leesie327 says: Okay, bad idea. BUT you've got to see this. I found a website for Reef Memorial. It's so perfect. I'm sending you the link. You won't believe it. They do services UNDERWATER, especially for divers.

liv2div says: an underwater funeral? you're kidding. that would be awesome. but hey, what happened to gram's doctor and your dive ban? Does this mean you think i SHOULD be underwater?

Leesie327 says: Moses found salvation on the top of a mountain. Why shouldn't you find yours at the bottom of the sea?

MICHAEL'S DIVE LOG—#8

DIVE BUDDY: Solo

DATE: 01/09 — ~~DIVE #:~~

LOCATION: Teacup — DIVE SITE: Gram's

WEATHER CONDITION: dark — WATER CONDITION: not snowing

DEPTH: still deep — VISIBILITY: better than you'd expect

WATER TEMP.: ??? — BOTTOM TIME: 39 minutes

COMMENTS:

i open the link Leesie sent. Reef Memorial is amazingly perfect. i can't believe she found this for me. Maybe she does have magic powers. This is so right. This company stirs a diver's ashes into a special concrete mixture and molds it into a sphere or an obelisk or a number of different reef-shaped formations. Then they haul it out to a spot just outside of the marine sanctuary and let it sink in about thirty feet of water. i can buy a monument that will be a permanent artificial reef made out of my parents. They'll be part of the ocean. No worms. Coral. Fish. It's all so cool.

i click through pictures of the different shapes Reef Memorial can make. i go for the biggest and baddest—a narrow reef that mimics a coral finger. It's thirty feet long, with tubes for eels and a big ledge at the bottom where a friendly nurse shark might want to hang out.

As part of the underwater funeral, Reef Memorial attaches a buoy and gives the mourners a GPS tracking chart so the bereaved can dive their loved ones anytime. In a few decades, my parents will be covered in coral growth, a home for fish. i can see it sitting on the ocean floor, covered with algae and flowing fans, yellow and purple juvie fish. All of it not far from the condo. i could take my kids diving there. i think about Leesie, our kids. i'm never letting her get away again.

i fill in Reef Memorial's online reply form. It asks for a date. i flip through the calendar Leesie marked for me when we started going out. MLK day? Too soon. Spring break? Too far off. Presidents' Day weekend? Too short, but we'll make it work. A solid, whole feeling that this is right comes over me. My face gets hot and my throat aches, but i feel something new. Beyond misery. Strong. Maybe i *can* be strong for them. Take them home, forever.

chapter 38

BON VOYAGE

Kimbo69 says: Hey, chicky, have a good trip . . . you all ready?

Leesie327 says: I'm going crazy packing. I need a new swimsuit. I found some cool shorts on sale, but the swimsuits were too expensive.

Kimbo69 says: I'd loan you a few of mine if they'd fit.

Leesie327 says: Buying a swimsuit with a body like mine is tragic.

Kimbo69 says: Look for one that shows a lot of cheek . . . no one will notice the rest of you . . . next time you shop with me.

Leesie327 says: Cheek? I'm not even supposed to show my stomach.

Kimbo69 says: Your church even tells you what swimsuits to wear? That's pathetic.

Leesie327 says: You're nice tonight.

Kimbo69 says: Jealous . . . totally . . . pea green . . . no, lime green . . . no, turquoise green just like the Caribbean you'll be swimming in.

Leesie327 says: This from the girl who went to Cozumel for Christmas.

Kimbo69 says: I can't believe your dad agreed to go with you . . . is your mom even speaking to him?

Leesie327 says: Are you kidding? He's the hero. When Dad piped up that he wanted to support what Michael and I were planning—actually come with us—my mom squeezed his hand and got her dreamy total devotion look on her face. She doesn't like being the bad guy.

Kimbo69 says: What are you going to do with him while you're there?

Leesie327 says: He's speaking at the service . . . he's good at things like that.

Kimbo69 says: So you get to scuba dive? That's way cool.

Leesie327 says: Michael hasn't even brought it up. I think he wants to do this on his own.

Kimbo69 says: Of course he'll want you down there. Why else is he bringing you? It's his parents' funeral.

Leesie327 says: Don't go there, Kim.

Kimbo69 says: Whatever . . . so congrats on the scholarship! What did Michael say?

Leesie327 says: Since we got back together, he's been into planning this trip and the memorial service and getting all the particulars right for the artificial reef made out of his parents' ashes. He's so excited about diving again he's going to burst. He's doing much better, and it's because I'm with him. How can I jeopardize that?

Kimbo69 says: I can't believe it . . . you still haven't even told him you're going to BYU.

Leesie327 says: We're kind of finding our way back to each other.

Repenting is supposed to be tough, but forgiving is harder than anyone ever tells you.

Kimbo69 says: That I get. If Mark slept around on me, I'd dump his butt down the deepest pit I could find.

Leesie327 says: Nice. I'll let Michael know how lucky he is to just have a girlfriend who freezes up every time he tries to kiss her good night.

Kimbo69 says: You have to tell him about your scholarship soon . . . what's he planning for next year?

Leesie327 says: Nothing. It's like the future doesn't exist beyond this trip. I've researched schools for him. I think he'd like Seattle. There's great diving close by, but maybe he'll want to go back to Arizona or Florida. He could probably make a good claim for residency in either state.

Kimbo69 says: He's got all that money . . . he could go anywhere.

Leesie327 says: I don't think he should blow it.

Kimbo69 says: I can't believe you're going to throw that catch back into the ocean.

Leesie327 says: It makes me sick to my stomach just to think about it.

Kimbo69 says: What if your dad blurts out something on the trip?

Leesie327 says: Yeah. That makes me nervous. I'm planning to tell Michael everything after we get home. I've got to figure out how to do it without hurting him. I've been praying and praying about it, but I'm getting zip. I can't lose him again.

Kimbo69 says: But you're going to when you leave.

Leesie327 says: That's what I have to figure out. How we can stay together.

Kimbo69 says: Talking it over with him might be a place to start.

Leesie327 says: This weekend is not going to be easy. Diving again should be great for him, but what if it's not? And the memorial service. He's bottled everything up for so long. The whole thing might hit him hard. Who knows what he'll do.

Kimbo69 says: You should be celebrating instead of hiding all this and stressing out . . . four years, full tuition . . . people don't get that every day.

Leesie327 says: I know. They gave me everything I always wanted, but now—I want him.

chapter 39

TRUST

MICHAEL'S DIVE LOG—VOLUME #8

DIVE BUDDY: Leesie	
DATE: 02/14	DIVE #: 42 days back with her
LOCATION: Duck Key, FL	DIVE SITE: Hawk's Cay Resort
WEATHER CONDITION: sunny	WATER CONDITION: 2-ft swells
DEPTH: not yet	VISIBILITY: ??
WATER TEMP.: ??	BOTTOM TIME: lost track

COMMENTS:

i wanted to stay at the condo, but crazy Stan has it in the resort's rental program. It's like a hotel room now. Presidents' Day weekend. Of course it's booked. The guests check out Sunday, so we could have stayed in it for one night, but Leesie didn't think that would be cool. Maybe she's right. Just the airport freaked me. My parents were everywhere. Trapped in the mirrored ceiling over the escalator going down to baggage claim and the smoky doors that dumped us out into the honk and spit of Miami traffic. It was dark driving down, so i just got flashes of the miles of mangrove swamps we passed, but that was enough to set Isadore off.

We checked into the main hotel too whipped to care about

anything by the time we got to the rooms. Leesie's sharing with Gram. i get to bunk with her dad. He snores—sounds kind of like his pigs.

i'm up before the sun. Didn't really sleep. Slip out onto the balcony and breathe the salt air. At least we've got an ocean view. The sunrise should be nice.

i hear the sliding door on the balcony next to us open, bare feet tiptoeing, her breath.

i climb over my room's balcony railing, around the privacy screen, and onto Leesie's balcony like i used to sneak into Mandy's room to surprise her. That's how i found out she'd hooked up with a new guy at the resort's dive shop.

"You're good at that," Leesie's whisper greets me.

i don't share why.

i hug her close and kiss her good morning. She answers my kiss in a way she hasn't for a long time. Maybe we've outrun the shadows.

i pick her up, sweep her right off her feet like a bride, and carry her over to a chaise lounge. Gently settle her on it. She scoots over to make room for me. One knee bends over the side of the chaise so her right foot can rest on the floor.

She catches my hand and pulls me down beside her. Her lips settle on my neck.

My arms slip around her. "Good morning," i whisper into her hair.

"Do I have gross breath?"

i kiss her again. "You taste amazing."

"I feel amazing." She takes a deep breath of my Caribbean air. "I love you."

That's the first time she's said it since we got back together.

i don't reply. She knows why. i will love her. When she lets me. i will.

She dozes on my shoulder waiting for the sun to rise. i watch her sleep. She *is* precious like that. Long eyelashes resting on creamy cheeks. Forehead slack. Her mouth slightly open. i kiss it, and she rouses. "Our chaperones are useless."

"You know you can trust me."

"Yeah." She caresses my cheek. "I know."

We lounge together as the rosy glow in the east lights up my world. Palm trees, ferns, bright pink bougainvillea, red hibiscus. Shimmering turquoise water everywhere we turn. It comes to me out there on the balcony, like the gradual flush of pink that edges the horizon—in a few hours, i'll be back in that water again. i'm going diving—with Leesie. It's going to happen.

Diving.

Ocean.

Salt water all over me.

Tasting it.

Sinking in it.

With her.

LEESIE'S MOST PRIVATE CHAPBOOK

POEM #43, WILDLIFE ENCOUNTER

Pink sky flares orange magenta gold.
Settles down to startling, pure blue
as deep as the ocean
the sun reveals.

We hang over the balcony together.
He points to docks and black nets
strung between weathered green pilings
crisscrossing a lagoon.

You can see them from here.

What?

Keep watching.

A snubbed snout.
A round head.
The elegant curve of a dolphin
leaping free and perfect
into the air.

I leap, too.
Come down all over
him. I convince
him to get me closer.
He persuades me into going
in my jams and tee, my hair
a tangled mass.

Florida style, babe.

Elevator make out,
rushing past empty pool,
cushy loungers, expectant
umbrellaed tables,

along a boardwalk dripping
with blooms and vines and
palm fronds.

He finds the magic key, jiggles
the secret latch, and
open sesame.

I can't believe this.

Shhh. Come here.

We kneel at the dock's edge.
His playmate bobs up, nods
squeaks and chatters.
I can't contain a tiny squeal.

Excuse me—you're not supposed—Michael?

A tan blond body packed
in a bikini top and boy shorts
flies at him, captures him,
glues itself all over my
guy.

She talks fast and cries
against his cheek
over Johnny, and
emails, and
          drowning.

Sorry. She soaks up tears
with her fingertip.
*I do this a lot. The dolphins
don't mind. Damn, you're pale.*

I try hard not to hate her—even
when she turns to me with her arm
draped too low around him
and says, her fingertips drumming his thigh,
Hey, you guys cousins?

Girlfriend. Leesie.

Mandy. Nice to meet you.

She assesses my wild hair, jams,
my flat, bra-less T-shirt.

*Hey, girl, you owe me—I
taught him everything
he knows.*

I can't smile at this girl,
who took him where I can't,
make friends, pretend it's all cool.
*Gotta go, my dad, Michael's gram,
memorial service.* Prissy overload.

*Right. Tomorrow. And we're all diving
today.*

Diving?

Later, babe—at least he's
talking to me now instead
of ogling her cleavage—
I'll fill you in.

Her teeth glow, large and white
against her tan as they flash
in my direction.

Your dad? His gram?
Gotta cramp your . . . style.
My room's yours anytime.

I panic to get out—the latch
sticks, pinches, traps—Michael
flicks it open too easy, too practiced.
I can't look at his face,
which reads way too clearly.
I just hang down my head
and flee.

MICHAEL'S DIVE LOG—VOLUME #8

DIVE BUDDY: Leesie	
DATE: 02/14	DIVE #: damn
LOCATION: Duck Key, FL	DIVE SITE: Hawk's Cay Resort
WEATHER CONDITION: sunny	WATER CONDITION: 2-ft swells
DEPTH: not yet	VISIBILITY: ??
WATER TEMP.: icy	BOTTOM TIME: lost track

COMMENTS:

After Leesie bolts, Mandy wrinkles up her nose, fits herself around me again. "She doesn't seem like your type. Not like—"

"i need to go find her." Especially with Mandy breathing hot on me like that. "She's kind of sensitive about—"

"I'm sorry." Mandy looses her grip. "You tell her she was your one and only?"

i back away, out of arm's reach. "She's a Mormon."

"Enough said." Mandy turns away, sits down on the dock next to the dolphin.

i run up the boardwalk and find Leesie sitting at one of the tables by the pool. i try to help her up, but she bats away my hand. "The next time we meet one of your old girlfriends, can I at least get dressed, brush my hair, maybe?"

"i had no idea she'd be there. She used to just come summers."

"You're going diving with her."

"The club is diving today." i close the distance between us. "She's in the club. We're going, too. You and me."

Leesie eyes the water out past the resort's protected beach. "Me?"

"That's the cool part." i put my arms around her. She's tense.

i rub her back while i explain. "i brought your gear. Mitch is going to meet us at the resort's pool. You'll like him. His ponytail's as long as yours. He'll run through the preliminaries for the resort course, and you get to actually strap on some tanks and scuba dive with me."

i wish she would jump all over me, excited, like she was when she saw the dolphin, but she shakes her head.

"You're rushing this, Michael." She backs out of my embrace. "Please stay here with me." She turns and studies the water. "I don't want you to go off with that girl. She looks . . . hungry."

i want to grab her, spin her around, and shake some sense into her, but i won't win a fight. i move beside her, put my arm around her waist. "Babe"—she relaxes into me when i say that—"please. i'll need you down there tomorrow. What happened to trusting me?"

"You're right." She lets me pull her into a hug. "I'm sorry." She lets me kiss her. "I do trust you."

i kiss her again. "You're not acting like it."

She buries her face in my shoulder. Doesn't speak while i comb my fingers through her wild hair, trying to tame it just a bit. "Please, babe. You don't know what it took to set this all up."

She tips back her head and locks my eyes with hers. i sense terror behind her calm expression, but she whispers, "Okay, I'll do it."

i move in to celebrate, but she holds me off. "In case I don't survive, I need to tell you something." Her forehead knots up. She licks her lips. "More trust." She swallows. "I got some news before we left on the trip." She stares at the water again, then back at me. "Brigham Young University is offering me a four-year, full-tuition scholarship."

My gut muscles get tight. "Why would they do that? You didn't even apply."

"I did."

My grip on her tenses. "You said the place is impossible to get into. Are you that smart?"

She nods. "I kind of blew away the ACT."

"You're not going to take it, though, right?" i'm shaking my head, denying what she's telling me. "That's great that they want you, but i'm not a Mormon. i can't go there."

Leesie's head drops.

"You are going to take it?"

She won't meet my eyes.

"You're leaving?"

"Not until August." She still can't look me in the eye.

i take her face in my hands and tip her head back so she has to see the pain that must show. It's ripping all through me like an electric current. "You've known this all along?"

"Nothing was for sure."

"All those times i held you and said i needed you, and you promised you'd never go *anywhere*"—i can barely speak around the stone lodged in my throat—"you were planning this?"

"I've dreamed of going to BYU my whole life. It's my great escape."

i let go of her at the sting of that. "From me?"

"Of course not. From Troy and his creeps, the small town where I'm trapped, my stupid brother. Not you. I planned this way before you. I do not want to escape you." She clutches at the front of my shirt.

"Leesie." My brain spins. My arms go back around her. i clutch, too. "You don't need a scholarship. I'm going to be loaded. We can go anywhere you want. Name the school. i'll do it."

"They do let nonmembers into BYU."

"Like that's going to work. We both know what my GPA was like last semester." In some distant life i took the SAT, visited a few campuses, talked about marine biology. i can dredge up college plans if that's what Leesie wants. "Let's find a school that works for both of us."

"I worked harvest with my dad summers—saved every cent—killed myself at school—took the ACT three times to get that score." She loosens her grip on me and her voice gets kind of dead. "You want me to give that up?"

"Look what i've given up for you. No sex since—"

"DeeDee?"

"Freak, Leese."

"It's not the same."

"Yeah. It's way worse." How can i go back to the darkness of those days we were apart? "So you're just going to abandon me?" My voice throbs.

"This is killing me. That's why I didn't tell you sooner." She's on the edge of tears. "I wanted to wait until the memorial was over and I could figure something out." She's clutching again, speaking fast and frantic. "Look. We won't have to break up. We'll be online all the time. You can come visit whenever you want."

"That would last until some BYU do-gooder asks you out."

"Now you need to give me some credit." She lets go of me, smoothes down my T-shirt, and steps back.

"What am i supposed to do?" i take her hand, feel the scars on the back of it. My prints on her. The brand that says she's mine and can't leave. "Sit at Gram's staring at the stupid crack in the wall?" i suck in fresh sea air, but the bitter taste of anger floats on the breeze.

"I think you'd like Seattle. The University of Washington is a great school. It's not too late to apply."

"i'm supposed to just go there by myself? i don't think i can hack more school for a while. If i'm not going with you—"

"But you have to go to college."

"Why?" The anger starts to tingle my fingertips and pop in my brain.

"I'm sure that's what your parents want."

i drop her hand—burned. "Don't tell me what they want. They're dead. They don't want anything anymore."

"They still want what's best for you." She tries to recapture my hand, but i pull it out of reach.

"Don't go there, babe. Your heaven isn't mine."

Her face gets red. "Wouldn't it be better if it was?"

"My parents are ash. Thanks to you, they're mixed up with cement and molded into an artificial reef. We're sinking them tomorrow. My parents are finished. i'm on my own." My words echo in the pit of my guts as i realize i won't even have Leesie.

"You're wrong." She won't quit. "They still love you. They want you to be happy."

"Just stop. No. If you're so eager to ditch me, why don't we start now." i put my hands up to ward her off. "Stay away from me. Forget diving. Forget the whole damn thing. Stay away from the service. Keep your dad out, too. No way i want you guys there preaching at me. i'm trying to say goodbye."

"I have to go. That's why I came."

"i thought you came for me."

"You can't mean this." Her arms wrap around her stomach, and she's hunched over like i hit her. "I know it will be hard when I leave"—her voice wavers and dissolves—"but we'll figure it out." Her face crumples.

Good. She can hurt, too. i want her to hurt more. i want to crush her right out of existence. "i'm going diving. Maybe you're right about Mandy. Time i hang with a chick who appreciates what i can offer. She'll enjoy how much i've improved." i turn to leave.

Leesie doesn't move. "You can't just walk away."

i spin around. "Why not?" i advance on her with all that anger flushing my face into a menace. "Isn't that what you're planning to do to me?"

She doesn't back off. Meets my anger with, "Please, Michael. I love you."

That doesn't cool the blast. It just makes her desertion worse. Fuels the fire. Fans the flames. i bend over her, get smack in her face, and seethe, "Prove it," into her crying eyes.

chapter 40

TEMPTATION

MICHAEL'S DIVE LOG—VOLUME #8

DIVE BUDDY: Mitch

DATE: 02/19   DIVE #: 750

LOCATION: Key Largo   DIVE SITE: Spiegel Grove

WEATHER CONDITION: sunny

WATER CONDITION: 2-ft chop, strong current

DEPTH: 108 ft   VISIBILITY: 30 ft

WATER TEMP.: 68°F   BOTTOM TIME: 47 minutes

COMMENTS:

Leesie's out, so we ditch the wimp beginner dive we were going to do and cruise up to the *Spiegel Grove*. Gutsy. Dangerous. Testosterone-pumping wreck dive. The club just bought scooters, and Mitch is eager to test them out. It's so good to see these guys. The ones who booked too late to make the Belize trip or couldn't get off work or didn't have the cash. Survivors like me. Even Mandy.

i get an intense rush simply setting up my gear and testing a tank of nitrox. i hunker down on deck savoring the sea spray. This is what i came for. Forget Leesie. How could she lie to me again? Act so loving and tender and then wham, rip my heart out. Here i am dreaming of diving forever with her, and all along, she's packing her bags.

Mandy enjoys being the only chick on the boat. She gets Mitch to set up her gear. She interrupts me testing my second tank. "Where's Lisa?"

"Leesie." i stumble over her name. "She doesn't dive."

"Too bad."

"Yeah." Really bad. i'm stuck toting around a bag of useless pink chick gear.

"Can you help me with this knot?" Mandy turns around and lifts her hair. "I'm going to work on my tan before i change." She goes commando under her wet suit.

i stand up and work on the knot.

"I always tie it to tight." She giggles. "Wouldn't want anything falling out."

We both know she's famous for falling out.

My fingers are useless on the tiny knot and slippery strings. i bend down and loose it with my teeth. She smells familiar, slick with coconut tanning oil. "Thanks." Her lips are close enough to my ear to bite. "Come on up when you're ready."

That's Mandy. Never wastes time. i go back to my nitrox tank as she slinks around to the bow, holding her loose bikini top up with one hand.

Flesh. All i want. A few feet away. Waiting for me. And nobody's going to call recess.

i fill in the nitrox log and pass the gauge on to Mitch. He looks at me like i just won the lottery.

i hook my first stage to the tank. Turn the gas on. Check my fill. Sit on the bench in front of my gear and reset my computer.

i finish.

Don't move. Stare out at the ocean to where it curves into the horizon. No clouds in sight, and the swells are only a couple of feet. Calm for February.

Mandy on the bow, waiting, wanting me again—tugs on me like the current pulling on a moored sailboat we pass.

Trust. Respect. Predator.

No matter how angry i am with Leesie, how much i want to hurt her, how easy Mandy's making it—i loathe that girl. i don't want any kind of closeness with her. She took me too young, too far, too fast. Kicked me aside. Taught me, sure, but were her lessons worth the pain? How can she think i'd get tangled up in her tentacles again? Sure, it would soothe this rage Leesie brewed in my guts. Hurt Leesie worse than anything else i could do. Destroy everything there ever was or will be between us—

Do i really want that?

What about me?

i got to survive.

i turn my face up to the sun and salt spray and close my eyes. The roar of twin outboards remind why i'm here. i'm going to dive. Sink beneath the surface. Return to the world i'm drowning without. Will Isadore be waiting? i don't care. She can come, too. i'm going under. Nothing else matters.

We get to the *Grove*, and i sit on the boat's side and roll backward into the ocean. The current's ripping. Knocks my mask off. The salt water stings my eyes and gets up my nose. Freak. Where's the sweet embrace of my daydreams?

i fight to the back of the boat where Sammy hands me a yellow, torpedo-shaped scooter. i descend hanging tight to the line so the current doesn't wash me away. Ten feet. Twenty.

The vis sucks. i can barely make out the giant conning tower in the gloomy murk. Sadness wells up in me, and i have to stop. This was Dad's favorite dive. What am i doing here without him?

i hang onto the line, frozen like an idiot. Mitch finds me, leads me to the group scootering down around the massive prop blades. i follow them across the decks. Memories chase me all the way. Mitch leads us out around the bow. The current hits us, but the scooters can hack it. We all begin broad U-turns to head back to the *Grove*.

Halfway through my turn, my BC's inflator hose gets tangled in the prop of my scooter. i let go of the power button, and the scooter stops. Everybody else keeps going. It takes me about twenty seconds to untangle the hose.

When i look around, i'm in a desert of murky water and white sand. No divers. No wreck. The current swept me downstream while my scooter was off, and i'm living my dead-body nightmare—except Leesie's gone. She'll never pull me out again.

i scan the water like a crazy man. Where are the salmon riders hiding? i breathe in and out too quick. Not good at this depth. i could be out of air in minutes.

Isadore pulls. My mother is screaming for *me* to come to *her*. And i stand on the deck. Ignoring her. A surge of regret threatens to sweep me downstream.

Let it go. Let it go. Isadore's black oily voice is as enticing as Mandy's. *Come with me, Michael. I'm here.*

i could go to them—right now.

Fear jabs my guts. i'm so not strong. Big cowardly freak. i point the scooter into the current and get my butt out of there.

chapter 41

IN MEMORIAM

LEESIE'S MOST PRIVATE CHAPBOOK

POEM #44, CEREMONY OF TEARS

I am the uninvited, the intrusion,
the traitor.

Reef Memorial's catamaran is crowded
enough with divers for me to hide
from the stone gray glare he's turned
on me since my premature confession.

A flat barge carrying the reef
made of his parents leads us forth.
Small brown seabirds cry out.

Silver scuba tanks flash in the sun.
Michael, with his wet suit pulled just to his waist,
Hovers, his face set hard as the concrete monument.
I long to take his hand.
He was supposed to need me.

Chains clank, cranes lower ash reborn
into the glassy Caribbean blue.

My dad's voice crackles on the sound system:
Carry their love with you.
Cherish it. And I promise you,
when you need a parent's hand,
their hearts will guide you.

Michael turns away from the power
in my dad's eyes to find
faces aching for the story
only he can tell.

He eases the valve open, lets it flow,
feeds them crab legs,
pelts them with rain,
drowns them in the storm surge,
plucks them out in time to see
a row of bodies covered in white sheets
lined up along the dock
at a place called Monkey River.

Then tanks clank, fins flap—
divers, one by one, stride over the side
as a final tribute.

Michael disappears with them
leaving me behind going
crazy.

I lean far over the side, but all I
see are bubbles that whisper,

Prove it, Leesie. Prove it.

Maggie finds me snorkel gear.
I jump and the ocean swallows
but spits me back up.
I fight the mask until it yields a keyhole
to this mystery he loves.
Black-suited divers glide below me.
A feathery fish close-up zooms me into panic.
I give it up, turn back, but wait,
there it is—

His parents glow spectacular white,
shimmering in the sun rays the water refracts.
I forget how to breathe—
it's him, swimming toward me,
surfacing beside me.

Your lips are blue, babe.

A shiver runs through me.
My teeth chatter—I hadn't noticed the cold.
He holds out his arm.
I hang on too tight.

Sorry I'm not down there—I messed
things up—again. My knees are jelly,
but not because I'm afraid of the water.

Let me take you back to the boat.
He's eager to leave me, get back
to his parents.

Please, Michael.

I take off my mask, so does he.
His eyes still storm.
But mine see clearly, at last.

I won't—I can't—leave you.
BYU can live without me.
I've got a new dream.

He musters a smile and kisses me
while the ocean swells under us.
My heart seethes like it will break.
A piece of me dissolves
and floats away.

Do you trust me?

He glues me to the front of his scuba vest,
puts his regulator in my mouth.
When your ears hurt, pinch
your nose and blow.
Don't forget to breathe.

My heart dances to his bubbles.
The power of his body
drives me under, his legs
kick behind mine, panic seeps inside my mask
as he swims me down
to meet his
parents.

Calm. Breathe. Calm. He has me.

I touch the plaques that
bear their names.
Wonder steals over me
at the beauty of the blue beneath
as he swims me to the surface.
Overcome.

MICHAEL'S DIVE LOG—VOLUME #8

DIVE BUDDY: **Mom and Dad**

DATE: **02/15**	DIVE #: **751**
LOCATION: **Marathon**	DIVE SITE: **Mom and Dad's Reef**
WEATHER CONDITION: **sunny**	WATER CONDITION: **still**
DEPTH: **40 ft**	VISIBILITY: **70 ft**
WATER TEMP.: **68°F**	BOTTOM TIME: **79 minutes**

COMMENTS:

i bring Leesie back up, and she's trembling like crazy. It's a good thing she doesn't know how massively illegal that was. i want to stay with her, get her back on the boat, convince her she's made the right choice, but she makes me go back down to my guests.

The dive mourners circle my parents, converging in haphazard slow motion on the artificial reef. And me. i shake neoprene-gloved hands and show them the plaque with my parents' names on it. i didn't realize i knew so many divers down here, didn't know how many loved my parents. Cared. They retreat in buddy pairs as tanks run low until i'm alone—but i'm not. She's still up there, watching me. She'll be way cold, but i'll never call her ice again.

i ascend a few feet to join her before she's hypothermic, but something draws me back to my parents. i let my body sink onto the top of their reef, stretch out, pressing my cheek to the surface, knowing i'll kill growth if i touch it when i return months from now. The white will be gone, too—replaced with yellow-green algae.

i peel off my gloves and run my hands over the smooth cement. A school of blue tang fly over me, circle back around the east end of the naked reef, and disappear, returning the way they came.

As i lie there, i imagine what Mom and Dad will look like in twenty years. Coral coating every inch. Purple-veined sea fans. Gorgonians, pale green. Soft feathery corals. Velvet pillars. Orange sponges. Wrasses, grunts, chromis. Tiny damselfish picking at the rich garden. Queen angelfish trailing wisps of peacock blue tinged purple. Long thin trumpet fish. A flounder hiding in the sand, its bulging eyes watching for trouble. A moray living in the tube, feasting on the fish. And on the special shelf, a nice big nurse shark.

It's so clear, almost as if i'm really at the lush reef in the future. Mom and Dad come, too. i see them in my mind. Mom has on her pink and black gear. Dad's strapped into his oversized BC. i hear Mom whisper my name, feel the warmth of her breath on my neck, Dad's hand on my back, and love familiar, strong. Tangible.

i open my eyes to catch a glimpse of them. Find just me and water. And a gleaming white monument made of their essence. Their presence lingers—a scent i can't quite catch—like the gardenia perfume my mom used to wear. Overcome, i close my eyes and let it flow through me again. i want to go to it, join it, stay with it. But they won't let me.

As i lie on their monument, awash in waves of their love, my mind starts to whirl. Not frenzied ideas or frightening images. No questions. Only answers. A perfect plan flowers in my brain.

But it leaves one detail out.

Leesie.

chapter 42

SUNSCREEN WITH
GARDENIAS

MICHAEL'S DIVE LOG—VOLUME #8

DIVE BUDDY: **Leesie**	
DATE: **02/15**	DIVE #: **752**
LOCATION: **The Keys**	DIVE SITE: **plunge pool**
WEATHER CONDITION: **too sunny**	WATER CONDITION: **flat**
DEPTH: **3 ft**	VISIBILITY: **to the horizon**
WATER TEMP.: **steaming**	BOTTOM TIME: **lost total track**

COMMENTS:

Post-launch, me and Leesie head out to the pool. She needs a good soak in the hot tub. The place is jammed. "Follow me."

i lead her over to the canal. Vacation homes with big boats tied up in front lounge across the canal. The resort side is lined with pastel town homes. i open the back gate of a pale pink one, hold it for Leesie to walk through.

"This is yours?"

i nod.

"It's gorgeous."

The plunge pool in the corner is perfectly clean, still hot

and bubbling. Somebody got the rust stains off the shell fountain. The palms are trimmed and the bougainvillea blooms magenta. i have to swallow the lump that grows hard in my throat.
"It's just the patio." An empty patio.

We slide into hot water. My thigh touches Leesie's. She
floats to the other side. "This is even worse than being in a
house alone."

i study her creamy arms and throat. "You're going to fry."

"I forgot to pack sunscreen."

"Be right back."

The spare key is still under the cement garden turtle my
dad hated. i let myself in. Expect them—Mom at the sink, Dad
on the couch with the remote in his hand—they were so real
this morning.

The place is empty. Hotel room sterile. Fresh-painted white.
The furniture is the same, but all the pieces of our life here
are gone. Mom's dive log scrapbooks, the paperback novels she
only read here, Dad's sandals by the front door, my pool towel
drying on the back of a kitchen chair. i'll kill Stan for doing
this. For cleaning up.

i race up the stairs, retrieve the key to our owner's closet
from under the bathroom sink, slip the key from its magnetic
metal box, replace the box, and take the stairs down two at a
time. i skid to a stop in front of the owner's closet, slide the key
in the lock, and open the door.

It's all here—the books and clothes and knickknacks. Even
the toiletries from the bathroom. Okay, Stan can live.

Sunscreen. Leesie. She wants sunscreen. My eyes go to the
jumble on the shelf. i rummage through the junk looking for a
high SPF. i knock a bottle with my hand.

It tips—

My mom's gardenia-scented perfume stronger than i ever smelled it before spills all over my hand.

i right the old-fashioned bottle, frantic to save the stuff. i freeze, stare at the bottle, then pull the leaky stopper out, pick up the delicate glass container, cup it in my hands, and breathe it in, hold gardenia Mom in my head, blow her out, suck my lungs full of her again, venting, cycle after cycle. i pack for a peak vent, close my eyes, hold her in me, wishing i knew the words to the incantation that would conjure her up long enough to thank her for putting up with my crap, long enough to tell her i love her, long enough—

i hold my breath three minutes, four. My mom screams again, and i finally hear her. Not the beautiful essence i found under the water this morning, but the terrified woman facing a storm alone. She called me. And i did not answer. Kept the camera going until Isadore washed it all away.

i could have saved her. Should have saved her.

"i'm sorry, Mom. i'm so sorry." A sob that shakes my core breaks free. "i didn't mean it. Come back. Please come back. Next time i'll be there. Just come back."

The door creaks, and it's Leesie. She puts her arms around me, holds my head to her shoulder. "Its okay now," she murmurs, "you're going to be okay." She massages my back, running her hands along the muscles, loving me with her fingertips.

Hot tears sneak out of the corners of my eyes, slide down my face. "i didn't save her, Leese. It's my fault."

"No, that's not true. You would have both drowned."

"She buddied me all the time. But when she needed me, i was a snot. How can you love me like you do? i'm a disease."

She whispers, "Cursed, I guess," and smoothes my hair back from my forehead.

i hide my face in her lifesaving Sweet Banana Mango hair. A fresh sob rips through my body. "Why didn't i grab her? Hold on?" The tears flow and mount until wrenching, cleansing sobs i can't control shake me to the core. "i just saved myself. What good is that?" Regret, remorse, shame, and the simple ache of missing them consume me.

"It was a hurricane, Michael." Leesie's voice finds me in the storm. "A miracle you lived. God saved you for me."

And then we're both crying. i sink to the floor, cradle her on my lap. i look down at her face, blotched and swollen with tears shed for me. "i'm so, so sorry." i don't even know who i'm apologizing to anymore. i rest my forehead on hers, let the peace of her flow into me.

An overpowering emotion i never felt before rises on a tide of hope. "i love you." i whisper it at first, then say it louder. "Leesie Hunt—I love you." It's not the same as the love I've known before, but it's there, as strong and beautiful as she is.

Our tears blend. Our lips meet. We kiss as deep and wrenching as we cried. I can't stop telling her I love her. She says it back over and over, and I think I'm going to die. My heart is breaking with emotion.

Leesie was right all along. Saying goodbye, I found my parents. She made that happen. And here in this bleak valley of desperation and guilt, she found me. And somehow, holding her, kissing her, loving her, the guilt fades. I believe every word she says. I didn't kill my mother. I couldn't save her. It's going to be okay now.

My parents are dead.

But I live.

I want to live.

I can't hold back how grateful I am to Leesie. And how much I love her. We pass the no-tongue boundary without even noticing. We're wrapped together in sorrow that surges to passion.

Her slender body yields.

No recess.

No feet on the floor.

Just her under me and swimsuits between us.

I ease back to undress her and glimpse her face, stained with my tears, lost in love—

I barely recognize her.

A vision of her standing in front of her white temple with snowflakes falling around her—pure, untouched, holy—fills my soul.

I can't take that.

She moans and reaches for me, eyes closed, not seeing where we're heading.

"Stop. Leese." I roll off her. "We have to stop."

LEESIE'S MOST PRIVATE CHAPBOOK

POEM #45, ANSWERS

Curled tight in a ball
on the cool tile floor
with my *No* in shreds,
I spiral into choking,
tearful remorse—and then

divine love fills me,
whispers comfort and hope—

I'm not condemned.

Michael caught me, saved
my body, my soul, my life.
He has the answers today.

This morning, underwater,
like your poem,
like you said—
my parents.

Not me. Never me.
I couldn't save him.

When they left, I had answers
I didn't want to hear. Stay
in the Keys. Go to dive school.
Start my own gig.
Keep Gram close.

What about me? How do I fit?

He caresses the scars on my
hand for the last time.

Go to BYU. Marry
your Mormon guy.

I love you too much
to hijack your life.
You have your dream.

Now I have mine.

chapter 43

LESSONS

LEESIE'S MOST PRIVATE CHAPBOOK

POEM #46, DEPARTURE

> Standing in front of Dad's rental car
> Michael holds my scrawny, scarred
> hand to the light. *Don't take*
> *any crap at school,* he says,
> worried about me without protection.
>
> I shift closer to him. *It's all over*
> *in a few months.*
>
> He presses the pink bunny key mistress
> into my hand. *Friends?*
>
> *For life.*
>
> He kisses my forehead like we're just
> friends already—but then his salt soft
> lips coast down my face, searching for
> my mouth.

I try to memorize the gentle tug as he
sucks on the corner of my lower lip
until Dad's quiet, *Ahem*, reminds us
I have a plane to catch.

I don't cry on Delta flight 207 as I wait
for boils to erupt on my arms
and a plague of locusts to be
sucked into the jet engines.
I am the Eternal Ice Queen
until my dad pats my hand
and asks about the scars.

His shoulder is warm and smells of Old Spice.
He keeps the flight attendants at bay
until the cascade trickles,
and I'm locked in the economy class cubicle,
trying not to step in the urine on the floor,
patting my face cool with a damp paper towel,
stuffing my pockets with stiff airplane tissues,
staring at the new zit on my nose,
thanking God for handing me
a desolate heart that needed my
icicle chest to thaw,
to ache, to love,
and beat with it for a season.
I thank Him for the glory of the joy
and the revelations in the pain
of this exquisite test.

Pass or fail?
God only knows.
I cannot fathom why
He set my faith
this examination,
gifted me with a love
I'll cherish long after
the wheels touch down,
the bags roll out,
and I'm tucked safe under
my grandmother's hand-patched quilt,
crying my self awake,
night after long,
lonely
night.

chapter 44

NEW PROJECTS

LEESIE HUNT / CHATSPOT LOG / 03/12 10:18 P.M.

Leesie327 says: I really got into your last poem. The part where Mark's foot goes through the bathroom floor made me laugh out loud.

Kimbo69 says: I don't think we'll ever find a decent place we can afford.

Leesie327 says: It's weird. You and Mark can move in together this summer and nobody thinks anything of it. If I'd even considered marrying Michael . . .

Kimbo69 says: You're way too young to get married.

Leesie327 says: See what I mean. Did you look at my poem? Do you think it's too tragic?

Kimbo69 says: It made me cry.

Leesie327 says: Me too.

Kimbo69 says: You got to get over that.

Leesie327 says: I am. It helps if I keep busy. ChatSpot has three BYU new freshmen groups. I joined them all. Even started a new one.

Kimbo69 says: So you're into the BYU vibe? Good for you.

Leesie327 says: I'm looking for roommates. I need five, so it isn't that easy.

Kimbo69 says: Six girls in one room? That's dangerous.

Leesie327 says: It's an apartment. Three bedrooms, kitchen, our own bathroom. We'll be too busy praying together for catfights.

Kimbo69 says: Gag.

Leesie327 says: Course selection is coming up. I get priority because of my scholarship. I'm trying to decide which honors envelope to sign up for. I want to take them all.

Kimbo69 says: Did you ever decide on a major?

Leesie327 says: It was always going to be English—they have an intensive-writing major, but now I'm thinking about psychology. Counseling. Helping people.

Kimbo69 says: You need to be needed . . . what does Michael think about all this?

Leesie327 says: I haven't told him.

Kimbo69 says: You haven't heard from him.

Leesie327 says: His laptop crashed. He's been too busy to get a new one yet—has to go all the way to Miami for it.

Kimbo69 says: You could call him.

Leesie327 says: I did and had a nice chat with Gram.

Kimbo69 says: He was out?

Leesie327 says: He's really busy with his instructor training. Now he's studying dive resort management, and next week he starts getting certified to fix all the equipment. It's really tough and shoot, Kim, he can be out if he wants to be.

Kimbo69 says: I still can't believe he dumped you after everything you did for him.

Leesie327 says: It wasn't like that. We both agreed.

Kimbo69 says: If you write "it was for the best," I'm going to hurl.

Leesie327 says: Last time he emailed, it was all about strange places he wants to go work before he starts his own dive operation. He keeps sending me pictures of boats.

Kimbo69 says: I can't figure you out.

Leesie327 says: I don't have it figured out, either. I may not have made all the right choices, but I know I was supposed to love him.

Kimbo69 says: You still do.

Leesie327 says: I think I always will.

LEESIE'S MOST PRIVATE CHAPBOOK

POEM #47, SPRING CLEANUP

The third Saturday I sacrifice
to Gram's backyard jungle—
hacking, pulling, trimming—
the lines of her old garden begin to reappear.

Pleasing progress trickles down
my neck with the sweat I grow
from tackling a colossal
chrysanthemum needing division.
I dig and dig and dig,
deep around the root-ball.

I get my shovel under, strain,
and lift it all by myself.
I chop it up with care, replant,
confident the flowers will bloom
for Gram this fall.
I'll be gone, but maybe Michael
will be here, too, enjoying
the love I left behind.

I'm a muddy mess.
My eyes blur again.
I slip into their silent house,
wash the muck off in the basement sink,
search upstairs for a towel—
get stuck—

outside his bedroom.

His bed needs making.
The pillow lies on the floor.
I cross the threshold of this forbidden territory,
gather up the pillow, plump it, place it gently—
pick it back up,
smother my face in it.

It's him, trapped in the fibers,
the sweet taste of Michael.

I totally forget myself,
lie right on his bed, curl

around his pillow. I pull
his quilt up over my head
so he can permeate
my senses. I breathe deep,
like he taught me,
hold it in my head—
then try—
with all my soul—
to let
it
go.

chapter 45

BEGINNINGS

MICHAEL'S DIVE LOG—VOLUME #10

DIVE BUDDY: Leesie	
DATE: 08/21	DIVE #: 1,159
LOCATION: Washington	DIVE SITE: Kettle Falls
WEATHER CONDITION: some clouds	WATER CONDITION: placid
DEPTH: 30 ft	VISIBILITY: 20 ft
WATER TEMP.: 72°F	BOTTOM TIME: 3-4 minutes

COMMENTS:

Mid-August. Hurricane season. Gram wants to go home, and I have to get myself out of the Keys. We stop in Phoenix, pack up my parents' personal stuff, and ship it to Gram's. My junk's going, too. No room at the condo. I meet with the real estate agent and the woman who'll handle the estate sale. Then we get a direct flight to Spokane.

As soon as I unload the Jeep I rented for the weekend, I drive out to Leesie's farm. When I get there, I park the Jeep, have to nerve myself up to knock on the front door. Probably stupid to stir the embers, but I need to tell Leesie about my new job in Thailand face-to-face. Emails just don't cut it. And I have something for her that I wouldn't trust to the mail.

Her mom answers, surprises me with a hug. "Leesie's driving truck. They'll knock off for dinner in about an hour. Do you want me to get her on the two-way?"

I beg off, say I'll be back, return to the Jeep but don't leave. I recline in the sunshine, catch a whiff of dried pig stink as the breeze blows, and doze.

The sound of a truck engine, idling, sputtering off, wakes me. I get out of the Jeep, pull the gift I brought out from under the seat, and watch Leesie jump down from the driver's side. Tanned gold face. Hair hidden under my old black Eagle Ray Divers cap. My T-shirt, streaked with dust and sweat, hangs loose on her slight frame.

Her dad gets out of the passenger's side. They meet at the front. He says something to her. She laughs, shucks off her gloves, and whacks them against her leg. A puff of dust rises up. She pushes my cap back from her forehead and catches sight of me.

Her dad does, too. He meets me at the gate, shakes my hand. "Welcome back, son." He glances over his shoulder at Leesie, still standing in front of the truck. "We'll save you some dinner." His hand rests on my shoulder. "I think there's pie." Then he's gone.

I close my eyes and vent. When I open them, she's still staring at me from across the barnyard. I don't know who moves first, but we meet in the middle.

Up close, I can see how dusty she is from working all day.

"Hey." I ache to hold her, but we both hang back.

"You cut your hair." She touches my neck.

My hand goes to the place she touched. "Gram loves the garden."

She half smiles. "I'm glad." A muddy drop of perspiration runs down the side of her face.

I wipe it away. "She cried."

Leesie catches my hand before it leaves her face and wraps it in hers.

I bring her dusty hand to my lips, kiss the faint scars like I used to. "You recovered from that hell I put you through?"

She pulls her hand away, biting her lower lip to keep it still. "I don't remember it like that." She hands me my hat. "I borrowed it."

I don't take it, want it forever on her head. I hand her a small brown package. "Keep this safe for me, okay?"

She unwraps my dive log—can't speak. Her eyes are shining and wet. She eases the band off her hair, shakes it out, full and brilliant with sun-kissed streaks. I capture her in my arms and smother my face in that hair. It smells of dust and sweat and wheat chaff and Sweet Banana Mango shampoo.

Next morning Leesie's mom sends Stephie to a friend's house and drives truck so Leesie and I can spend the day together. That's all I have. Just this one day. Tomorrow I'm off to Phuket.

Last night, I showed her pictures on my laptop of the liveaboard I'll be working on, gleaming white outside, dark wood interiors. "Whale sharks, Leese. I'm going to be diving with whale sharks. Big as a bus, those suckers."

Leesie touched the screen and whispered, "It's so far away."

This morning we drive to Coulee Dam. Leesie's idea. "Back where we began."

We stop at the dam for a few minutes, and then she wants to go to Kettle Falls, the place where the Salmon People gathered for the real Ceremony of Tears. The falls aren't there anymore, just the Kettle River flowing wide and slow into dam-made Lake Roosevelt. We park by the tribe's visitors' center. Leesie drags me through it. I've never seen anyone get so pumped over old black-and-white pictures and a homemade tribal flag. She brought a couple of inner tubes. I have my free-dive gear and her pink mask and fins.

We hike up the road with the tubes, then float down the river.

"When do you leave for BYU?" I stretch out on the tube, savoring the smell of pines that meets me everywhere here. It reminds me of the pines at Leesie's lake and her hand drawing a line across my chest and how I stood there like a stone.

"Two weeks. Mom and Dad are driving me down." She dabbles her fingers in the water.

"I always thought you'd fly." I drag my foot in the cool river.

"My computer doesn't fit in a suitcase."

"You're not taking that piece of—"

"We can't all afford an upgrade." She tries to splash me, but I'm way out of reach.

I splash her back. "You better have fun there."

She laughs, wipes water from her face. "Well, it's not whale sharks"—her voice turns serious—"but it's *one* thing I've prayed for a lot."

I know the other. It makes me feel safer, going off to Asia with her back here chatting with her God-man about me.

When we get to where the river empties into Lake Roosevelt, we ditch the tubes. I lift the bag with my free-dive stuff out of the back of the Jeep.

I brought my BC for a raft. I bought a real raft for the condo. Black kayak. Room for two. I used it summer evenings when I didn't have to work, free diving at my parents' monument with a buddy from the club. A shrink joined the club last fall. He's been cool. Agrees it's good therapy. Isadore never found me there, but it didn't keep me from missing Leesie.

She and I put on masks and fins and float the vest out into the lake fifty feet past the mouth of the river.

"We should be right over where the falls were." Leesie sounds solemn. This is another ceremony for her. She's too caught up in it to be afraid today. She's changed. Maybe more than I want to know.

I blow into the BC's oral inflate hose to fill it up.

Leesie treads water as I set up my red and white diver-down flag. "Promise you won't go too deep."

"Sixty feet, max. Just keep your eyes on me. If I pass out, it'll be on the way back up—the last ten feet or so. Swim down and pull me out."

"Right." She still isn't freaking.

"It's easy." I pull an extra weight belt and a five-pound weight out of the BC's front pocket. "We'll practice just in case."

She hangs on to the floating BC and snugs the belt around her waist.

"All you do is hang on to the line and watch me."

"That won't be hard." Her tan cheeks tinge pink.

Months loading and unloading scuba tanks supplied me with ripped abs and pecs to rival Troy's. I like that she noticed. "Breathe through your snorkel. Keep focused on my eyes. If they roll back into my head—"

"Don't scare me." She slaps my arm. "How often has this happened?"

"Once. My mom saved me."

"And now I'm supposed to save you?"

I can't resist kissing her cheek. "You already did."

Her mask fogs up. She pulls it off and rinses it.

I swallow the lump in my throat, get busy as Mr. Diving Instructor, helping her get the hair out of her mask when she puts it back on. "Looks good. Now, if I slump on the way up, just duck dive." I make her practice a few. She dives down fifteen feet no problem—doesn't panic once. Then I show her the rescue position and dive so she can practice pulling me out. It's great to see her swimming down to me, feel her arms go around my chest, her slender body close behind me, her strong legs kicking against mine. She wants to practice again. So do I.

I dive twenty feet, level off, look up, and see her floating at the surface, the sun's rays refracted around her, long hair loose, fanned out in a circle. I remember my old blue water nightmare, see her coming through the water, fringe and long hair. My rescue. She pulled me out with both arms and didn't let go until I could breathe on my own.

LEESIE'S MOST PRIVATE CHAPBOOK

POEM #48, KETTLE FALLING

His chest expands, collapses
in patient cycles, waiting,
while the Salmon People
chant farewell,
my grandmother
whispers blessings,
and his parents don
their wet suits.

Kettle Falls hides in
the dark water below us.
He'll be safe with me
one more time.

The music wanes
and his body shakes
with the effort of packing
air on top of air.
He slips the snorkel from
those lips I've missed for months
and motionless transforms to
fluid, fast, silent, slow—
all at the same time.

So different from his scuba,
which hampered him
with a tank and BC,
bubbles, and me—

terrified and shaking,
holding him back.
It was nothing like
the resilient soul,
the hope in motion,
the lanky poetry
I watch as he dives
free.

Thank you . . .

Mom. She always believed I could do this, so I believed it, too.

All my sisters and brothers, their wives, husbands, and kids. My most enthusiastic fans.

My husband, Allen. He learned how to free dive with me, paid for my MFA, and worships the ground I walk on. I love you.

Rob and Andy, my oldest sons, who filled my head with teen guy voices. The next book will feature time-traveling space pirates and a troop of undead monkeys. I promise.

Shante, my caring daughter-in-law, for Baby Jack.

Rachel, my daughter, for taking my beautiful author photo—and forty ugly ones. And keeping me and the rest of the family fed while I revised.

Will, my youngest. Sorry I missed all those birthdays. Thanks for not milking it *too* much.

My first mentor, Mrs. Daniels, at Tekoa High School, who sent me off to CENTRUM fiction workshops where I met authors and, glory be, other teens who felt like me.

BYU for the scholarship, and all my professors, roommates and friends, who made my time there everything I'd prayed for.

Vermont College. You changed my life. Thanks, especially, to my brilliant advisors, Ron Koertge, Sharon Darrow, Louise Hawes, and Susan Fletcher, who helped me birth this novel, my talented critique buds, Joelle, Connie, Kathi, and Rhay, and my classmates, Le Salon—colleagues, sisters, soul mates.

My heroes, Ann and Erzi in Paris, who gave up their creative time to throw the SCBWI Sequester where I found the lovely, Lexa, my genius editor.

Thank you, Lexa, and everyone at Razorbill for all your hard work and taking a risk on an unknown author, a novel that had been rejected, rejected, rejected, and my faithful Mormon heroine.

And I must acknowledge and thank the Source of my story. He sent me these voices and compelled me to capture them and craft them into the novel you hold in your hands. I could not create without His guidance. Thank you, Father. I am most grateful.

Love can haunt you forever, like a beautiful, aching song.

Another luminous love story by Angela Morrison:

sing me
to sleep

sing me
to sleep

ANGELA MORRISON

prologue

Damn, she's ugly.

My bio-dad's first words when he saw me. It's my only image of him. A shadowy figure bending over Mom wearing a hospital gown, holding a flannel-wrapped bundle in her arms.

Damn, she's ugly, Tara. What did you do?

Like she ate or drank something strange that made me come out red and pimply with a purple blotch on my forehead. No hair. Cone head from the delivery. My baby face screwed up and screaming at him.

Mom didn't hate him enough to actually tell me that story. She doesn't talk about him—not to me. He played in a rock band. Not a big one. That's all I know. I've seen the picture, though. It's in our family album with the rest of my baby pictures. The only one that survived with him in it. But Mom did hate him enough to tell that story over and over to his sister, her best friend since high school, every time his name resurfaced between them.

It's my first clear memory. Stacking Cool Whip bowls and margarine containers on the kitchen floor, listening to Mom talk on the phone, tuning into the quiet intensity of her voice.

"*Damn, she's ugly.* Our beautiful baby. That's all he had to say."

I was her beautiful baby. She called me that all the time.

Beautiful? Now I knew the truth. I was ugly. *Damn ugly.* No wonder Dad took off. Never looked back. Not at his ugly daughter making a fairy-tale tower from white and yellow plastic bowls, singing the first song she ever wrote, quietly to herself.

Da-amn ugly, da-amn ugly.

At least I can sing. Got that from my mom's side. I may not look like a songbird—more like a song stork—but if you close your eyes, it's beautiful.

chapter 1

THE OFFERING

Crap. There's a naked freshman chained to my locker.

No. Not naked. Briefs. Not a good look, kid. Spindly white legs, wimpy chest, shaking arms. Black socks. Maybe his mom didn't do the laundry all spring break, and that's all he's got today.

A bike chain encased in lime-green plastic goes through my locker's handle down the poor kid's underwear and out a leg, loops up, locked tight. He could escape if he wanted to streak.

Sniggering behind me. I don't turn. That's what they want. The sound multiplies. Amplifies. Magnifies into an audience.

I didn't see it coming while I slumped into the hall traffic, sinking lower into my baggy sweatshirt and loose Levi's, my eyes tracing the regular lines in the floor tiles, as I hid behind my long brown frizzed-out mane, face rigid just in case.

My progress was strangely quiet. No guys darting in front of me telling me to "get my effing ugly face" out of their way. No one shouting, "Take cover. The Beast is loose." No dying animal moans echoing off the lockers as I walked by. Only silence. Deadly silence. I thought I'd escaped this morning. I should have known. The hunters are on the attack.

But I'm not the only one they attacked this time. I focus on the trembling kid. "Did they hurt you?" I accidentally brush his arm.

He jerks back, stares at the spot I touched like it will burst into flames or harden to stone and turn to dust. Can't blame him. I'm Beth the Beast. Too tall to ever stand straight. Bony body. Face full of zits. Bug eyes magnified by industrial-strength glasses. The braces have been off for three years, but no one sees my straight, white teeth. Just fangs, long yellow ones. Dripping blood.

"They said" —the kid shudders and swallows hard— "to tell you I'm the offering."

They. We both know who *they* are. Colby Peart, Travis Steele, Kurt Marks. The Horsemen. Aren't there supposed to be four? And I think that's biblical. Ironic. Nothing biblical about Colby and his senior ultra-jock following who hold Port High School in their grasp. Apocalyptic? That works. But the end of their reign approaches. Seniors graduate. Unless by some sick shake of fate's dice they fail, next year this place will be liberated. The Horsemen will ride off into the sunset. I hope warriors hiding behind the hills get them and tear them to pieces.

The kid's talking again. The press behind me seethes in close enough to hear. "They said the Bea—you—require a sacrifice." He shudders again and looks down at the floor. "Every full moon."

The crowd behind us roars. Laughter is supposed to be healthy, uplifting. Not in Port, Michigan.

"It's okay." I restrain myself from patting his shoulder. "We'll get Mr. Finnley to bring his bolt cutters."

The kid won't shut up. His head comes back up, and he grimaces at me. "They said you'd drag me into your lair—"

More laughter.

Heat pours into my face, and I mumble, "I don't eat freshmen for breakfast."

"Eat me?" Confusion knits the kid's brows together. "That's not what they said you'd do."

Riot levels break out behind us. It sounds like half the school has crammed into the hall.

I don't turn and look. "I'm not going to hurt you."

"Can you knock me out first?"

The laughter, mocking and harsh, bounces back and forth across the hall, off the metal locker stacks.

This kid must have swallowed every word of the Beast legend. I'm a giant. I'm hideous. But a crazed female rapist preying on skinny freshmen?

I hold up my hands and back off. "They got you, okay." My eyes sting. They got me, too. "You're safe." I turn and try to push through the wall of unyielding bodies to find the custodian. My eyes are blurry. Crap.

Don't lose it. Don't lose it. Don't lose it. "Excuse me. Please." The surging wall of cackling bodies solidifies.

Then I see Mr. Finnley's head. Scott's there, too—leading him through the crowd. I swallow hard.

"Sorry, Beth." Scott bites his lip. "I wanted to get this cleaned up before you got here—but the kid wouldn't leave his whities."

"That's enough, people. Don't you have classes to go to?" Mr. Finnley glares, and the masses scuttle off back to the cracks and drains they came from. The Finnster shakes his head and gets busy cutting the chain. "I'll have to report this."

That's all I need. Another session in the office. Questions I can't answer. "Who did this?" Silence. "Who do you think did this?" Who do *you* think did this? We all know. Colby and his clones are behind everything nasty that goes on here. Nobody names them. We have another assembly about bullying. Nothing changes.

I glance down at the binder I'm carrying for first period. I scribbled out the words, but I know what they say:

Your words—
Why do they define me?
Why do I believe you?
Your face,
Your lips, and your fingers—
Don't spill them on me.
I'm bones, blood, and flesh
Not clay to be pounded,
And scorched in the fire
That seethes in the hate you feel.
I bleed when you wound me
Just like the pretty girls do.

It needs some kind of hopeful chorus. Can't seem to squeak anything like that into the equation. No music, either. Just those thin lines that make me sound so angry. I guess I am—angry. But I don't want everyone knowing that. I do a lot of erasing, burning, shredding, hiding, hurting. I run back to *Da-am ugly* and stay there.

The end of the year can't come fast enough. If I tiptoe next year, I'll be able to breathe—like when they left junior high.

Scott reads my mind. "Only three months, eight days, thirteen hours, and twenty-nine minutes until they graduate."

"Why do you help me?" Scott and I were best friends in preschool, and then he was in my class again in third grade. He was skinny and had to go to the nurse's office for hyper drugs at lunch. I was already taller than everyone else and wore thick, round glasses that made me look like an overgrown bush baby. My hair was short back then. Cut it now? No way. Where would I hide?

Scott doesn't have to hide. Doesn't have to help me and doom himself to eternal loserhood. He's cute since his face cleared up. I don't think he sees it. He's still way short, Quiz Bowl captain, core nerd. Still my friend.

He grins, nonchalant, self-sacrificing, Clark Kent to the core. "I don't take gym anymore. They can't steal my clothes and throw them in the toilet."

"But they could hurt you."

"You're worried?" He pats my shoulder. "That's nice, Beth. See you in choir."

Choir. School choir. Not my real choir down in Ann Arbor. Not the choir I begged Mom to let me audition for when I was thirteen. Not the competitive *all-girls* choir where I sit unobtrusively in the back and anchor the altos. Not the one I have to drive a hundred miles to, through Detroit's rush-hour traffic down I-94 every Tuesday and Thursday to rehearsals in a freezing cold church. Not Bliss Youth Singers of Ann Arbor. The choir I live for. The choir that takes me away from who I am to what I long to be. Beautiful? I guess. Isn't that what everyone wants? They all probably want love, too. I live with so much hate that I'm not even sure what love is. Neither is on my horizon.

Scott's just talking about our struggling school choir. Kind of a joke. Marching Band is almighty here. But choir passes the time. Easy A. Music is music. Singing is singing. A respite from the madness. No jock senior boys allowed. Out of this school of nearly two thousand kids, there are only eight guys in the whole group, so I sit by Scott and sing tenor. I've got a decent low voice and perfect pitch so sight-reading parts come naturally. I can sing high, too. I can sing as high as anybody if I want. I help out the sopranos and altos when we run parts. They go to pieces when I go back to tenor.

Scott can't sing, but he tries. I asked him once why he takes choir. Any guy who signs up is instantly labeled "gay" by Colby and his jocks—and the rest of the school.

Scott turned kind of pink. "So I can hear you sing."

That was probably the nicest thing any guy had ever said to me. Not that Scott was serious.

I played along. "Be careful." I punched his arm. "You'll ruin your reputation."

He got serious then. "I'm not gay, Beth."

"Of course, you're not."

He was going to say something else, but he just shook his head and walked off.

I dare you to say I'm not ugly.

So, back to this morning. Scott's halfway down the hall, but I catch up easy. Long beast legs cover ground quickly. "Thanks, Scott. I mean it. School would be hell without you."

He puts out his arm like he's a prom princess escort. "My pleasure, ma'am."

A shuddery, weak laugh comes out of me. I rest my arm on top of his and let him lead me down the hall, grateful for the support.

He smiles up at me. No braces for him now, either. Teeth recently whitened. A bit dazzling. "I wonder what people think when we walk down the hall together."

I laugh, stronger this time. "Beauty and the Beast. Dr. Namar did a great job on your face." We go to the same dermatologist. So far the miracle of clear skin hasn't happened for me. Dr. Namar keeps trying. He says the scarring will be minimal. But I have eyes.

Scott stops and turns to me. He's got a dreamy look on his face. "Beauty and the Beast? So if we dance in the moonlight—"

"You better bring a stool."

"One of the wheelie ones from the library?"

"Perfect. Mind if I lead?" Then I feel dumb. This giant girl dwarfing sweet, little Scott. I let go of his arm and move forward, head down, withdrawing into myself again. My shoulders round to their usual downward curve.

Scott hustles to catch up. "What I want to know is," he grabs me by the elbow and makes me stop walking, "if I kiss you when the music stops," he stands on his toes and whispers in my ear, "will you be my Princess Charming?"

I snort. "Dream on. No magic's going to help this." I pull back, deeper into my beastly cave.

Scott smiles. "I wouldn't mind an experiment."

I don't like it when he gets like this. "You don't want to waste your virgin lips on me. You could dazzle a half–decent looking freshman into making out easy." I head for my class. "Look in the mirror."

He scurries along beside me, scowling. "I wish you'd get over the looks thing."

I scowl right back at him. "Look at me, Scott." I part my hair with both hands and pull it away from my face long enough to give him a frightening glimpse. "How could I *ever* get over the looks thing? I am the Beast."

"If you believe that, they win."

"Wake up. Look around." I wrap my arms across my chest, trying to control the delayed reaction that shudders through me. "They won a long time ago."